"You can____
no one ca____

Cait whispered brokenly, her voice little more than a sob. "He killed her. He killed my mother. And he's going to kill me."

"He's not going to get anywhere near you," Shay said with flat certainty. "That's a promise, Cait."

She shivered again, and Shay tightened his arms around her, starting to realize a little uneasily that she was all but naked, dressed only in briefs and his light cotton T-shirt.

Bad idea, noticing that. She moved just then, just a slight shift of her body that made him grit his teeth, and he was unsettled to realize he was becoming aroused, his body responding to the unspoken promise in hers.

Real bad idea.

Dear Reader,

Hot days, hot nights and hot reading—summer's really here! And we truly do have a hit lineup for you this month. For example, our American Heroes title is by Naomi Horton. *Hell on Wheels* is a very apt description of the hero, as well as the name of the truck he drives. But when he meets our heroine... Well, all I can say is that they'd both better prepare for a little taste of heaven!

Award-winner Justine Davis checks in with *Target of Opportunity,* a sexy bodyguard story with a hero who's absolutely scrumptious. Lee Magner's *Standoff* is set in the rugged American West, with a hero who's just as rugged—and a whole lot more romantic. Frances Williams brings in *Passion's Verdict,* with a hero on the run and a heroine who's along for the ride of her life. Christine D'Angelo's title says it all: *A Child Is Waiting.* But for the heroine, finding that child is going to take the help of one very special man. Finally, welcome new author Victoria Cole, whose *Mind Reader* has a psychic heroine and a skeptical hero on the trail of a missing child. Something tells me that you'll want to get hold of each and every one of these books!

And in months to come, look for more great reading from favorite authors such as Emilie Richards, Marilyn Pappano, Suzanne Carey and Linda Turner, to name only a few of the talents contributing to Intimate Moments, where excitement and romance go hand in hand.

Enjoy!

Leslie Wainger
Senior Editor and Editorial Coordinator

AMERICAN HERO

HELL ON WHEELS

Naomi Horton

Silhouette®
INTIMATE MOMENTS®

Published by Silhouette Books New York

America's Publisher of Contemporary Romance

SILHOUETTE BOOKS
300 East 42nd St., New York, N.Y. 10017

HELL ON WHEELS

ISBN: 0-373-07505-7

First Silhouette Books printing July 1993

Printed in the U.S.A.

Books by Naomi Horton

Silhouette Intimate Moments

Strangers No More #323
In Safekeeping #343
Dangerous Stranger #425
Hell on Wheels #505

Silhouette Desire

Dream Builder #162
River of Dreams #236
Split Images #269
Star Light, Star Bright #302
Lady Liberty #320
No Walls Between Us #365
Pure Chemistry #386
Crossfire #435
A Dangerous Kind of Man #487
The Ideal Man #518
Cat's Play #596
McAllister's Lady #630
No Lies Between Us #656
McConnell's Bride #719
Chastity's Pirate #769

Silhouette Romance

Risk Factor #342

Silhouette Books

Silhouette Christmas Stories 1991
"Dreaming of Angels"

NAOMI HORTON

was born in northern Alberta, where the winters are long and the libraries far apart. "When I'd run out of books," she says, "I'd simply create my own—entire worlds filled with people, adventure and romance. I guess it's not surprising that I'm still at it!" An engineering technologist, she presently lives in Nanaimo, British Columbia, with her collection of assorted pets.

This one's for Leslie Wainger:
for giving me the opportunity to write the kinds of
stories I love to read—and have a lot of fun doing it.

This is work?

Prologue

Running. Heart pounding, breath rasping in her throat...and fear. Always the fear. Tearing at her like something alive.

Behind her...they were behind her. Had to be by now. They'd have gone looking for the ward orderly when he didn't appear at the end of his shift. Would have found him in the storeroom where she'd left him, bound and gagged with strips of torn-up sheet.

Running...she had to keep running.

The wind tore at her, blinding her with ropes of her own hair, and the rain...God, so cold! Her feet...she couldn't even feel her feet anymore. Couldn't find shoes...they'd taken them, along with the rest of her clothes. Hidden them. To keep her there, they said. Until they could make her well again....

Running...she was sobbing for breath now, the stitch in her side getting worse. *Away,* she chanted in her mind. *Get away, get away, get away...*

If they caught her again they'd do things to her.

Electroshock, someone had whispered against her ear the last time she'd gotten out. *Do it again, and they'll strap you down and hook you up like a toaster and you'll never want to run again.* And the other things . . . the endless drugs, the restraints. And so she'd run . . . run . . . !

But it was so cold! She hadn't counted on that . . . and the rain, the whipping, freezing rain that seemed to suck the strength from her. And the wind, battering like hands.

Running . . . keep running! Stop and they'll catch you, and if they catch you this time, you'll never get another chance.

They were helping her, they said, their smiles full of lies. Helping her get well. Helping her understand that her rage wasn't at *him* at all, but at her mother . . . her dead mother.

Let us help you, they whispered in the shadows of her restless, crowded nights. *Trust us,* they said. *Trust us and we'll make you better. You're just confused . . . so confused and angry . . .*

Running . . . somehow managing to stay on her feet, to suck in one aching breath after another, to fight the darkness creeping around the edges of her mind. It was always there now, hovering like impending night, whispering coaxing things at her. It was getting harder and harder to hold it back and at times she wondered if it wouldn't just be easier to quit fighting it and let it take her down, down into dark oblivion. . . .

Run!

And then there were lights . . . streaks of brightness in the howling night, and she stumbled, fell, her hands skidding along asphalt, and she realized she'd reached the highway. The rain hammered at her, pressing her against the soaked grasses along the verge, and she fought to lift her head as sudden brilliance lit her world. Headlights. A truck's headlights . . .

She struggled vainly to get to her feet, to wave him down, to shout, but all she managed to get out was a hoarse croak. And then he was rushing by, booming past in a fury of noise and gritty water. She flinched as the backwash of wind and flying spray hit her and she stumbled back, slipped and fell again. And she realized suddenly that she was crying, so cold she could scarcely move, crouched by the side of the highway like a wounded, hurt thing drawn by the light.

And that's when she saw it...the other lights. Across the highway, swimming through rain, blurred, miragelike. But real, as real as the cold seeping into her bones, the danger behind her. Neon blinked hypnotically: red, red, red... *Amber Hills Truckstop Café.*

Somehow, she managed to get her feet under her again. To take one step, then another, focusing every atom of will on those distant, beckoning lights. Keep moving, something whispered at her. Stop and you'll die. Keep moving...you have to keep moving.

It would be warm there. And dry. And someone would be there. Someone would help her....

Chapter 1

"It's a real bad night out there." The waitress—Betty, according to the plastic name tag pinned to the swell of her left breast—smiled as she refilled his coffee cup. She had smooth ivory skin that looked almost translucent under the fluorescent lights, and hair like corn silk.

And a smile with enough welcome in it, Shay thought with faint amusement, that would make most men start thanking their lucky stars.

"How about some pie to finish things off?" Holding the coffee carafe with practiced ease, she leaned one slim hip against his table and smiled down at him, eyes as warm as the smile. "The cherry's good. Or the banana cream. You look like a banana-cream guy."

"No, thanks. I'll just finish this coffee and be on my way."

She made a moue of disappointment. "But it's awful out there—weather report says they've had freezing rain just north of here. There've been accidents all up and down the interstate. I've seen the highway patrol go by twice already, lights flashing." She looked at him evenly. "You *could* stay here for the night. You can park your rig out back—Barney won't mind."

Shay relaxed against the fake leather of the banquette and propped one booted foot against the table leg, raised knee bent comfortably, free arm draped along the back of the bench. Lifting the coffee cup, he took a long swallow, looking at her over the rim. "And what about you? You have far to drive tonight?" Knowing, even as he asked it, what the answer was going to be. And wishing, in that tiny part of himself that was still alive, that he could honestly say he gave a damn.

Her mouth tipped up in a slow, beguiling smile. "Barney keeps a couple of trailers in back, and he lets me rent one of them. It's...umm..." She blushed suddenly, as though shocked by her own bravado. "The blue one."

"My favorite color," Shay said easily, playing along simply because it was cold and wet outside and she was young and pretty and lonely, and what the hell...it didn't cost him anything. He taunted himself with how easy the rest of it would be, too.

Park the rig like she said, take that short walk through the blowing rain...she'd be as warm and welcoming as her smile, all silken skin and breathless giggles and soft whispers in the night. She'd come to him wanting nothing more than his arms for a little while, and in the morning she'd kiss him sweetly on the mouth and tell him that it was all right, that she understood, that maybe she'd see him again next time he was down this way.

Easy as breathing, and needing as little thought.

He let his own mouth curve in a smile as warm as it needed to be, and said, with honest regret, "You make me wish I could stay. But I lost half a day down by Napa, and I want to get in a couple more hours before I stop tonight."

She smiled a bit wistfully. "She must be something special."

"Who?"

"Whoever she is that keeps you on the straight and narrow." The smile turned mischievous. "Barney says you're in here regular, but you keep to yourself—no horsing around, no jokes, no loud talk. He figures that means you've got yourself a woman who keeps you happy."

Shay forced himself to smile, trying to ignore the vivid little memories his mind tossed at him. "Barney sounds like quite a philosopher."

But she didn't smile back, her face a little sad. "You want to know what I think?"

"What do you think, Betty?"

"I think you're hurtin' bad," she said softly. "I think you keep to yourself 'cause some lady broke your heart and you're afraid of it happening again."

It hit closer than he'd expected and he winced before he could catch himself, laughing at his own unexpected vulnerability. "And I'd say you're dangerous to be around, reading a man's mind like that." He kept his tone teasing, ignoring the shadows taunting him from the back of his mind.

"If you ever want to just talk..." Her blue eyes held his seriously. "I've been there. I know what it's like."

No, you don't, he told her with silent brutality. You don't know what it's like at all, watching the woman you love dying a little more each day until she's finally just gone and there's nothing left but the emptiness and the memories. You can't possibly know that kind of pain....

But he just nodded, his face feeling oddly stiff, and forced himself to smile again as he reached for the coffee mug. "I'll keep it in mind, Betty. And I appreciate the offer."

She smiled, suddenly self-conscious, and reached up to smooth her hair. One of the men seated at the only other occupied table leaned back and caught her eye, making a pouring gesture over his empty coffee cup, and Betty nodded and shoved herself away from Shay's table.

"You think about staying tonight," she said firmly, giving him the no-nonsense look of a woman with a mission. "I give a real good back rub, and we can talk as long as you want. And we don't have to...well, you know. I mean, I'm not saying I wouldn't if you wanted to, but...well, we don't have to or anything."

"Hey, sweetcheeks," the other man complained. "Can we get some coffee over here, or what?"

"Hold your horses," she snapped. "Coffee's not going anywhere, and neither are you."

A grin broke across his beefy face. "McKittrick don't want none of what you're trying to give away. But Mikey and me..." He nudged his companion. "Whattaya say, Mikey? We got a few minutes, don't we?"

"You wish," Betty said with studied boredom. "What's the matter, Hank? Wife kick you out again?"

Shay smiled to himself as he watched Betty sashay across to the table by the window, her repartee barbed. It was slow tonight. The weather was keeping the locals off the roads and the tourists in their motels, and except for a hardy few trying to make up time or get home to warm beds and warmer wives, most of his fellow truckers would have stopped for the night.

Which he should probably do, if he had any sense. Sure, he was behind schedule, but nothing he couldn't make up over the next few days. The real reason he wasn't ready to stop for the night—not counting the fact he didn't want to have to deal with a well-intentioned but potentially awkward invitation from a lonely waitress—was that it was still too early.

Too early to go to bed, even if he could sleep. Which, most nights, eluded him for hours until sheer exhaustion

dragged him down. With luck, past where the dreams were
waiting. When he was tired enough, he could go most of the
night without waking more than two or three times. And the
dreams, if they came at all, were disjointed and unfocused
and usually pretty harmless.

But on the bad nights—and for some reason, this felt like
it was going to be one—well, on the bad nights, he could go
clear through to dawn without ever closing his eyes.

He'd just lie there staring into the darkness, listening to
the slow rhythms of his own heartbeat and thinking it was
the loneliest sound in the world. Thinking of the bottle of
whiskey, still sealed. Of the revolver. Of the dreamless sleep
both offered...

Shay took another swallow of lukewarm coffee and
glanced at the clock above the counter. He'd drive for another couple of hours tonight. Having too much time on his
hands was just a little too dangerous.

A gust of wind hit the big front windows like a fist, making them shudder, and the door rattled against its catch as
though something was trying to get in. Rain sluiced down
the glass and Shay squinted through it, barely able to make
out the blurred lights of the gas pumps out front. It was going to make for bad driving, the wind pushing his big rig all
over the road, the blowing rain playing havoc with visibility
and traction.

He let his gaze drift across to where Betty was still talking with the other two truckers, standing with one slim hip
canted to one side, head tossed back as she laughed at
something, the lights glinting in her thick, honey-blond hair.
And found himself wishing he could stay...

The wind caught the door again just then and blew it open
with a shuddering crash that made everyone jump. A curtain of icy wind-lashed rain swept in, glittering from the
parking-lot lights, and it was only when the slender form
caught the door and slammed it closed, cutting off the

wailing of the wind, that Shay realized someone had come in with the storm.

In the sudden silence, everyone stared at the newcomer. And Shay, slowly lowering his coffee mug, felt the hair prickle along the back of his neck for no reason at all.

She was young, mid to late twenties maybe, average height, slender, pale. Too slender, Shay found himself thinking. Too pale. Her dark rain-soaked hair hung almost to her waist, tangled and knotted by the wind, and she was dressed in white cotton slacks and a matching shirt that were both too large for her, as though she'd grabbed someone else's clothes and bolted out into the night without a coat or even shoes.

She'd rolled the cuffs of the slacks to midcalf and her legs and bare feet were splattered with mud and bits of wet grass, and she was shivering, Shay realized. Shivering so badly, he could see the tremors running through her from clear across the room.

Water dripped off her and was forming a pool around her feet and she stood there staring back at them as though she expected to be attacked, back tight against the closed door, chest heaving as though she'd been running hard and fast. Her eyes were huge and dark and her gaze darted around the café like a trapped bird.

"My Lord!" Betty recovered first, putting the coffeepot down and walking quickly toward the newcomer. "What in heaven's name are you doing out on a night like this without even a coat? You must be frozen! Did your car break down? Do you need a tow?"

The woman stared at Betty uncomprehendingly, then shook her head. "N-no."

"Well, for heaven's sake, don't just stand there! Come in and get warmed up. Give her a coat," she added, looking around at one of the truckers she'd been talking with. "For

Pete's sake, Hank, give the woman your coat! Can't you see she's half-frozen?''

"But she's wet...." he mumbled unenthusiastically.

"You're a genius, Hank, you know that?'' Betty reached across and whipped his wool plaid coat off the back of his chair, then walked across to where the woman was still standing. "Here, honey, you get into this. Stinks of diesel fuel, but it's warm.''

"No.'' The woman stepped past Betty's outstretched hands and the proferred coat without even looking at her, her gaze flickering around the room, pausing on Shay, then on the two other men. "T-that eighteen-wheeler outside. The black-and-s-silver one. Whose is it?''

"That's McKittrick's rig,'' the brawny one said plaintively, nodding in Shay's direction. "Can I have my coat back?''

The woman fastened those wide, frightened eyes on Shay and walked across to him, stiff with cold, leaving a trail of rainwater that glittered like ice. "P-please,'' she said in a half whisper, teeth chattering. "Please, I need a ride....''

There was something about her, about the look of desperation in her eyes, the way she seemed to be struggling against some deep, unnamed terror, that made Shay's eyes narrow slightly.

Runaway.

The word was written all over her and Shay eased his breath out. Running from what, God only knew. Father. Husband. Some other problem, real or imagined. Whatever had driven her out into the night, it sure as hell was trouble he didn't need any part of.

"Sorry,'' he said quietly, trying not to see her fear, to think of what might have caused it. "Union rules. No hitchhikers.''

"Rules, my—!'' Betty strode across impatiently. "You look like a man who's broke a few rules in his day,

McKittrick. She's just asking you to give her a ride, not marry her and raise her kids!''

"I c-can pay." The woman stepped closer to the table, arms clutched across her chest as shiver after shiver racked her. "Please! Th-they're trying to kill me. . . ."

"Kill you?" Betty blinked, looking alarmed. "Who's trying to kill you? Look, honey, maybe I'd better just call the cops and—"

"No police!" The woman looked around at her in panic. "Th-they're in on it. They're all in on it!"

Betty's eyes narrowed slightly, her expression going oddly blank. "Honey, are you . . . umm . . ." She gave the woman a warm, reassuring smile. "You're not staying up at Amber Hills by any chance, are you? The . . . umm . . . hospital?"

For a heartbeat, Shay was certain the woman was going to bolt. She seemed to go even more pale than she already was, and he could see her swallow as she stared at Betty as though trying to decide something. "I need your help," she said finally, fighting to get the words between chattering teeth. "I'm n-not a patient, I swear it. They're keeping me there because it's the only p-place they can keep me quiet without arousing suspicion. And they're going to k-kill me if I don't—"

The whoop of sirens cut her off and Shay could hear her breath suck in as she wheeled toward the front of the café, nearly stumbling on half-frozen feet. She gave a low moan as headlights cut across the rain-washed windows and a moment later two highway patrol cars slewed to a screaming stop just outside the door, tires screeching on wet pavement.

"Well, for crying out loud," Betty said irritably, striding toward the door as blue and white lights strobed the night. "What do they think they're doing, driving in here like that!"

Another siren came screaming in just then, this one on an ambulance that careened across the wet parking lot like a banshee, headlights bouncing crazily as the driver brought it to a skidding stop just behind the cruisers. The doors flew open and Shay could see two white-uniformed attendants start to get out, then, before they'd even hit the ground, yet another vehicle slewed to a stop, this one a long, black car with no markings.

"You've got to help me!" The woman spun around to face Shay, her eyes wide with fright. "Please, you've got to get me out of here. I—I've got money. Please . . . !"

"Look, lady," he said quietly, "I've got problems of my own. The cops will help you."

"They'll take me back!" Her gaze darted to the door, back to him. "I'm not crazy, I swear it," she said in a low, frantic voice. "They've kept me locked up for weeks, drugging me, tying me down. I've got friends in Sacramento. Money. If I can just get to Sacramento, I can—"

"I'm headed north." He said it brusquely, not wanting to hear her story. Even if it was true—which he doubted—there was nothing he could do to help her. Besides, odds were she was just another mixed-up resident of Amber Hills with a fuzzy grasp on reality. And he, God knows, had enough problems handling his own these days.

"Please. . . ." She reached toward him, one slender, pale hand, bloodless with cold. "Please help me. It's not what you think, I swear it. I'm not sick. . . ."

Her pupils were dilated, he realized suddenly, and her eyes had that slightly glazed, fevered look that spoke of some kind of drug. Nancy's eyes had held that same look, he recalled numbly. Near the end, when the pain had been so bad and she'd finally given in and—through tears of anger and shame at her own weakness—had let him give her the morphine the doctor had prescribed.

But the shame had been his. The drugs had been as much a retreat from pain for him as for her, and he still felt sick when he thought of the relief he'd feel each afternoon when she'd finally slip into drugged sleep and he didn't have to sit there with her as she fought the pain and fear. Didn't have to watch the fierce struggle in her eyes as she clung to his hand, her breathing tight and ragged, and know what she was suffering.

"... told them I'm crazy and they believe him!" The woman's voice broke on what sounded like a sob. "The medical staff at Amber Hills are all in on it—he's paying them. And the police can't—"

The door of the café pushed open just then and two large highway patrolmen came in, water pouring off them. They looked around the room with hard, assessing eyes, taking in everything, everyone.

Then those cool gazes stopped on the woman. The taller one started walking toward her. "You'd better come with us, miss."

"Leave me alone!" She backed up a step, one hip grazing Shay's table. "He's trying to kill me, don't you understand? He killed my mother and now he's—"

"Now look, miss," the patrolman said wearily, "we've been through all this before. Your father is—"

"He's not my father!"

"Stepfather, then." He sounded less patient. "We've been looking for you half the night. Your fath—stepfather called us right after they found the orderly in the closet where you left him." He gazed at her disapprovingly. "*He's* going to be all right, no thanks to you. It's a wonder you didn't kill him when you hit him with that footstool."

"I didn't hit him with anything. I tripped him and he fell—if he says otherwise, he's a damned liar!"

"But you tied him up and stole his clothes and—"

"They took mine." She took another step backward.

"Look, lady," the other patrolman broke in. "We're all cold and wet, and it's late as hell. Come on back with us, and—"

"No! I'm not going back there!"

"Is she under arrest?" It took Shay a moment to realize it was his voice, and he cursed himself silently as the patrolman's cold gaze narrowed on him.

"Not officially. Her stepfather called us in to find her and take her back to the hospital before she hurt herself." The cold gaze held Shay's. "Your name?"

"McKittrick."

"That your black-and-silver semi out there?"

"That's right."

"Heading south?"

"North. Eugene, Oregon."

The officer nodded. "I take it your load's been inspected and that all your papers are in order."

"They're in order," Shay said evenly. It wasn't quite a threat, but it could be. One wrong step, and he could find himself hung up here for days while someone went through his shipping documents looking for imaginary transgressions.

He held himself firmly in check, not needing the grief. And wondering, a little coldly, just what the hell was going on.

The door pushed open again and the two ambulance attendants came in, looking wet and angry, followed closely by two other men, both dressed in business suits.

"You've given us quite a little wild-goose chase, Caitie," one of the attendants said, his smile cool as he looked the woman up and down. "Frank's got a knot on his head the size of a baseball where you hit him." The smile widened and he started toward her slowly, holding up a syringe. "Come on now, Caitlin. Make it easy on yourself, okay?

You know I hate having to chase you and hold you down...."

"Touch me, Crushank, and I swear I'll kill you." She spun around and—before Shay could stop her—had snatched up his steak knife and brandished it.

"Hey, hey!" He grinned, his eyes brightening with what could have been anticipation. "I love it when you fight, Cait, honey. But you never win, you should know that by now. We—"

"Shut up, Crushank," one of the other men snapped. "You, Ricchio." He gestured impatiently for the other attendant, who stepped forward holding what looked like a straightjacket. "I doubt we'll need that, but stay alert." Then he looked across at the woman, his expression one of bemused indulgence. "Caitlin, you know you're only hurting yourself with this behavior—I can't possibly keep it out of your file now we've had to call in the police. Why don't you call it a day, put down the knife and—"

"Hey, just what the hell's goin' on in here, anyway?" Barney, owner and cook, came striding in from the kitchen just then, hoisting his trousers over a broad expanse of stomach.

One of the patrolmen stepped in front of him. "It's under control, sir. Just sit down and stay out of it."

Barney's expression turned belligerent. "Now, look—"

The man who had been talking to the woman looked around impatiently. "I'm Dr. Richard Angstrom, Chief Psychiatrist at Amber Hills Care Center."

"The nuthouse, you mean," Barney muttered.

The man managed a tight smile. "I'm in charge of Miss Sawyer's case. She's suffering from paranoid delusions, drug abuse, severe depression and—"

"They're trying to kill me!" The woman's voice rose through the room. "You can't let them take me!"

You can't let them take me.

The words went through Shay like a knife and he gritted his teeth. The voice was a stranger's, but the words...God, the words were Nancy's! He could see her tear-glazed eyes as they held his, her outstretched hand as she pleaded with him...

"Now, Cait, you know that's not true." The doctor smiled a reassuring medical smile and started slowly toward her, a not-particularly tall man with gray hair who, for some reason, reminded Shay of Nancy's doctor. He'd had the same kind smile, the same air of reason and competence about him. "You'll feel better after a good night's sleep, Cait," he went on soothingly. "You've given us all quite a scare, but now it's time to—"

"I'll bet I did." She managed a harsh sob of laughter. "I'm the only one who knows the truth about my mother, after all. How much did he pay you to lock me up, Angstrom? How much is he going to pay you to kill me?"

"For heaven's sake, Caitlin, you've got to stop this!"

There was pain in the words, and it was only then that Shay bothered to take a close look at the other man who'd come in with the doctor. He was tall and fit and handsome, with well-styled silver hair and a yachting tan and the unmistakable air of someone for whom wealth and position and power were as natural as breathing.

He gazed at the woman—Cait, they called her—with an expression of concern and parental anguish. "Darling, I'm not trying to kill you. And I didn't kill your mother. You're confused, Caitlin, that's all. And sick. That's why I took you up to Amber Hills in the first place, to make you well. To—"

"You're a liar and a murderer," the woman choked out, stumbling back as he started to take a step toward her, the knife still raised in her fist.

"Caitlin, I wish I knew how to convince you how wrong you are." He held one hand out to her, then let it drop to his side. "Cait, darling, I know it's been hard. But they'll help you at the hospital. They'll make you well again."

While he'd been talking to her, distracting her, the two attendants had started to slowly circle. One of them, the one Cait had called Crushank, had a narrow-eyed expression of brutal anticipation that made Shay bristle instinctively.

It was none of his business, he told himself ruthlessly. Everything was under control.

Or was it? He looked at her arms again, at the bruises on her wrists, her legs, the side of her jaw.

Don't let them take me. Nancy's voice this time, crying out to him. Begging him . . .

He stood up suddenly, easing himself between the woman and her assailants. "I know this is probably all on the up and up," he said quietly, ignoring the way the patrolman's hand dropped to the gun at his hip. "But I'd like to see some identification. You *say* you're from Amber Hills, but . . ." He shrugged.

The doctor smiled easily. "Very prudent of you. And you're right, of course." He took a thin leather wallet from an inner pocket in his raincoat, opened it and handed it to Shay. "Feel free to look through it. And you might want to call the hospital. Anyone there can give you a description of me . . . and of Mr. Dalkquist here. And Cait, of course." He smiled at her as he said this, a benevolent, gentle smile that set Shay's teeth on edge. "We all know Cait."

"Don't let them take me," the woman said in a half sob behind him. "Please, take me with you, at least as far as the state line. They'll kill me if they get me back there!"

Except there was nothing he could do, he realized with a chill as he wordlessly handed the wallet back to Angstrom. The cops wouldn't be here unless Angstrom was on the up and up—and they sure as hell weren't going to let him walk out of here with the woman in tow.

Besides, what were the odds that things weren't exactly the way Angstrom said? A million to one? *Five* million to one? She was probably just some rich kid burned out on any one of a hundred drugs, caught in some nightmare only she could see.

One of the cops started toward him and Shay held his hands up and gave his head a shake, backing off. Telling himself he was doing the right thing, that the best way to help her was to get out of the way and let these people take care of her. Telling himself that he'd done the best he could for her, as he had for Nancy...that there was nothing else he could do...trying not to hear the fear in the voice that, somewhere behind him, sobbed a plea for help.

"All right, Cait, this has gone on long enough." Angstrom's voice was brisk and authoritative. "We've all been more than patient with you, but it's late and you've entertained these people with your dramatics for quite long enough. Now put that knife down and come quietly or—"

"I'll get her," Crushank said with a grin, stepping around a table.

"Back right the hell off," Shay growled, stepping in the man's path. "Call your boy off, Angstrom. This guy's enjoying himself just a little too much."

"Now look, buddy," Crushank started menacingly, "this isn't—"

"Look out! She's going for the door—!"

Shay glanced around in time to see the woman fling the knife down and bolt for the kitchen at a dead run. She grabbed a huge tray of glasses sitting on the end of the counter and pulled them into her path behind her. There was a bellow of profanity as the other orderly tripped over the tray and went flying, glasses shattering around him like artillery.

The woman was through the swinging doors and into the kitchen like a shot and Shay swung around clumsily, hitting Crushank in the solar plexus with his elbow in a move he would have sworn to every judge in the land was purely accidental. Crushank staggered to one side with an explosive groan and collided with one of the patrolmen and Shay eased himself out of the fray, meeting Crushank's murderous look with one of his own.

The patrolman got himself untangled and went after the woman and Crushank took a step toward the kitchen, pausing long enough to step close to Shay, teeth bared. "You'd better hope you and me never cross paths again," he said in a vicious undertone.

"Actually, I was kind of looking forward to it."

"Is that a threat?"

"If it needs to be."

"She's nothing to you. What the hell do you care what happens to her?"

"I don't like bullies."

"Oh, yeah?" Crushank gave a snort and checked the syringe he was still holding. "Well, I don't like civilians who get in the way, McKittrick. So if you have some sort of problem . . ." He grinned, showing yellowed teeth. "Maybe we can talk about it one day."

"Like I said, I look forward to it."

Crushank's lip curled, then he gave another snort and wheeled away, heading out the door after the others.

And, very suddenly, it was dead silent. Shay glanced around and found they were alone again, Hank and his companion looking a little stunned, Betty looking as though she was on the verge of tears. Barney was walking through the ruin of what had been his café, broken glass crunching underfoot, swearing in a monotone as he surveyed the damage.

"Someone's goin' to pay for all this," he proclaimed loudly, glowering out the window where the ambulance was heading for the highway in full voice. "I'm calling my lawyer first thing in the morning. People can't just come in like that and break up a man's place and not even *pay* for it!''

"You don't suppose..." Betty hugged herself as though chilled, looking out into the storm uneasily. "You don't suppose she was telling the truth, do you? I mean...you don't think...?"

"Naw." Hank downed the rest of his coffee as though nothing unusual had happened at all, then fumbled in his pocket, hauled out a handful of bills and tossed one down. "Hell, Betts, she ain't the first one to break outta that place and come wanderin' in here. Remember that old man last summer? Swore he was Abraham Lincoln. And that kid a coupla months ago—higher'n' a kite on something. Figured he could fly and got up on the roof...remember that? Had half the fire departments in the county trying to talk him down."

"This was different," Betty said quietly, rubbing her arms. "She was scared, Hank. Scared to death. I'm going to lie awake all night, worrying about her. It's so cold out there...."

"They'll find her," Hank said reassuringly. "Get a sedative into her and tomorrow she won't remember any of it."

Shay stared out through the rain-washed window at nothing, only half listening. Thinking of the terror and desperation in the woman's eyes as her gaze had held his.

He swore suddenly and wheeled back toward the table, grabbing his fleece-lined jacket and pulling it on, then settling his worn cowboy hat over his hair. It was over. In another hour, this café and the woman and everything that had happened would be sixty miles behind him and in another day, he wouldn't even remember the color of her eyes.

Although at the moment, he could remember them all too clearly. Brown, his mind taunted him. The warm russet of good brandy...

He shook it off and stalked across to the cash register with his bill.

It was raining even harder, although he hadn't thought it possible. The wind caught the door when he pulled it open and nearly wrenched it from his hand and he swore and turned his jacket collar up as a gust of blowing rain hit him in the face, sharp and bitterly cold.

Grabbing the brim of his hat to keep it from being swept off, he tucked his head down as he walked around into the shadows at the side of the restaurant where he'd parked his rig, clutching the thermos he'd had Betty fill with coffee and the bag of turkey sandwiches she'd pressed on him.

"In case you get hungry," she'd said with an effervescent smile, refusing to let him pay for them. She'd slipped in a slab of apple pie wrapped in waxed paper, "to keep you sweet," and although he knew he was a damned fool to lead her on, he hadn't had the heart to hurt her feelings by turning her down, either.

His rig glowed with reflections from the flickering neon sign above the restaurant and he stepped into the lee of its sheltering bulk gratefully. Out of the wind, he lifted his head and could see, off to one side, the dark silhouette of one of the highway patrol cars.

It rolled toward him, lights still off, and the driver's window eased down. "Bad night to be driving." The patrolman squinted a little against blowing rain.

Shay nodded. "Any luck finding the woman?"

"Not yet." He gave his head a disgusted shake. "Damn waste of everybody's time, you ask me. I don't know why he doesn't just lock her in a padded room and toss the key away."

"She seemed pretty upset."

"She's been on her step-daddy's case for years, but it's got real bad this past year." He gave his head another shake.

"Has some crazy idea he murdered her momma—well, you heard her."

"Any chance he did?"

The patrolman's cold gaze met his. "Brenton Dalkquist is one of the richest men in the county. *And* he's running for governor. Man like that don't go around murdering people."

"So you're saying his stepdaughter imagined the whole thing?"

"I'm saying she's a fruitcake."

"You sound like you're on Dalkquist's election committee."

The cold eyes got even colder. "I just don't want you jumping to no wrong conclusions, is all, McKittrick. Situation got a little tense in there, I'll admit that—I saw that slick move you pulled on Angstrom's boy. Figured he deserved it or I'd have done something about it. But that's the end of it, hear? The girl will be okay. She's just drugged up some, and confused as hell. Be fine in a few weeks."

Shay nodded slowly. "No need for me to lose sleep worrying about her, is what you're saying?"

"That's what I'm saying." He smiled tightly. "Just didn't want you leaving here with the wrong idea, is all."

"Appreciate it," Shay said dryly.

"You have a good trip up to Eugene now." The patrolman touched his hat, then the window rolled closed and the car moved off through the sheets of blowing rain, lights still off.

Eyes narrowed, Shay watched the cruiser until it vanished, then he gave his head a shake and reached up to pull open the driver's door. Damn strange. But then, the whole night had been one damned strange thing after another.

Still thinking about that, he pulled the heavy door of the truck cab open—and found himself staring into a pair of wide frightened eyes the color of good brandy.

Chapter 2

He swore grimly, not even knowing why she'd caught him by surprise. She was huddled under the dash on the passenger's side, small and wet and shivering, her face the color of wet bone in the reflection of the parking-lot lights.

Setting the thermos and sandwiches aside, he pulled the flashlight and tire iron out from under the seat, not even looking at her. "I'm going to check the rig. This would be a real good time for you to get the hell out of my truck."

Not waiting for a reply, he let the door swing closed and started to walk back along the trailer, pulling his hat low against the blowing rain as he checked the connections and lines. He gave his tires a cursory look, then hunkered down on his heels to play the beam of the flashlight along the underside of the rig to make sure everything was secure.

He was half-drenched in minutes, icy water running down the back of his neck, the legs of his jeans soaked. By the time he'd worked his way back to the driver's door he was in an even worse mood than when he'd started out, and he wrenched the door open with a growl of profanity, knowing damned well what was waiting for him.

She hadn't moved, except maybe to draw a little deeper into the shadowed darkness under the dash. He could hear the sound of her breathing, quick with fear, and he stood there for a hostile moment, thinking about just reaching across and hauling her out bodily and getting the hell out of there before that patrolman came back and arrested the both of them.

He didn't need the trouble, damn it.

There was a whisper of tires on wet pavement just behind him and he glanced around to find the cruiser there again, window down. The cop eyed him curiously. "You still here?"

Shay looked across, seemingly casually, into the depths of his truck, seeing nothing but her eyes in a stray reflection cast from the blinking neon light. They held his in silent desperation, and he swore to himself and shoved the flashlight and tire iron back under the seat, shifting slightly so the cop couldn't see into the truck.

"Just checking my load," he said evenly, sweeping his hat off and shaking the rainwater from it. "On my way right now."

To his relief, the patrolman didn't seem inclined to sit there with his window open any longer than necessary. Shay waited until the car had eased off into the rain and darkness again before stepping up into the cab and slamming the door closed.

"Give me one good reason why I shouldn't throw your tail the hell out of here." He pulled his hat off and tossed it onto one of the hooks behind him, raking his wet, tangled hair back with his fingers. Still refusing to look at her.

He didn't think she was going to answer. Then: "I'm not crazy." Just a whisper, a sigh of sound that could almost have been the wind. Almost.

He sat there for a moment or two, staring out the rain-blurred windshield, and let his shoulders slump under the weight of the wet rawhide jacket. Then he swore wearily and started to shrug the jacket off. He tossed it down to her. "Lady, I don't know what your story is and I'm not sure I want to know. But you're in my rig now, and that makes you illegal cargo. Keep your head down and your mouth shut, and I'll give you a ride to the nearest town. Then you're on your own."

He turned the key and the big engine turned over with a growl and a cough of diesel, then settled into a rumbling roar that shivered through him like another heartbeat, as familiar as home. Not even bothering to look at his passenger, he slid the truck into gear and pulled out, wheeling slowly through the driving rain and the eerie red pulse of neon and the moan of the wind toward the exit. And as he pulled the big rig out onto the access lane and started to pick up speed, shifting through the gears smoothly, diesel belching, he saw a pair of headlights suddenly pull out and settle in behind him and knew it was going to be a long, hard night.

Warmth.

So exhausted that her eyes kept sliding closed, she burrowed into the dry, soft sheepskin depths of the heavy rawhide jacket, the shivers almost nonstop now, racking her from head to foot. The coat folded around her like sheltering arms and she breathed in the musky, warm scent of the man who'd given it to her, wondering if she'd thanked him aloud or had just said the words in her mind, too weary to force them past her throat.

Water had pooled around her, soaking the rough carpet, but she hardly felt it. Felt only the shudder of the big truck easing through gear after gear as it picked up speed, snorting and rumbling, taking her away . . . away. The engine vi-

bration trembled through every cell of her body, filling her
embracing her, and she relaxed into it as gratefully as she
had the jacket.

Safe. She was safe ...

That damned cruiser tailed him for a good thirty min
utes, the headlights glowing in his rearview mirror for mile
after wet stormy mile. He ignored it for the most part, con
centrating on staring through the rhythmic sweep of the
windshield wipers into darkness and blowing rain. The wet
pavement unrolled ahead of him in the tunnel of his head
lights like a glistening ribbon of silk, deserted for the mos
part. Aside from the headlights in his rearview mirror, he
more or less had the road to himself, the only other traffic
a couple of cars and a truck or two heading the other way.

Usually he would have welcomed the solitude, but tha
cruiser tailing him made him jumpy and he kept glancing a
it, wishing it would make a move. What was it doing—jus
making sure he actually was heading for Oregon as he'c
said? Or was he being set up somehow? Had someone seer
the woman getting into his truck and was waiting until he hi
the Oregon state line before grabbing him? And if so
why ...?

But finally, just before he reached the Oregon border, i
pulled around in a U-turn and headed back, and he breathec
an oath of relief as he watched the red taillights dwindle and
then vanish into the rain.

It took another half hour before he found the turnoff he
was looking for, nearly missing it in the pelting rain. He
eased the big rig off the pavement and down the narrow mud
road cutting through a stand of dense trees, the engine
growling as he dropped it into the lowest gear. As he brough
it around and the headlights swept across the small parking
area adjacent to the picnic area, he was relieved to find i
deserted.

She hadn't uttered a word the entire time, hadn't even moved except to shift slightly now and again as though to ease cramping muscles, and he wondered if she'd fallen asleep or was just afraid of him.

"What the hell am I going to do with you?" He muttered it more to himself than to her, not expecting an answer. Not getting one. He heard more than saw her move in the shadows under the dash, sensed that she'd lifted her head and was watching him. "You all right?"

He heard her swallow, saw a movement of black within black that may have been a nod.

"Well, come on out so I can get a look at you." He flicked the cab light on and she winced, squinting slightly, and then, very slowly, as though too stiff and cold to even move properly, she eased herself out from under the dash and up onto the passenger seat.

She still had his jacket wrapped tightly around her, the collar turned up around her ears, and she looked even colder and dirtier and more waiflike than he'd remembered. Her long hair had dried in thick, tangled ropes and she was as pale as milk in the dim light, the skin under her eyes looking almost bruised from exhaustion and strain.

She didn't say anything, didn't even look at him, just sat there huddled in the depths of the jacket as though even that took all the strength she had.

A flicker of irritation shot through him. She was too compliant, damn it. Too trusting. As though she'd simply put herself into his hands, and now it was up to him to take care of her.

Except he wasn't taking care of anybody but himself these days. He was through with having people count on him. "Hasn't it even occurred to you that you should be scared? That you just *might* have jumped from the frying pan into the fire?"

Slowly she lifted her head to look at him, her eyes slightly glazed. "Fire?" Her voice was just a rasp whisper.

Shay smiled a little grimly. "You don't know me. You're sitting in my rig fifty miles from nowhere in the dead of night, in a roadside stop most people don't even know is here." He let the smile linger on his mouth. "There *are* plenty of men who wouldn't let an opportunity like that just go by...."

He held her gaze, wanting to scare her. Wanting her to think about what she'd done. What she was doing.

But she just gazed back at him, seemingly unafraid, not even curious. "Are you saying you're that kind of man?" Still, it was little more than a hoarse whisper.

Her apathy irritated him. "I could be, damn it. I *could* be more trouble than you ever dreamed."

To his surprise, she smiled very faintly, just a lift to one corner of her mouth that held more bitterness than amusement. "There's nothing you could possibly do to me that's worse than what's waiting for me back in Amber Hills."

Shay found himself thinking of Crushank...the cruel little smile on his mouth as he'd stalked her, the anticipation on his face. A chill wound its way down his spine and he shrugged it off, suddenly ashamed of taunting her.

He reached back and pulled open the curtain to the sleeper. "Come on back here," he said quietly. "I'll find you some dry clothes, for a start. Are you hungry?"

That did get a reaction. He felt a jolt of satisfaction when she lifted her head and nodded with the first sign of interest she'd shown, and he realized with some surprise that he'd been more worried about her than he'd let on even to himself.

Which was fine, he reminded himself, as long as he didn't let any of this hero business go to his head. She was *not* his responsibility. Fall into the trap of seeing himself as some sort of "rescuer," and he was going to find himself in a world of trouble.

He helped her into the sleeper and she sat on the bed, shivering as he helped her out of the jacket. "The l-light," she whispered. "Won't s-someone see the light?"

"I doubt it—it's late, and we're pretty well hidden." But the precaution sounded like a good one, and he reached through and turned the cab light off, then drew the sleeper curtain tightly closed before turning on the small battery-operated reading lamp over one end of his bed.

Watching him, Cait found herself thinking a bit stupidly that it was a relief to discover that she hadn't imagined him after all. For a while, curled up under the dashboard drifting in and out of a reality she wasn't even sure was there, she thought she might have just dreamed the tall, broad-shouldered trucker in the café.

But he was here. And he was—undeniably—real. Just as tall and broad-shouldered as she recalled, radiating a healthy, warm male vitality that banished the shadows and made her feel, for the first time in months, almost safe.

"Where—" A sudden shiver racked her and she had to clench her teeth to keep them from rattling. "W-where are we?"

"Rest stop." He didn't bother looking around at her as he started rooting around in a tiny built-in cupboard.

The brusque reply didn't even start to answer her question, but just the thought of trying to ask it again—more clearly this time, perhaps—took more energy than she had.

"That damned cop followed us right to the state line," he growled after a moment.

The words seemed to mill around in her mind before they finally took shape and made some sense. "We—we're...out of California?" She asked it hesitantly, almost afraid to hope.

"We crossed into Oregon about thirty miles back."

"Oh, thank God." It was little more than a sob of relief and she closed her eyes, feeling tears well. "Thank God…"

"I'd save some of that prayin', if I were you," he drawled, still rummaging through the cupboard. "Won't take more than a radio call or two to bring the Oregon police after us. After *you*," he corrected, sounding irritated.

She managed to lift her head to look at him. "Do they know I'm with you?"

He spared her a sidelong glance, impatience flickering across his face. It was a good face, ruggedly handsome with straight, clean features, a good chin and a solid jawline. But it was a little cold at the moment, hard-edged with shadows, and the eyes holding hers were remote and unwelcoming.

"I doubt it. I figure that cop just wanted to make sure I wasn't going to hang around being a problem."

He went back to his search and a moment later found what he was looking for. Giving a grunt of satisfaction, he tossed a wrinkled white cotton T-shirt onto the bed beside her. A pair of faded, ragged jeans followed, then a heavy cable-knit sweater that looked at least three sizes too large. But warm, she thought as another shiver made her teeth chatter. And dry.

"Why are you d-doing this?" she whispered, hugging herself.

"As I recollect, you didn't give me much of a choice."

"You stood up to Angstrom and my stepfather," she whispered, fighting another shiver. "And you didn't turn me over to that policeman when you had the chance. You could have ended it right there in the parking lot. But you didn't…."

He went very still and she found herself holding her breath, wondering if she'd jeopardized sanctuary with that one careless question. Then he reached across and gripped her wrist in a large, tanned hand, his fingers folding around her with incredible gentleness as he drew her arm out in front of her.

"This is why," he said tightly, turning it to reveal the livid bruises on her forearms. "And this." He rubbed one of the strap marks on her wrist with his thumb, the bruised welt already fading but still visible. "And this." He reached up to touch the side of her jaw where Crushank had lazily hit her two days ago.

His eyes caught and held hers, and she read anger in them, and bleakness and despair and a dozen other things. Her heart gave a little leap of hope. "So you believe me?"

"I believe you've been pretty damn roughly treated," he said shortly. "As for the rest of it . . ." He shrugged.

The hope died almost before it was fully formed, and Cait let her shoulders slump. "Oh . . ."

Then, abruptly, he dropped her wrist and eased himself away from her as though suddenly aware of how close he was sitting. "Just don't get the wrong idea," he growled, dropping a pair of heavy gray wool socks on the pile of clothes beside her. "I'm not any kind of damned hero. If your step-daddy brings the law down on us before I can cut you loose, I'll turn you over to him without even having to think hard."

He eased himself out of the sleeper and back into the cab of the truck without waiting for a reply, pulling the curtain closed behind him. And after a minute or two of indecision Cait started peeling off her still-damp clothing, wondering if he was watching her through some secret spy hole. Too tired to give a damn if he was.

She shouldn't complain, she reminded herself wearily. He might be one of the most reluctant knights in shining armor she was likely to meet, but he got the job done and that's what mattered. Whatever his problem was, it didn't have anything to do with her. Once they hit the nearest town and she could get to a bank, she was history.

Shay stretched out on the cab seat and rubbed his eyes with his hand, wondering how in hell he'd managed to mess up his life so thoroughly in such a short space of time. Jail, he found himself thinking disconsolately. That's where he was going to wind up, sure as hell, if Dalkquist put two and two together and figured out where his wayward daughter had gotten to.

Damn it, why couldn't he have just stayed out of it? He was no hero; he hadn't lied about that. He'd proved that with no shadow of a doubt with Nancy, especially at the end when things had been so bad for her. A hero would have been there. A hero wouldn't have crept off to the bar and crawled into the bottom of a bottle of whiskey and stayed there while his wife was dying.

He should have been there for her. The words, so familiar they were almost a catechism, ran through his mind, taunting him, and his stomach pulled into a tight, hard knot. He hadn't been there for her. Not when it had counted the most. She'd lain in that hospital bed and had called for him, and finally she'd died there, surrounded by strangers and machines and cold, sterile walls.

He poked around the tenderest memories as he might a sore tooth, almost relishing the pain. It was an old friend, with him every waking hour and as often as not following him into sleep. Idly he thought of the sealed bottle of whiskey tucked under the far edge of his mattress. It had been there for two years now, and there hadn't been a night in those two years that he hadn't taken it out and held it in his hands and stared at it, taunting himself with the peace it promised, the oblivion.

And the deeper oblivion of the other thing he had stashed under there, the Smith & Wesson. Two years, and he'd never found the courage to use either of them. It would be too easy that way. Too easy to forget. It didn't seem right, somehow, that Nancy should be dead and that he should be allowed to forget.

"Are you still there?"

The quiet voice, edged with nervousness, broke into his thoughts like a stone dropped into water and he started slightly. So complete had been his retreat into the past that for those few minutes he'd all but forgotten his unwanted passenger, and he swore under his breath as reality—*this* reality—intruded all too vividly.

"Yeah," he muttered unhappily. "Yeah, I'm still here."

His thermos and the bag of sandwiches that Betty had given him were still behind the seat, and he dug them out before slipping back into the sleeper.

It took him a disconcerted moment to equate the almost-pretty stranger sitting on his bed with the terrified creature who'd crawled into his rig no more than an hour ago, soaking wet and half frozen and telling anyone who'd listen that her stepfather was trying to murder her.

The clothes were too big for her although she'd done her best, rolling up the legs of the jeans and shoving the sweater sleeves up to free her hands. She was sitting cross-legged on his bed, trying to work damp knots out of her long dark hair with her fingers, and she glanced up as he came in, sparing him a faint smile. "You saved my life, and I don't even know your name."

The smile was fleeting, but real. For some reason, it made him take a second, longer look at her. Seeing her, really, for the first time—a person now, not just something running scared and frightened in the night. It was hard not to notice that she was damned attractive, for one thing. Cleaned up a little, she'd be a knockout with that flawless skin and those wide, dark-fringed eyes and that torrent of near-black hair falling around her like a curtain of silk.

This Caitlin Sawyer looked almost normal—if you didn't look too closely. If you didn't notice the ugly bruise on the side of her jaw, or the welts and bruises on her wrists and ankles or the hunted expression in her eyes.

As before, anger flirted through Shay. Something was wrong at Amber Hills. Even if she was messed up emotionally, even if she was in there receiving legitimate treatment, the bruises didn't fit. And if by some stretch of imagination they could explain them—if she'd turned violent and they'd had to restrain her, if she'd fallen against something and bruised her own face—that still didn't explain the sadistic satisfaction Crushank had obviously gotten from taunting her. It was a little too familiar, a little too... comfortable. As though it was a game they'd played before.

Finally he remembered she'd said something, and shook himself free of his troubling thoughts. "McKittrick. Shay McKittrick. Coffee?" Unscrewing the cap from the thermos, he poured her a generous mugful of still-hot coffee without waiting for her reply.

As the aroma of hot, strong coffee wafted around her, Cait lifted her head, still not entirely convinced she wasn't dreaming. She took the mug carefully, her hands still trembling so badly from cold and leftover fear, that she was afraid of spilling it. She wrapped both hands around it, as thankful for the warmth as the coffee itself, and lifted it to her mouth.

He watched her speculatively as she sipped the coffee, his eyes troubled. They were blue eyes, she noticed idly. Or maybe gray. And they didn't give much away about the thoughts ticking away behind them. A gambler's eyes, she found herself thinking, always tallying up the odds and thinking of a way out, even when he held a winning hand.

"You think I'm crazy, don't you?"

"Jury's out on that, as far as I'm concerned." He gave her an even, forthright look. "Although, for the record, are you?"

"No." It was just a whisper, and she shivered violently.

"I can live with that for now." He started rummaging under the end of the mattress, and when he drew his hand out he was holding a bottle of whiskey. It hadn't been opened, and he looked at it for a long, thoughtful moment. And then, as though making up his mind about something, he broke the seal and twisted the cap off, then reached over to pour a healthy splash of the liquor into her coffee.

She thought he'd pour some out for himself, but he capped the bottle again, tightly, and returned it to its hiding place as though wanting temptation out of reach. Which may have meant something, she thought wearily. Or may have meant nothing at all.

She took a sip of the doctored coffee and its heat started to seep through her almost at once, banishing the worst of the chills. God knew what was going to happen when it hit the mélange of drugs that were probably still floating around in her bloodstream, compliments of Angstrom and his cohorts, but at the moment just getting warm seemed more important.

"Here."

She looked up and stared disbelievingly at what he was holding. "Is . . . is that for me?"

"Turkey on whole wheat, by the look of it," he said mildly. "Lettuce, mayo, Lord knows what else."

She reached out almost hesitantly, wondering if the sandwich were some sort of whiskey- and drug-induced delusion that would vanish the instant she tried to touch it. But it stayed wonderfully whole when her fingers closed on it, and in the next instant she had a mouth full of bread and turkey and mayo and decided that if it was a delusion, she didn't even care.

McKittrick watched her for a moment, then stretched his legs out, back against the wall, one foot drawn up. He draped his arm across his upraised knee, looking very relaxed and at ease, if you didn't notice the watchfulness in his eyes, the hint of tension along the square jaw.

Which wasn't surprising, Cait thought. For all he knew, she could come at him with a razor the moment his back was turned. Or go into a screaming rage for no reason at all, or simply break down and beg to be taken back to Amber Hills.

It took courage to do what he'd done tonight. And trust. She had to be very careful not to give him any reason to regret bringing her with him. Or worse yet, any reason to think she was so unstable—or out-and-out deranged—that he called Dalkquist to come and take her off his hands.

She was all too aware of the picture she must have made in the café tonight, wild-eyed and pale, lank ropes of hair hanging around her face, feet bare, dressed in nothing but stolen hospital garb, babbling that someone was trying to kill her. Was aware of the picture she made now, a little drier and warmer and calmer, maybe, but no less desperate.

Very aware of him watching her, she concentrated on eating the huge sandwich, trying not to get crumbs on his bed or dribble mayo down the front of his sweater or do anything else that might annoy him enough to toss her out into the rain . . . or think she wasn't even competent enough to feed herself.

"I really appreciate your help," she said calmly, trying to sound rational and logical. And sane. "Not many—"

"As I said, you didn't give me a hell of a choice."

There was an undertone of irritation in his voice and Cait swallowed a mouthful of sandwich, wondering what he wanted from her: apology, explanation, both, neither? Fleetingly, she recalled what he'd said about jumping from the frying pan into the fire . . . wondered, slipping him a sidelong glance, if it was possible she really *was* in danger.

It would be ironic to escape certain death at Amber Hills only to fall victim to some deranged trucker who filled his lonely hours by systematically murdering any woman he could lure into his rig....

In spite of the situation, Cait had to smile around a mouthful of sandwich. More than likely he was probably wondering the same thing about her. What he'd seen of her so far would hardly inspire a man's confidence.

"Out of curiosity, where were you heading tonight?"

He asked it casually, as though the answer hardly mattered at all, and Cait shrugged, concentrating on licking a smear of butter from her finger. "Away. Just... away." It sounded crazy, she knew that the instant she said it. Which was the last thing she wanted.

"So you didn't have any kind of... plan."

"It..." She looked up at him bleakly. "I had an opening, and I took it. Frank—one of the orderlies—came in while I was asleep. He... he started touching me. And then he unstrapped my hands from the bed railing so he could..."

She drew in a deep, careful breath, aware that Shay had gone very still, his expression closed and private and hard. "I don't even remember what happened, exactly. He tried to pull my gown off and I kicked him and he stumbled back. There was something behind him, a footstool I think, and he tripped over it and fell and hit his head."

She looked at Shay evenly. "He went out like a light and I didn't take the time to come up with a *plan*. I just knew he'd given me an opening I might not get again, and I wasn't going to waste it. I stripped him, then tied him up and gagged him and dragged him into the closet. Then I put his clothes on and I ran... and I didn't stop running until I reached that café. And you know the rest."

Shay eased his breath out tightly. "This Frank..." he asked carefully. "Was he anything like Crushank?"

She shuddered, staring down at the sandwich. "Worse."

Rage blossomed like something white hot inside him and Shay fought it down, reminding himself that it might not even be the truth. She could be making it all up, deliberately manipulating him, his emotions. She could have misinterpreted the entire incident with Frank, seeing danger where none was intended. Hell, going by what Angstrom and Dalkquist claimed, she could have imagined the whole thing!

He stared at her, wishing her story—and she—were just a bad dream that would go away. Wishing he'd never stopped at that damned café in the first place. Wishing he didn't have a deep and persistent feeling that there was more to this than met the eye.

Swearing, he raked his fingers through his hair and hit her with a hard, impatient look. "Okay, honey, it's time you started talking. Just what kind of trouble have you got me in, anyway?"

She licked a smear of mayonnaise off her lower lip, frowning a little as she looked at the rest of the sandwich in her hand. Then, as though she'd lost her appetite, she set it aside. Taking a deep breath, she closed her eyes and rubbed her forehead with her fingers as though to rally her thoughts, then looked up at him with that same bleak expression. "It's a waste of time trying to explain it," she finally said in a dull voice, shoulders slumping. "No one else believes me. Why would you?"

"Try me."

She looked at him for a long, doubtful moment, then a ghost of a smile brushed her mouth, just a fleeting touch of wry humor that caught him by surprise. "Why not?" The smile widened slightly. "Do you want the unabridged version, or just the highlights?"

The smile did things to her eyes and mouth that he liked, and his thoughts went wandering suddenly into erotic directions they'd not been for a while, which surprised him even more.

Careful, McKittrick, he told himself. You're in enough trouble already. "The highlights. For now."

She nodded slowly, and the smile gradually faded until it was just a memory. Distracted, Shay wished he could think of something to say that would bring it back.

"The highlights are that my father died six years ago, and eight months later my mother married Brenton Dalkquist. Last April, he murdered her. And now he's trying to kill me."

"Why?"

"Because I know he killed her." She looked at him calmly. "And because I won't quit trying to prove it until he's in jail. So far he's managed to discredit me and everything I say by maintaining—with Angstrom's help—that I'm...emotionally unstable." She spat the words out, her eyes going hard. "Angstrom's telling people I'm angry with my mother for dying and that I'm transferring that anger onto Dalkquist—he jazzes it up with a lot of technical psychobabble, of course, but he manages to get the meassage across. Dalkquist plays the role of benevolent, concerned father, and I come across as the crazy stepdaughter."

Shay nodded, his mind worrying her words, trying to see what shook loose. "If that was working, why put you in Amber Hills?"

The smile was back, but bitter now. Angry. "He wants to be governor and he's not going to let anything—least of all me—get in his way. He's managed to discredit me with family friends, the lawyers, the police—everyone who counts. But he knows I won't give up. And there's always the chance that I'll dig up some piece of proof that will *make* people listen to me. Or that someone who doesn't want to see him in the governor's mansion will start taking me seriously just on the off chance they can dig up some dirt."

Put like that, her story was almost believable. Almost.

"And Angstrom? Where does he fit in?"

"I figure Dalkquist either just bought him off, or Angstrom owed him some kind of favor and this is payment."

"Seems to me it would be pretty hard to carry off a scam like this for any length of time."

Cait gave a snort. "Between them, Dalkquist and Angstrom know everyone worth knowing in this state. A lot of people owe their jobs to Dalkquist—they're not going to jeopardize their livelihoods by going against him. And Angstrom is a very big cheese in his circles. If he says someone is crazy, no one's going to put his career on the line by saying otherwise."

"What about the rest of the staff at the hospital? You'd think someone would have caught on by now."

"Angstrom is God at Amber Hills." She ran her fingers through her long, tangled hair. "It's privately funded. Having someone of Angstrom's stature on the board more or less guarantees the money will keep rolling in, so no one is going to make waves." She let the bitter smile touch her mouth again. "As I said, if Angstrom says I'm crazy, then I *am* crazy."

It *was* possible, Shay thought uneasily. "And you're saying all this started because Dalkquist murdered your mother."

"Yes." It was little more than a whisper, and a flash of raw pain crossed her face. "He..." She swallowed, looking down at her hands where they lay in her lap. "He married her because of the money, and—"

"What money?"

"My father was a very wealthy man—part of it family money, part from his own business. And then there was my mother's money." She looked up at him. "Her father was Simon Ivarson."

Shay gave an involuntary whistle of surprise. "Ivarson Oil?"

"As long as my mother controlled the money, he had to keep her alive. But when he finally managed to get the last of it transferred into holdings under his name..." She shrugged, toying with a small ragged tear in the knee of her borrowed jeans. "He didn't need her anymore. So he killed her."

The silence between them grew. Shay watched her finger the raveled tear, trying to convince himself that Angstrom was right and that she was in Amber Hills because she needed to be. That she'd transferred the anger, hurt and bewilderment she'd felt at her mother's death onto Dalkquist, convincing herself he was responsible because it somehow made her loss more bearable.

"It was partly my fault." She said it softly, and tears glimmered in her eyes as she lifted her head to look at Shay. "I'd been against the marriage right from the start, but after two years I got tired of trying to convince my mother he was using her and went to Italy to finish my degree. If only I'd *stayed* in California!" She hit her knee with her clenched fist, and the glimmer in her eyes dissolved and spilled into tears. "He couldn't do anything while I was there. So he waited until I was away, and he—" The last word was a sob and she bit it off fiercely.

Shay felt a little cold suddenly, his mind flickering unbidden to all those times he'd heard himself say those two same words: *If only*.

"What happened?" He asked it as much to distract himself as anything.

"According to the police reports, she lost control of her car and went off the road." Her eyes glittered again, but with anger this time. "My mother was a careful driver. There is no way—*no way*—that she'd have gone over that embankment. Not without help, anyway."

"It happens," Shay said mildly.

"Not this time." Her voice was hard. "The man who reported the accident to the police said her car was in Neutral when he found it, and that there were fresh scrapes on the rear bumper—as though another car had pushed it. But the official police report never mentioned either of those things. The officer who was first on the scene failed to produce his notes at the inquest, and his original accident report had somehow gone missing, so he testified from memory. And the medical examiner's report said she had high levels of a common sleeping pill in her bloodstream."

She lifted her head slightly, her chin set at an obstinate angle. "My mother was terrified of sleeping pills. She'd seen two of her friends get seriously messed up on them, and she wouldn't touch them. I remember right after Dad died, her doctor gave her a few just to get her through the first few nights. I was with her when she walked into the bathroom and washed them down the sink—she wouldn't even keep them in the house!"

"You said you were in Italy. . . ."

"I talked with her every week," she said with certainty. "She . . ." She lifted her hand, then let it fall back into her lap again, eyes filling. "She was very childlike at times. She seemed to need my approval—I guess the fact I hated Dalkquist so much made her even more sensitive to that. I was so against her marrying him, and when she went ahead and did it anyway. . ." She shrugged, wiping her cheek with the back of her hand. "Anyway, it's as though she wanted to make up for that. So she'd call me up for my advice before she did anything—we talked all the time. If she'd started taking sleeping pills, I'd have known about it."

Unless she was afraid of her daughter's disapproval, Shay thought.

"She told me he was trying to kill her."

It took Shay a split second to realize what she'd said. "She *told* you?" He leaned forward a little, looking at her intently.

"There had been a series of what she called 'funny little accidents'... the brakes on her car stopped working, she woke up one night and found the gas in the bedroom fireplace had been turned on but not lit, she was standing at a curb waiting for the light to change and someone shoved her out into traffic—that sort of thing."

"You told the police this?"

"They said she was... confused." She smiled faintly. "That's one of those generic catch-all phrases they use, like *emotionally disturbed.*" Then the smile faded and she took a deep breath and rubbed her forehead, frowning. "Angstrom says he'd been treating her for depression, which is a lie. He made it sound as though she'd been drinking too much and taking pills and imagining things."

"And you don't."

She glanced up, and for a moment the exhaustion glazing her eyes vanished and there was nothing in them but pure fury. "Brenton Dalkquist murdered my mother. And if he gets his hands on me, I'm going to be just as dead."

Chapter 3

Shay didn't say anything. It sounded crazy as hell, all of it. And yet...

And yet there were moments when he'd been listening to her that he could have sworn she was as lucid and logical—as *sane*—as he was.

He swore wearily and rubbed his face with his hand, late-day stubble scraping against his fingers. He should be in bed, he thought irritably. And if he'd resisted that uncharacteristic urge to play hero tonight, that's exactly where he'd be. Instead of sitting in his rig in a road side rest stop in the pelting rain listening to some crazy story about murder and kidnapping and God knows what else.

She was just sitting there, head bent forward slightly, long hair partly shielding her profile, hands in her lap. Then, as though shaking off her memories, she straightened slightly and scooped her hair off her face with one hand, turning to look at him with a weary, wry smile. "You don't believe me."

Shay didn't say anything right away. Wordlessly, he leaned across and picked up one of her hands and turned it toward the light, then pushed the sleeve of the sweater up past her elbow. The sharp focus of the small reading lamp made the ugly scars across her inner wrist and the bruised needle tracks on her arm stand out in stark relief.

"They gave me the drugs," she said quietly, making no effort to pull away. "And they made those cuts on my wrists to make it look as though I'd tried to kill myself."

"To explain why you'd been committed in the first place." He didn't bother trying to keep the skepticism out of his voice.

"To make it look as though I was suicidal. So when I was found dead of an overdose no one would be surprised. Or ask for an investigation."

For some reason, the quiet way she sat there bothered Shay more than the ragged scars on her wrists. He'd half expected her to be defensive, embarrassed, angry… instead, she simply waited for him to release her wrist, as though too tired and dispirited to even argue anymore.

"Hell," he muttered, dropping her wrist and pushing his fingers through his hair. "I don't know what your story *really* is, lady, but I know it's more damn trouble than I need. I told you I'd take you to the next town, and I will. But then you're on your own."

"Which is all I wanted in the first place," she reminded him with a slight edge to her voice. "It was your idea that I tell you about Dalkquist, not mine—I already knew it was a waste of time. No one else believes me. Why would you?"

"I didn't say I didn't believe you," Shay said mildly. "I'm just saying I don't give a damn."

Her shoulders seemed to slump slightly and Shay felt a pang of guilt at his brusqueness. But he shrugged it off. There was no point in giving her false hope, he told himself bitterly. He'd do this much for her—give her a head start and some dry clothes and safe refuge for the night—but that was it. He wasn't running a rescue service. And this particular rescue mission had trouble written all over it. The kind of trouble no man in his right mind took on if he didn't have to.

"You can bunk down in here for the night." He reached across and picked up one of the pillows and his leather jacket. "I'll sleep in the cab."

"Sleep?" She looked up, eyes wide and frightened. "But we can't sleep. We have to keep going. We've got to get—"

"It's late and I'm tired," Shay told her bluntly. "I'm hauling over a half million dollars' worth of computers, and it's not going to do them—or us—any damn good if I drive off the road." The fear in her eyes reminded him of something trapped, and he found himself thinking of Crushank.

"Look," he said more quietly, "we're safe here. As safe as it gets, anyway." He reached out and put his finger under her chin, lifting her face so she was looking at him. "If your stepfather's figured out you're with me, he'll have notified the State Police and given them a description of this rig—every patrol car on the road will be looking for us. It's even possible they'll have roadblocks up. We'll have a better chance of not being spotted if we just mosey along with the rest of the traffic in the morning."

She nodded after a moment, still looking uncertain and scared, but not particularly inclined to argue, as though she didn't like what he was saying, but trusted his judgment and was willing to go along with it.

Which—again—didn't fit the profile Dalkquist had painted of her as an irrational and wildly paranoid woman who was a danger to herself and anyone close to her.

None of it added up worth a damn, Shay told himself irritably. Her whole story had more loose ends than a cut-rate retread, yet there was something about it…something about her…

Swearing under his breath, he shoved his hand under the mattress and pulled out the small handgun, his stomach knotting slightly at the sight of it. The chamber was empty—he knew himself too damned well to risk keeping it loaded—and he had to rummage through one of the tiny storage lockers for the box of ammunition. It fit his hand just a little too comfortably and he idly thought of the hours he'd sat here with it, toying with the idea of just ending it once and for all.

And hadn't. So far, anyway. Although he couldn't have said whether it was cowardice or bravery that had kept him from pulling the trigger.

He became aware suddenly that Cait was looking at the gun with an odd expression on her face. Before he could say anything, she looked up to meet his gaze, a faint, bitter smile touching her mouth. "You don't need that, Mr. Mc-Kittrick. I may be straitjacket material, but I'm not dangerous."

"You wouldn't be in my truck if I thought you were," he told her bluntly. "And it's not you I'm worried about."

She looked startled, and then, for just a moment, the veil of exhaustion and caution in her eyes gave way to gratitude. For what, he wasn't sure—maybe just trusting her even that much—but it made the knot in his belly unravel, and for a moment or two the night seemed to recede just a little. And he found himself thinking that even glazed with exhaustion and drugs and despair, she had the most expressive eyes he'd ever seen.

And beautiful, he mused. Damned beautiful.

It was only when she started to look a bit uneasy that he realized he was still staring at her, and he drew away from her casually, wondering how they'd wound up sitting so close. Wondered, too, just when he'd stopped thinking of her as an abstract irritant and had started thinking of her as a real and extremely attractive woman.

Or why he hadn't noticed until now how graphically intimate the sleeper was, all bed and nothing else, its purpose
glaringly enhanced by the rumpled blanket and pillow beside them. Or why he was noticing *that* at all, come to think
of it, his mind flirting with an idle idea or two that were
anything but heroic.

Two years, he thought remotely. Nan had been dead now
for two years....

He caught the rest of his strangely wayward thoughts and
reined them in, showing Cait how to turn off the small
reading lamp. Then, muttering a terse good-night, he took
the pillow and a spare blanket and retreated.

He settled himself none too comfortably on the seat of the
cab, pulling his heavy leather jacket over himself for warmth
and swearing under his breath as he gave his knee a crack on
the steering wheel.

He was crazy, he told himself as he shoved the pillow under his head and gave it an angry punch. He'd be asleep in
a real bed in a warm motel room right now if he hadn't suc-
cumbed to a sudden urge to play hero.

An urge he still didn't fully understand. Although part of
it had to do with Crushank, he knew that. And part of it had
more to do with that arrogant, self-assured bastard Angstrom than he liked to admit. There'd been something about
him that was just a little too reminiscent of Nancy's doctor
for Shay's taste. He had been just as slick and impatient and
convinced of his own infallibility.

And maybe part of it had to do with Cait Sawyer herself—hell, you couldn't help but admire her, standing up to
Angstrom, Dalkquist and the California Highway Patrol
with nothing but a steak knife and more brass than he'd seen
in a long time.

Rolling onto his back, he managed to bang his shin on the
wheel and he whispered a rough oath, trying not to listen to
the sounds coming from the sleeper. The sound of clothes

coming off, of soft breathing. She was silhouetted against the curtain and he watched her pull the sweater over her head, the curves of her breasts clearly outlined against the light behind her as she lifted her arms. Then he watched as she rose onto her knees and unzipped the borrowed jeans and eased them over her hips and started wriggling out of them—

Gritting his teeth, he rolled onto his side, trying not to hear the sound of her wriggling into the sleeping bag—*his* sleeping bag—and pulling the zipper closed.

How the hell had he gotten himself into this mess? He should have turned her over to that cop when he'd first found her in the truck. The whole thing would have been long behind him by now and he'd have nothing on his mind but delivering those damn computers and picking up the load of plywood that would be waiting for him at the warehouse. A quick haul up to Seattle, then across to Spokane with a flatbed loaded to the limit with plywood. From there to Butte, then maybe on to Denver.

His whole life was just a road map and he liked it that way. No responsibilities beyond getting his freight to its destination on time, no one else to worry about, no one expecting things he didn't have to give. Just himself, his rig and an open road.

Until he'd screwed it up trying to help a woman he'd never seen before and would never see again.

For that matter, he might not be helping her at all. What the hell gave him the idea that he was qualified to know if she was telling the truth or not—or if the truth she believed even existed? Maybe she was simply one of those people who lived in her own confused version of reality. Maybe she'd been in therapy for most of her life and he'd managed to set her treatment back years in the span of one night. Maybe she did this all the time, running away and snaring some unsuspecting stranger into "helping" her, the story

changing when and how it suited her. Maybe he'd be doing
her a favor if he called Amber Hills in the morning and told
Angstrom where he could find her. Maybe... Hell, there
were a thousand maybes!

And none of it mattered, when you got right down to it.
Because he was getting rid of her in the morning. By noon
tomorrow, Cait Sawyer was going to be nothing but a
memory.

They were waiting for her when she finally fell asleep:
Dalkquist, Angstrom, Frank, Crushank...all of them,
smiling. It was no use, those cold smiles seemed to say. She
couldn't run far enough or fast enough to elude them for
long. No one believed her. No one would help her. She was
alone and defenseless, and she was theirs.

It was a scream that woke Shay, a high sound of sheer
terror that snapped him up out of sleep before he even fully
understood what it was. He sat bolt upright, heart hammering, trying to figure out where the hell he was and why
he was holding a gun. Then he figured out the *where* and
recalled the *why,* but still couldn't remember reaching under the truck seat for the gun. And yet he must have grabbed
it as he'd been coming out of sleep, reacting on pure instinct before his brain had even had time to separate reality
from dream.

His first thought was that they'd been discovered—but
the black-velvet night around them was broken only by the
moan of the wind and the hammering sound of rain on the
cab. And then he heard her again, whimpering this time, her
voice soft with fear as she pleaded with someone to let her
go.

He was in the sleeper in the next instant, gun cocked, not
knowing how anyone could have gotten past him but
knowing only that someone *was* there, threatening her,

frightening her ... and realizing then that it wasn't anyone at all. Anyone real, that is. Although her fear, even in sleep, was real enough. She was thrashing around now, fighting whoever was there in her nightmare with her, one arm up as though to protect herself from a blow.

He reached through and put the gun in the cab, not wanting her to wake up and see it unexpectedly, then sat gently beside her. "Cait ..."

"No!" She recoiled back against the pillow. "No more!"

"Cait ... hey, it's okay. You're okay...."

She whimpered again and rolled onto her side, trying to crawl away from the sound of his voice, and Shay felt dull anger burn through him at whoever had done this to her.

"Cait ..." He gently caught her shoulder. "Wake up, Cait. It's just a dream."

"No!" She wrenched back and around and in the next instant she was sitting up and fighting, clawing and pummeling at him as she tried to untangle herself from the sleeping bag and get away.

Shay swore as one of her fists caught his unprotected cheek and he caught both her hands and held them, giving her a shake. "Cait! Wake up. Wake up!"

And then in the next breath she was awake, her eyes wide and filled with terror.

"Cait, it's just me—it's Shay."

She stared at him uncomprehendingly, panting slightly, trying to twist her wrists out of his grip.

"Cait!"

She blinked. "It ... Dalkquist ... he was here!"

"No one was here. You were just dreaming, Cait."

"No, he was here! I saw him! H-he tried to grab me and—"

"He's not here, Cait." Shay pulled her toward him without really thinking about what he was doing until he had his arms around her. She was all stiff and angular and unyielding, and he could feel her heart hammering against his chest like a terrified bird. "Relax, Cait—it's over. It was just a nightmare. No one's here but me."

"But I—I saw him," she protested thinly, starting to shiver now. "I saw him."

"I know you did. But he wasn't real, Cait. He wasn't real."

He could feel her disbelief like a tangible thing, as tangible as the fear still coursing through her. Her breath was warm and rapid against the hollow of his throat and she nestled more deeply into the sheltering curve of his arms as though seeking warmth and safety.

"It . . . I saw him so clearly, just standing there l-looking down at me."

"No one's here but me," Shay murmured against the top of her head. "Dalkquist's not going to hurt you again."

"You can't stop him," she whispered brokenly, her voice little more than a sob. "He killed her. He killed my mother. And he's going to kill me. . . ."

"He's not going to get anywhere near you," Shay said with flat certainty. "That's a promise, Cait."

She shivered again and Shay tightened his arms around her, starting to realize a little uneasily that she was all but naked, dressed only in briefs and his light cotton T-shirt. And she wasn't wearing a damned thing under it, either, that was pretty obvious. Her small firm breasts were round and warm, and he could feel the imprint of her nipples against his chest as she huddled against him.

Bad idea, noticing that. She moved just then, just a slight shift of her body that made him grit his teeth, and he was unsettled to realize he was becoming vitally aroused, his own body responding instinctively to the unspoken promise in hers.

Real bad idea.

"I think," he said softly, "that I'd better go. You'll sleep fine now."

"No!" She clutched the front of his shirt. "No, please . . . don't go. Not yet."

"Cait . . ."

"Please." It was just a warm breath of sound against his throat and Shay felt his belly muscles pull tight as she shifted again, turning more fully toward him. "Please . . ."

"For a couple of minutes," he managed to whisper hoarsely, clenching his teeth so tightly they ached.

Her breath curled around the side of his neck like warm smoke and he tried not to think about that, about the way she felt in his arms, about the way her skin smelled. Her long hair hung around her like a curtain, still scented of rainwater, and he tried not to think of that, either, the feel of it incredibly erotic on his bare arms.

She was relaxed now, sitting quietly within the curve of his arms and body, and he could feel the slow rhythm of her breathing, her heartbeat. He could hear her swallow, felt more than heard her take a deep, almost experimental breath. And then, incredibly, felt the touch of her fingers on his face.

And without even thinking of what he was doing, he turned his head slightly and captured her finger in his mouth, felt her lift her head to look at him, knew with a certainty more deep than he'd ever felt before that things were suddenly getting out of hand. It was impossible, of course—maybe *he* was asleep.

But no . . . he sucked on the delicate, exploring finger and felt his pulse starting to race, heard her breathing catch very slightly as she moved against him, deliberately this time, lifting up until her mouth was against his cheek, his mouth . . .

She drew her finger from between his lips and he turned his head slightly and her mouth was there, lips parted, the nectar of her breath warm against his. Tentatively, he kissed her, still convinced he was indulging in an erotic, forbidden dream; except the taste of her was too real, the way she shivered slightly as he settled his mouth over hers too vivid for a mere dream.

She whimpered something against his mouth and Shay put his hands on her shoulders and pulled her against him, wondering in a dim, shocked way what the hell he was doing ... what she was doing....

It was insane, impossible. He tried to pull away and found he couldn't. Tried to convince himself that it wasn't right, that she was troubled and frightened and neither of them was reacting normally, and found he didn't care.

And then suddenly he was pulling the T-shirt over her head and she was naked in his hands, whimpering his name against his mouth as he filled his hands with her breasts, caressing them, teasing them, running his hands up and down the long, smooth sweep of her back. She arched and moaned softly and he kissed her again, tasting the salt of tears, and tried one last desperate time to stop whatever madness was happening before it was too late.

But then suddenly it *was* too late and he was shrugging out of his shirt and jeans, the blood pounding in his ears like pagan drums, and she was touching him and whispering to him and he was losing it....

Her briefs had disappeared without his having any memory of removing them, and when he touched her she gave a broken sob of encouragement and he realized with dim surprise that she was as ready as he was, as slippery and welcoming as hot wet silk, and as he teased her and explored her and readied her she gave a soft needful cry that echoed his own groan.

Somehow, he managed to reach over her to fumble around in the small storage locker until he found the package of contraceptives, silently thanking the jokester who'd tossed them into the cab of his truck a couple of months ago with an earthy suggestion that it was time he found himself a woman. He'd nearly thrown them out, breathed a silent prayer of thanks now that he hadn't. And in the next heartbeat he was pressing himself between Cait's long, slender thighs and any last-minute hopes he'd had of stopping before he got this far were long gone.

She gave one softly indrawn breath, and then he was moving downward and inward and was through, sinking into her warmth, too deep, too fast, too urgent, feeling her shiver and knowing he hadn't a hope in hell itself of holding back to wait for her. It had been too long and he was too far-gone and she was sweet-scented and soft as velvet and just the taste of her mouth and the feel of her taut, trembling thighs tightening on his was enough to take him that final, plunging distance.

It lasted long enough and yet no time at all, and he sank against her, trembling and panting, the pounding in his temples like the pounding of heavy surf. He continued to move gently within her even after he was spent, not wanting the impossible magic to end…hoping against hope that he had somehow managed to please her even while knowing he couldn't have.

And yet she seemed content, panting against his throat as though she'd been running, her slender body dewed lightly with perspiration. Her legs were wrapped around his and he relaxed against her, supporting himself on his forearms so as not to crush her, and lay there silent and confused in the musky darkness, afraid to move in case he awoke and discovered it wasn't a dream at all, but reality.

After a long while, he pulled the sleeping bag up around them both, closing out the chill, and settled against her, still cradling her in his arms. He found himself thinking he should say something to her, but had no idea what. And so he said nothing at all, just lying there in the still darkness

holding her and listening to her breathing, feeling the soft
ness of her skin, the slow, steady thump of her heart as it
beat in counterpoint to his.

He must have slept, because he awoke sometime later with
a start, discovering that Cait, too, was awake, lying quietly
in his arms. He lay there, thinking he should get up and go
back to his rough bed in the cab, but he never did get around
to it. And after a moment he lowered his mouth to her
again, and then it was too late anyway.

They made love in silence, and this time he made it last a
long, long time, until, finally, he drew a soft sob of sound
from her, half protest and half pleasure. And as he col
lapsed panting into her arms a few minutes later, he thought
with grim amusement that for a man who'd sworn to keep
trouble to a minimum tonight, he'd messed up in a singu
larly spectacular fashion.

He eased himself out of the sweet tangle of her arms
sometime just after sunrise and left her sleeping, pausing to
gaze down at her thoughtfully. Seeing her lying there in the
half-light filtering through the cab curtain, dark hair spilled
across the pillow, her face relaxed, almost serene, it was
hard to believe she was the same wild-eyed, knife-yielding
woman who'd stumbled out of the storm and into the cab
last night.

Harder to believe he barely knew her name, knew noth
ing about her—nothing he could swear was true, anyway—
and yet had made love to her, the last time no more than an
hour ago. Had touched and explored and caressed and
tasted and pleasured...still had the taste of her in his mouth,
could still feel the perfumed damp of her naked skin on
his...

Swearing under his breath, he wheeled away and ducked
into the cab of the truck, sliding a little stiffly behind the
wheel and sitting there staring out into the cold dawn, feel
ing chilled and oddly empty.

Deliberately, he thought of Nancy. Of the last time they'd made love. She'd been in pain, although he hadn't known that until much later. At the time, all he'd known was that it had been sweet and gentle and exquisitely tender, and that they'd both known without admitting it that it was probably the last time. It had been good for her—he'd made certain of that—but bittersweet, too. And when it was over he hadn't been able to tell if the tears on his lips had been hers or his own.

Although the heart he'd felt breaking had definitely been his, he recalled numbly. He'd lain with her cradled in his arms for hours that afternoon, trying to convince himself that the most recent diagnosis had surely been wrong, that doctors made mistakes, that lab tests got mixed up, that she was too healthy and vibrant and just too damned *alive* to die.

But the diagnosis hadn't been wrong, the doctors hadn't made a mistake. And a few months later Nancy was dead and he was alone, and that's all they wrote, Jack.

Which didn't have a damned thing to do with the woman lying asleep in his sleeper behind him, Shay reminded himself coldly. Those few fevered hours they'd spent in each other's arms hadn't been about love, or even about sex. They'd been about need and want, about give and take, about reaching out for someone in the darkness and holding the terrors of the night at bay with the more urgent demands of the body.

And it had worked for both of them. Cait's nightmare hadn't returned and she'd slept curled up against him as if she belonged there, stirring once or twice to murmur something in her sleep but never fully waking. He, too, had slept without dreaming. For the first time in over two years. And when he'd awakened this morning, it had been out of physical desire, his body reacting to the naked woman in his arms before he'd even shaken himself free of sleep.

And he'd found himself making love to her that last time
the same way, more asleep than awake, not saying anything, not even kissing her. She'd drawn in a startled little
breath as he'd pulled her to him and had slipped deeply inside her, as though totally caught by surprise, and he'd
wondered for an uneasy moment if she'd awakened without remembering him or any of what had happened between them.

But she'd shuddered suddenly and had moaned very
softly, her body softening, melting, opening around him
and they'd made love with a silent, almost desperate urgency, breaths mingled, slippery bodies straining and moving with unrestrained need until she'd given a low, breathless
sound of surprise and her thighs had clasped his convulsively as she'd arched under him, head falling back, eyes
tightly closed.

And in that heartbeat of time, it had become suddenly
vividly real. Until then it had been more erotic fantasy than
reality, just warm female need in the darkness without even
a distinct face to give it form. But in partial daylight, seeing
her sleek golden body taut beneath his, upthrust breasts lush
and dark-tipped, the muscles in her belly rippling as she
moved her hips rhythmically against his . . .

It had been real and vital and erotic and he'd growled her
name then and had lifted onto his braced forearms and had
driven himself against her again and again, relishing the
silken, wet feel of her all around him, the hot musky scent
of sex, the sound of her breathless little moans. He'd shut
out past and future and had concentrated only on the hot
urgent *now,* making it real, reveling in it, slaking himself.
And, all too soon, it had been over.

Teeth gritted a little at the suddenly too-vivid memories,
Shay scraped his fingers through his unruly hair, then dug
the keys out of the pocket of his jeans. Last night had
been . . . hell, he didn't even know what it had been. Some

thing unexpected and wild and the stuff every man's fantasies were made of. But fantasies—even ones as good as this one—came to an end. And only fools tried to pretend they didn't.

Swearing again, he jammed the key in the ignition and gave it a twist, suddenly angry for no reason he could think of. The engine snorted and snuffled, then caught with a powerful, smoky roar that settled into a smooth rumble that vibrated right through to the bone, as comforting and familiar as the voice of an old friend.

It seemed to relax him slightly and he blew a tight breath between his teeth, feeling better now that he was underway. This at least was something he understood. Something he had control over. He'd get this load of computers to Eugene before noon, pick up the plywood that was waiting for him and be back on the road by three, putting fast, hard miles between him and last night.

And Cait Sawyer?

The question caught him unawares, and he muttered a rough curse as he wheeled the rig out of the rest stop and into the acceleration lane. There was no traffic and he swung out onto the highway, running the truck up through its gears as it picked up speed. Cait Sawyer would be just fine. She was smart and shrewd and had courage to burn . . . and last night didn't change anything.

No ties, he told himself clinically. He didn't owe her a thing beyond getting her to the next town safely. He'd promised her that much; he wouldn't go back on his word now.

But that didn't keep his mind from wandering all over the place for the next hour or so, until, more in frustration than hunger, he pulled into a big roadside restaurant. As he parked his rig between a white Freightliner cab-over and a metallic blue tanker with Canadian plates, he wondered if

Dalkquist had figured out yet how his prey had eluded him. He hadn't heard anything on the CB, but that didn't mean anything. Every cop in five states could be looking for his silver-and-black rig—the fact he hadn't been intercepted before this might be no more than blind luck.

In the restaurant, he gave his thermos to the waitress, then ordered a couple of muffins to go. If he'd been on his own he'd have stopped for a proper breakfast, but he couldn't risk bringing Cait inside and he didn't like leaving her in the truck by herself any longer than necessary. Not that he thought she'd do something reckless, but the longer they stayed in one place, the more dangerous it was. He was taking enough of a risk stopping like this, even with half a dozen other rigs outside acting as camouflage.

To his relief, the waitress was too busy trading hostilities with the cook to pay more than passing attention to him, and as he waved off the change, he doubted she'd remember him five minutes from now. He paused long enough to shove a handful of creamers and sugar packets in his jacket pocket, then pushed open the door and strode across the parking lot, gravel crunching underfoot.

It was still overcast and cold and he glanced at the brooding sky assessingly, wondering if he was going to hit snow before the day was out. Wondering, too, if the black car that had parked in front of the restaurant while he'd been inside belonged to Dalkquist. Or if the guy in the tweed jacket standing beside the telephone booth, looking cold and annoyed, was looking for Cait.

He pulled the door to the cab open and swung up into the driver's seat, pausing to tuck the thermos into its customary niche and toss the bag of muffins onto the other seat. He was just going to slide the key into the ignition and get underway when it occurred to him that he should check to see if Cait was awake yet. The restaurant facilities were hardly first-class, but he had an extra toothbrush and a clean towel he could lend her if she wanted to freshen up a bit.

He leaned across and pushed the curtain to the sleeper aside—and swore in surprise. It was empty.

Chapter 4

His own reaction surprised him even more: he was out of the truck in the next heartbeat, gut knotted, scanning the parking lot for some sign of her.

The black car was still in front of the restaurant, tinted windows secretive and mocking, and he gave it a hard stare. California plates.

It may mean nothing, he reminded himself. Hell, maybe she'd just decided she didn't want to face him this morning and had taken off. He glanced at the handful of big transports parked behind him. She could be hiding in any one of them. Or maybe she'd already caught a ride and was ten minutes in either direction, glad to be rid of him.

He should be relieved, he told himself angrily. Damn it, she was nothing but trouble—he should be *glad* she was gone.

"Hey, buddy—you lookin' for your gal?"

The voice made Shay turn on one heel, eyes narrowing. The trucker looked vaguely familiar, although Shay didn't

know his name. He was a big man, not too tall, but solid
and barrel-chested, with meaty shoulders and a benign,
friendly expression at odds with the scarred fists and fighter's stance.

He turned his head and spat a stream of tobacco juice into
a nearby pot of flowers. "Seen her head for the Ladies' a
few minutes back." He nodded toward the rear of the service garage attached to the restaurant. "Couple other guys
noticed, too."

Shay's gut gave a sharp twist. "Other guys? What other
guys?"

Heavy shoulders lifted indolently under red plaid. "Came
in a few minutes ago, while you were inside. Looking at all
the rigs, askin' questions."

Swearing under his breath, Shay gave the man a nod of
thanks and headed for the washrooms at a fast lope. It may
have been nothing, just two strangers asking directions or
checking out road conditions or looking for someone they
knew. Odds were it was nothing.

The door to the ladies' washroom was closed and Shay
knocked on it loudly. "Cait? Are you in there? It's me—
Shay." Silence answered him. He thought he heard water
running but couldn't be sure. "Cait? You okay?"

Still no answer. He rapped on the door again, then tried
the knob. It turned in his hand and he pushed the door
open.

It was dim inside, lit only by two windows high on the far
wall, and it took a moment for his eyes to adjust enough for
him to see that the figure standing by the vanity and sink was
indeed Cait. And another moment to realize she was more
naked than not, wearing only her white cotton briefs and a
startled look.

She was standing on a makeshift bath mat of paper towels and was giving herself a rough sponge bath with what he
recognized as one of his towels. Her skin shone like satin

where it was still wet and he found himself unable to take his eyes off her for a moment, his mouth going suddenly dry.

Her breasts were small and perfect, nipples pebbled as the sudden draft from the open door hit her, and he let his gaze slide over them, down to the sleek indentation of her midrift and waist, the taut, flat belly, remembering . . .

She recovered first. Calmly she picked up the towel lying on the vanity and held it against herself. "Sorry. I thought I'd locked the door."

"It . . . uh . . . didn't catch. I guess." Shay licked his lips, drawing in a careful breath. Her eyes locked with his and for a heartbeat he knew she was thinking the same thing he was: that they'd made love, had touched and tasted and caressed and yet, for all that, were still strangers.

There was something strangely erotic about it and he could feel the awareness between them grow, the unspoken recognition that passes between a woman and the man who has touched and satisfied her, has cleaved her flesh with his in that ultimate act of possession, has heard her soft intimate outcry of pleasure. The room seemed suddenly filled with it—and with her—and for one impossible moment, Shay felt himself responding.

He'd actually taken a step toward her before he caught himself. Her eyes widened very slightly and something shifted in them. Sexual awareness turned, suddenly, to self-consciousness, and just like that the moment crumbled and vanished.

Easing a taut breath between clenched teeth, Shay eased his weight back, uncomfortably aroused and knowing by the way she kept her eyes averted that she knew it. It irritated him, his body's response a betrayal somehow, and he glowered at her, as though by turning desire into anger he could somehow undo what had already been done.

"I should have been on the road five minutes ago," he growled ungraciously. "You're costing me time, lady. Get a move on, or find a ride with someone else."

She turned her head and gave him a cool look. "I would have been dressed and back in the truck by now if you hadn't come crashing in here looking for me."

Shay had his mouth half open to tell her about the men he'd thought might be looking for her, then closed it again. The last damned thing he needed was to have her think he was worried about her. "Just get a move on," he barked, turning on one heel. She may have said something under her breath, but Shay didn't bother asking her to repeat it, pulling the door open and stepping out into the cold morning air without looking around.

They were waiting for him. Two of them, one heavyset and solid, the other tall and pale with narrow cold eyes and a thin smile. Shay didn't say anything. He just leaned against the wall by the door, arms crossed, and smiled benignly. " 'Morning."

"You always hang out in the ladies' washroom?" The taller of the two smirked a little.

"Not as a rule," Shay said calmly. "What about you?"

"Is she in there?"

"Is who in there?"

"Look, buddy," the taller one said softly, "this isn't—"

"Mr. Dalkquist wants her back," the other man put in with a friendly looking smile. "We understand what happened, McKittrick. She got in your truck, she soft-soaped you into believing that crazy story of hers about her mother, you thought you were doing the right thing by giving her a ride—hey, it's understandable. And Mr. Dalkquist says he won't press charges. He doesn't want any trouble at all, as a matter of fact. He simply wants his daughter to come home and continue her treatment."

"Charges?" Shay lifted a questioning eyebrow. "Last time I looked, this was a reasonably free country. If Dalkquist's daughter wants to sign herself out of Amber Hills and hitch a ride to Oregon, that's her business."

"No, Mr. McKittrick, that's *our* business." He smiled more widely as he said it, his eyes as cold as agate. The taller man flexed his shoulders and shifted his weight slightly. "You see, Miss Sawyer isn't responsible for her actions. Her father booked her into Amber Hills because of her drug dependency and severe emotional problems. You had no way of knowing that, of course, so—at the moment—you're innocent of any wrongdoing." He paused to let the words sink in. "But try and stop us from taking her back, McKittrick, and we'll run you over."

"As I see it, what you're doing is kidnapping," the tall man put in companionably. "That's pretty heavy stuff, McKittrick. So why don't you just walk back to your rig and forget you ever saw Cait Sawyer. She's just using you. No need for you to ruin your life because some nut case decides to—"

The door opened behind Shay just then and before he could bark a warning, Cait had stepped out, towel and soap in hand. She stopped dead when she saw the two men and he could hear her suck in a startled breath.

"Get back inside, Cait," he said quietly, not taking his eyes off his opponents. "And lock the door."

"Miss Sawyer, your father sent us to bring you back to—"

"Dalkquist is not my father, and if you think I'm going anywhere with you, you can both go to hell."

The taller one took a step closer, eyes narrowing. "Look, you little bitch, you're coming with us whether—"

"Back off." The two words snapped through the air like a bullwhip and Shay shrugged away from the wall, balancing himself on the balls of his feet, muscles tightening across s shoulders as he clenched his fists. "Unless she says the ord, you're not taking her anywhere. Cait? Do you want go back with these two men?"

"No."

Her voice was steady, but Shay could hear the fear in it. e shrugged and smiled at the heavyset man. "Sorry. You ard the lady."

"Get the hell out of the way, McKittrick," he grated, fists nching as he stepped forward. "Cross us, and you're in world of trouble. You have no idea what you're messing ith."

"I have a good enough idea," Shay said evenly. "Now ck off, or—"

"You go back and tell him he's not going to keep me iet," Cait said with quiet savagery, stepping by Shay to ce the man. "I'm going to prove he murdered my mother. e's—"

The taller man took a step toward her and Shay moved tween them, pushing Cait behind him. "I said 'back f'!"

"You're dead meat, McKittrick," the man said softly. 'm going to—"

"You having some kind of trouble over here?" The cker Shay had spoken with earlier appeared around the rner suddenly, looking very large and very solid.

So did the tire iron in his right hand. And so did the three her men who stepped from around the corner behind him, e carrying a short length of chain, another balancing what oked like a baseball bat, the third unarmed except for a ir of scarred fists the size of coal scoops.

"No trouble," Shay said calmly. "These gentlemen ought the young woman behind me wanted to go back to alifornia, that's all. But she doesn't. So they were just ving. Isn't that right, fellas?"

"We *are* taking her back with us, McKittrick," th
heavier of the two said, taking a folded piece of paper fror
the inner pocket of his jacket. "This is signed by Dr. An
strom, Chief Psychiatrist at Amber Hills Care Center, ar
it authorizes us to—"

"What about you, little lady?" The trucker turned h
head to fire a stream of tobacco juice into a patch of da
delions, his eyes never leaving Cait. "Seems to me you ha
a say in this."

"My stepfather sent them after me," Cait said quietly.

"And McKittrick? He helpin', or gettin' in the way?"

"Helping." She swallowed, looking cornered and scare
"My stepfather is trying to—" She stopped, glancing
Shay. Then, suddenly, she gave him a sweet, shy smi
"Shay and I are getting married," she declared a litt
breathlessly. "My stepfather's trying to stop it, you see, :
we decided to run away and—"

"That's a damned lie," the heavyset man said imp
tiently. "She's—"

"McKittrick, why don't you and your little gal get in yo
truck and head on out?" The trucker smiled beatifically.
think your two friends here are going to be busy for a whi
Got four flat tires on that big car, for one thing. And a co
pla busted headlights."

"There's nothing wrong with my car," the taller m
snapped.

"Well, sure there is," the trucker told him gently. "A
four tires flatter'n hell—strangest thing I ever did see. Ai
that right, Billy?"

The trucker with the bat just grinned. "Can't say as I s;
it myself, Sonny. Maybe I'll just go around front right n
and check."

"And take a look at them headlights, too, hear?"

"Headlights, too."

"You touch my car, you—"

"Hey, now," the man with the chain said quietly. "You just take it easy. Wouldn't want anyone getting hurt, would we?" He glanced at Shay. "Better hit the road, friend. Four flats ain't goin' to keep these gents away from a phone. And I expect if her step-daddy sent these two after her, he can send others."

"I owe you," Shay said, slapping the man's shoulder. "Come on, honey—we've got a wedding to get to." Grabbing Cait by the hand, he pulled her past the men and headed for the parking lot at a run.

He pulled the truck door open and, settling his hands around Cait's slender waist, lifted her up into the cab and gave her an unceremonious shove inside, then slammed the door behind her. He swung up into the driver's seat a moment later, giving her an appraising glance as he stabbed the key into the ignition. "You can think damn fast on your feet, I'll say that much for you. Although I could have done without the marriage bit."

"It worked, didn't it?" Cait's heart was still jackhammering against her ribs and she reached up and shoved a handful of tangled hair back from her face, trembling slightly. Close. Too close. If Shay hadn't been there...

"For the time being." He turned the key and the engine roared to life, belching smoke, the whole truck vibrating. "Did you know those two?"

"No." She glanced at Shay speculatively. "You knew they were around, didn't you? That's why you came storming into the washroom—to see if I was all right." He didn't say anything, apparently intent on threading the big truck and its trailer through the parking lot. "Did they believe us? Your friends, I mean?"

"I never saw any of those guys before in my life," Shay growled without looking at her. "And they believed as much as they needed to."

"I don't understand."

"They may have believed you, but it wouldn't have mattered if they hadn't. You were with me, that's what counted. And it didn't matter what our story was. They saw a fellow trucker in trouble and they gave him a hand, that's all."

Cait smiled faintly. "So, I've fallen into a brotherhood of heroes, have I?"

"I already told you I'm no damn hero."

"So you keep reminding me." Again, a hint of amusement lifted her mouth. "Although I'm curious why you call your rig Hell on Wheels."

His eyes may have narrowed slightly as he maneuvered the truck toward the exit. "It was my wife's idea."

It startled Cait so badly, she simply stared at him, fleetingly thinking of waking up and finding herself in his strong arms last night. Of how, without even knowing how or why it was happening, they'd made love.

"Wife? You're married?" She heard the faint accusation in her voice.

So did he. He turned his head and gave her a hard stare. "I was."

"Oh." She glanced thoughtfully at him, surprised that it made a difference. She hadn't given it any thought at all last night. Hadn't given thought to *anything* last night. Except being with him. Feeling his arms around her, holding out the night. "Divorced?"

"She died."

Cait winced slightly. "I'm sorry."

"So am I." He bit the words out, warning that she'd gone too far already.

She slipped him another sidelong glance. He was staring out the windshield as he turned the truck onto the acceleration ramp and then out onto the highway, his profile as hard-edged as an effigy cut from stone, jaw muscles tensed, eyes narrowed slightly. It was the face of a man used to doing things his way, stubborn, a little hostile, unbending.

Was he always like this, she found herself wondering. Or was he just reacting to her—reacting to finding her unexpectedly in his life, his bed, his thoughts? And who was he, this tall wide-shouldered man who'd stood face-to-face with Dalkquist and Angstrom, had put himself in peril to spirit her away from Amber Hills, had loved her last night with such gentleness and skill?

The original mystery man, this Shay McKittrick. All hard angles and rough edges, with hot sullen eyes and a magician's touch.

She thought of last night, the images flickering through her mind like a videotape on fast forward. She remembered dreaming...a frightening dream filled with threat and fear. And then Shay had been there and she'd clung to him as though drowning, terrified that if he let her go she'd fall back into the nightmare and never resurface.

And he hadn't let her go, had lain beside her in the darkness, with her listening to the drum sound of the rain above them, and then...

And then? Cait managed a grim smile. She didn't know what had happened then. Except that they'd turned to each other like two desperate, lost souls and had made love as though it was the only thing that could save them.

Although love hadn't had much to do with it. It hadn't been about love or even sex, but about needing another's warmth in the cold night, about holding off the demons for just a little while through the magic of another's touch, about just being *alive*.

He'd been gone when she wakened in the morning, and she'd lain there wondering if she'd dreamt that, too. But the sleeping bag had been redolent with the warm male scent of him and her skin had still tingled with his touch, and after a while she'd stopped trying to analyze it and had just accepted it for the unexplainable magic it had been.

"He's not going to let you go, you know that, don't you?" Shay's voice broke into her thoughts. "How long do you think you're going to be able to hide from him?"

"As long as it takes." She hugged herself, feeling suddenly chilled. It was raining again, and she stared through the rhythmic sweep of the windshield wipers at the wet, gray road unwinding in front of them. "He's got the bank in his pocket, of course, so I can't get at my money. But I've got some squirreled away under a different name. Not much, but enough. All I have to do is stay out of his hands long enough to get some proof, something that will *make* the police listen to me." She sensed Shay give her a sidelong glance and she smiled wryly. "You still don't believe it, do you? Even now."

"It doesn't matter what I believe."

"Then why are you helping me?"

He was silent for a moment or two. "Maybe I just don't like his attitude."

Cait nodded, glancing at him speculatively. "I... um... think there's something we should deal with before... before we go much further."

He gave her a wary look. "Is this going to be something I'll wish I hadn't heard?"

"I don't know. It's just that... well, I'm sorry for getting you mixed up in all this. Dalkquist isn't the kind of man who likes people getting in his way."

"Too bad you didn't think of that last night when you were stowing away in my rig," he growled.

"I didn't have a choice last night," Cait said tightly. "You were my only chance, and I grabbed it. But now..." She shrugged, rubbing her arms, chilled. "I think I'd better make something clear, Mr. McKittrick. I'm not crazy, and I'm not—" She felt herself flush slightly, finding it difficult to say what she needed to say with him looking at her like that, his gaze direct and steady and as clear as lake wa ter. "What I mean is, the other…part of last night wasn't… Under ordinary circumstances I'd never…"

His gaze hardened fractionally. Then one corner of his mouth lifted in a humorless smile and he turned his attention back to his driving. "What you're trying to say is that you're not that kind of girl."

Cait gave him a sharp look. "What I'm saying is, don't take the situation—or me—for granted. If you expect—"

"Honey, I don't expect a damned thing, okay?" He turned his head and have her a hard, cool look, his eyes shuttered of all emotion. "You're just dangerous cargo, far as I'm concerned. And the sooner I get you off-loaded, the better."

Oddly enough, his casual dismissal of the entire episode hurt. She hadn't expected tenderness and platitudes, but some acknowledgment that it had happened would have been nice.

Although it was probably just as well, Cait told herself wearily. Last night had been special and strange and wonderful, but it could have turned into a complete nightmare. Some men would have taken for granted that last night's intimacies were just the beginning of a good time, and convincing them otherwise could have been difficult. Even dangerous.

So she was lucky that Shay recognized those magical few hours for what they had been and was content to leave it at that, comfortable enough with his masculinity, with his sexuality, that he didn't need to pursue it further.

Not bothering to say anything, she rested her head against the back of the seat and closed her eyes. She wasn't feeling very well suddenly, cold one moment and hot the next, and she was finding it increasingly difficult to ignore the queasiness in her stomach.

And over the next hour or so it only got worse. She started shivering for one thing, and her skin felt as though she'd been flayed alive, every nerve ending exposed and raw. She couldn't sit still, filled with a desperate, nerve-racking tension, wanting something but not knowing what it was. She couldn't concentrate, her mind flitting around like a moth in a bottle, and she felt restless and on edge and so fidgety she could scream.

Shay kept looking at her, frowning a little, and she tried as hard as she could to sit still, to pretend nothing was wrong. She was more trouble than he'd counted on; if he thought she was sick, he'd more than likely just toss her out by the side of the road and leave her.

The nausea hit her a couple of miles later, along with an attack of chills that left her shivering like an aspen leaf, her entire body clammy with icy perspiration. She drew her legs up and wrapped her arms around them, telling herself it was just shock and exhaustion. That she'd be all right in a little while.

Shay glanced at Cait uneasily, but she was huddled quietly in the corner, eyes closed, and he decided maybe he was wrong about her after all, that she was just worn-out and needed some rest. Her skin was pasty and damp and the hollows under her eyes looked bruised and Shay wondered what in the hell they'd been doing to her in Amber Hills. And why. Always, the why—

"Stop the truck."

Jarred out of his brooding, Shay gave her an impatient look. "Here? There's nothing here but—"

"Stop the truck!" She grabbed the dashboard, swallowing, her face the color of chalk dust. "Please . . . I'm going to be sick. Just . . . just stop the truck!"

Shay swore and started gearing down, easing the rig onto the wide shoulder to get out of the way of traffic as he slowed as quickly as he could without jackknifing the trailer. They finally rocked to a stop, air brakes hissing, and Cait pushed the door open and was gone.

He found her just by the edge of the asphalt, half lying in the dusty weeds, and he held her as she retched emptily and then, finally, sank sobbing into his arms.

"Flu," she got out between clenched teeth. "I think I've got the flu."

"Flu my foot," Shay growled, lifting her to her feet and giving her a none-too-gentle shove toward the truck. "Quit trying to con me, lady—I know drug withdrawal when I see it. What are you on, anyway? And just for curiosity's sake, how long were you going to wait before asking me to get you something to take the edge off?"

Cait looked up at him in confusion, seeing the disgust and anger on his face and not even realizing for a groggy moment or two that it was at her. And then, finally, it hit her. She felt her cheeks flare scarlet and she pulled away from him violently. "Damn you, I am *not* a junkie! I told you, the needle marks on my arms are so people will think—"

"Give it a rest," he said roughly. "You've really had me going, I'll say that much. I was almost ready to believe everything you've been telling me."

"I'm telling you the truth!" Leaning against the truck's fender, she looked up at him miserably. "Th-they were giving me pills all the time and injections, and putting heaven knows what in my food."

He looked skeptical, but at least he was still listening. Cait drew in a deep, unsteady breath. "Please, you've got to believe me. If I'm coming down off something, it's from all the stuff they were giving me at Amber Hills. I swear I'm not using. I *swear* it!"

He looked at her for a long, undecided while, then he swore under his breath and took his hat off, wiping his forehead with his arm. He resettled the hat, tipping the brim down to shade his eyes. But she could see his mouth clearly. It looked hard and a little grim, and she wondered if he ever smiled. Doubted it somehow. It didn't look like a mouth used to smiling.

"What kind of pills?" he finally asked, his voice angry, as though he hated weakening enough to even ask that much.

"I don't know." She shivered violently and hugged herself, stomach roiling. "Dozens of them. Red ones. Blue ones." She scooped her hair back from her face, her hand trembling. "They used to hold me down and force them down my throat, but Angstrom was afraid I'd choke to death."

"I thought the whole idea was to kill you."

"It had to look as though I killed *myself*. If I died while being given medication, there'd be an investigation. Dalkquist can't afford even a hint of trouble. And neither can Angstrom."

"That's when they started the injections."

She nodded. "I fought and fought but they'd tie me down..." She shivered, closing her eyes to shut out the memories. "Sometimes they'd leave me in restraints all day. My wrists would be bleeding from trying to get free. That's what gave Angstrom the idea of making it look as though I'd tried to cut my wrists in a suicide attempt."

"How long were you in there?"

"I...I don't know. Time got so muddled...run together. They kept me locked in a room with no windows, so I didn't know night from day. I kept track of the days at first by the staff rotation. But then they put me in the special treatment wing and..." She looked at him questioningly. "Dalkquist and Angstrom came to my apartment to get me on the fifteenth of January." She shivered again, violently. "What...what's the date today?"

"March fifth."

"Seven weeks," she whispered. "Seven weeks..."

Shay got her cleaned up and back into the truck finally, swearing in a dull monotone the whole time at her, at himself, at Dalkquist. Even at Nancy, because if Nancy were still alive, damn it, he'd have been at home in bed with *her* last night instead of in the Amber Hills Truckstop Café!

But he *had* been in the Amber Hills Truckstop Café, and somehow in the intervening hours he'd managed to get himself into more trouble than he would have believed possible.

Trouble, he quickly figured out, that was going to get a hell of a lot worse before it got better. Because in the next little while, two things became unpleasantly clear: Cait was going into full-blown withdrawal from whatever arsenal of drugs they'd been pumping into her at Amber Hills, and he was *not* going to get to Eugene with those damned computers anytime within this lifespan.

Finally he gave up any pretense at having things under control and left the Interstate, cutting over to 101 and following the coast until he found a likely looking place to stay. There was a motel at the front, small and going to seed, but it was the rented cabins that Shay was interested in, a handful of them tucked away in dense forest overlooking the sea, completely hidden from the highway, the motel office and even each other.

He booked them in as husband and wife, dropping enough hints about weddings and honeymoons that the aging and nearly deaf proprietor beamed at him and assured him that they'd have complete privacy and solitude and that he would personally ensure that *no one* bothered them. And if he thought it a little strange that the groom was taking his new wife on her honeymoon in a trailer-rigged eighteen wheeler, he didn't mention it. He just handed Shay an armful of freshly laundered sheets and towels with a reminiscent little smile, and wished him and his new wife a pleasant stay.

The cabin was larger than Shay had anticipated, and although simply furnished, it was comfortable and clean and private. The main room was spacious, with a big stone fireplace on one wall and a scattering of rustic, well-worn pine furniture. There was a small kitchenette at one end, complete with dishes and cooking utensils, and a door off the other that led to the bathroom and a surprisingly large bedroom. The honeymoon suite, Shay found himself thinking humorlessly as he took in the big bed and another fireplace, this one with a ratty bear rug in front of it.

He paused long enough to make the bed and turn on the small electric heater to get rid of the dampness, then headed back into the living room. Cait was wandering around aimlessly, looking upset and bewildered and pale, shiver after violent shiver racking her slender frame. Swearing under his breath, he took her into the bathroom and told her to get into a hot shower, then—disabling the lock on the inside and jamming the door closed from the outside with a chair—he risked leaving her alone long enough to make a couple of hurried phone calls.

He'd barely gotten a snapping log fire going in the living room fireplace when he heard the sound of breaking glass coming from the bathroom. The sound sent a chill through him and he was on his feet with a savage oath, suddenly remembering the ragged scars on her wrists. Damn it, he should have known better than to turn his back on her for even a heartbeat!

Kicking the chair aside, he wrenched open the bathroom door, half expecting to find her lying in a pool of blood with her wrists slashed and a look of triumph on her face . . . and instead found her sitting on the floor sobbing, glass from the broken tumbler scattered around her.

Her hand was bleeding from a gash on her palm and she recoiled when he burst in, looking frightened and disoriented. "I—I didn't mean to break it."

"I know you didn't, honey." Shay knelt beside her and gently looked at her hand, relieved to see the cut was only superficial. He stood up slowly, trying not to alarm her, and lifted her to her feet. "How about a shower, Cait?"

"Th-they're trying to kill me," she sobbed, starting to shiver suddenly. She stared at her bleeding hand as though unable to fully grasp what had happened, then looked up at him again, the beginnings of panic in her eyes. "W-who are you?"

"A friend," Shay told her quietly, praying she wasn't going to lose it entirely . . . and wondering what the hell he was going to do if she did. "My name's Shay, Cait. I'm your friend, remember?"

She frowned, looking doubtful, and watched the blood drip from her hand to the floor.

"I'm going to get some help," he told her, not knowing if she understood anything he was saying but hoping just the sound of his voice would calm her. "I have a friend who can help us, Cait. He's better at this sort of thing than I am."

"I'm cold. . . ."

"Yeah, I know." He started tugging the sweater over her head, thinking fast. Food . . . they were going to need food. A couple of days' worth, anyway. He'd passed a small convenience store a couple of miles back, but he couldn't risk leaving Cait for even that long. And toiletries . . . he had the basics in the truck, but three years of marriage had taught him that his idea of basics and a woman's idea of basics weren't even in the same ballpark.

He got her into the shower finally, although not quite the way he'd intended. Not wanting to leave her alone, he ultimately just stripped down and got in with her, telling himself she was too spaced out to even know what was going on. Telling himself he was too damned weary to care . . . and promptly discovering that he wasn't too weary at all.

It was an odd feeling, touching her, remembering having made love to her, yet looking at her and seeing a stranger. Problem was, his body didn't think of her as a stranger. His body knew her intimately, in fact, and responded to that fact with a vigor that made even breathing painful. Which didn't make it any easier to keep his mind on the business of soaping her down and getting her hair shampooed and washing away the last traces of Amber Hills.

He had the sudden and unpleasant thought that if she chose this precise moment to snap out of her drug-induced fog there was going to be some serious hell to pay. But she didn't, to his intense relief, and he wasted no time in getting her out of the shower—and temptation's reach—and into the depths of a big bath towel.

She seemed dazed and strangely tractable, making no protest as he led her back into the living room and sat her on the hearth with her back to the blazing fire, then started toweling her long, thick hair dry. And it was only after he'd finally gotten her into the big double bed in the other room and she'd fallen into a deep but troubled sleep that he made the one phone call he didn't want to make.

He wasn't even sure he still had the number. But he found the business card still tucked under a flap in his wallet and he sat turning it in his fingers for a long while, remembering. They'd parted on anything but good terms, both of them bristling with too much anger and grief, accusations flying like chafe. They'd come within inches of actually trading blows, had stood eye to eye, evenly matched in height and weight and fighting trim, the tension between them so taut it hummed.

It had been Rick who'd come to his senses first. Who'd backed away and apologized for his hostile words. Who'd said, as he walked out of his sister's house for the last time, that if Shay ever needed anything, he'd be there. For

Nancy's sake, he'd added bitterly. Because he'd loved his sister, even if her choice in husbands was damn poor.

Swearing under his breath, Shay dialed the numbers on the card, wondering if anyone would answer. He'd always had his doubts about Rick. And about that mysterious government agency he supposedly worked for. But to his surprise someone did answer, someone who not only knew Rick Jarvis and how to get hold of him, but also seemed to know who Shay McKittrick was.

Rick had explained the routine, so he wasn't surprised when the voice on the other end of the phone told him to hang up and wait for "Agent Jarvis" to call him. He did so—grudgingly—wondering what *Agent Jarvis* and the rest of his cloak-and-dagger buddies were doing now that the cold war was over.

The phone rang a few minutes later and Shay grabbed it up, knuckles white. "You said to call if I needed help," he said without preamble or greeting.

There was a taut silence on the other end of the phone, then a soft oath, edged with a wry laugh. "Nice of you to stay in touch, McKittrick."

Shay's fingers tightened around the receiver. "You still in the business?"

"I answered your call, didn't I?" The amusement was gone, replaced by thinly veiled impatience. "I take it this isn't a social call, then."

It was Shay's turn to swear, rubbing the back of his neck wearily. "Look, I'm...sorry. For not staying in touch. But I didn't think..." He didn't bother finishing it.

"I don't give a particular damn one way or another," Rick said with quiet anger, "but Mom and Dad don't understand why you just dropped out of sight. She was their *daughter,* damn it. They miss her, too. Losing you hasn't made it any easier. Personally, I figure it's better this way. But they liked you for some reason."

Shay gritted his teeth so hard his jaw ached. "Can you save the lecture for later, Jarvis? I've got this... situation. And I could use some of your super-agent expertise."

Jarvis muttered something colorfully obscene. "Going to give me a clue?"

"I think you'd better see for yourself."

"Where are you?"

Shay told him. "And I need some... things."

"Things?" Rick sounded suddenly alert. "Weapons?"

"A bra, for a start."

The silence crackled. "A... bra."

In spite of everything, Shay found himself grinning. He held up Cait's white cotton bra, squinting at the label. "Make it a 34B. And panties, of course. Small."

"Of course," Rick said mildly.

"Jeans, a couple of shirts, size ten, maybe. Shoes. About a six, six and a half. Socks. Toothbrush, hairbrush. And groceries. Enough for two people for three or four days. Maybe more."

Again, the silence pulled as tight as wire. "This... uh... problem..."

"Like I said, I think you'd better come out here and see for yourself."

"No kidding," Jarvis said blandly. "Bro, you couldn't keep me away. I'll be there by morning." He paused, then added, "And if you need help before I get there, call this number." He rattled off an Oregon phone number. "Tell whoever answers that I've authorized whatever action they deem necessary. Got that?"

"That include air strikes?" Shay asked dryly.

There was another silence. "If necessary." Rick's voice was cool, without even a hint of amusement, and Shay felt the back of his neck prickle. "See you in a few hours, McKittrick. And try to keep a lid on whatever you've got brewing down there, okay? Because I don't think I like the sound of it at all.''

And then he was gone, and Shay was listening to a dial tone.

Chapter 5

It was one of those nights he'd never thought he'd have to face again. One of those nights that turned up now and again in his nightmares and left him shaking for hours, wondering if he had the strength—or even the will—to go on.

It had been worse with Nancy. Nancy had been dying; Cait only thought she was.

But much of it was the same: the tears, the pleas to help her end it, the hours of holding her and arguing with her and cajoling her and, at times, of just having to listen to her screaming and knowing there was nothing he could do.

For the first hour or two, he thought he had it under control. Cait had wakened as restless and jumpy as a cat, convinced she had to leave...not knowing where or even why, just that she had to go. She'd tried reasoning with him at first, gazing up at him earnestly as she tried to explain that she *had* to leave right now and why wouldn't he understand? When that didn't work, she got angry, then coy, slyly insinuating herself into his arms and promising him wondrous things if he'd just let her go.

When he still refused to drive her into town, she retreated into sullen anger that abruptly escalated into full-scale rage. Not even trying to restrain her, Shay just let her work it off, making certain she didn't hurt herself but otherwise not interfering. Until she came after him with a rusty butcher knife, that is, and he caught her in a bear hug and wrestled her into the bathroom and under an ice-cold shower, suffering a gash on his forearm and a deep set of scratches down his left cheek for his trouble.

The cold water knocked the fight out of her, at least temporarily, and she huddled in the bottom of the tub, shivering and sobbing and asking why he was trying to kill her. And then they started the whole cycle again....

But by sunup, Shay decided that maybe they were both going to make it. Numbed with fatigue, he sat sprawled in a chair by the bed, watching over Cait as she slept. She'd finally simply collapsed about an hour ago and although she was doing a lot of tossing and turning and mumbling, she seemed down for the count.

It was hard, watching her like this, not to think of Nancy. He'd sat like this by her bedside, too, night after night. Had smoothed her sweat-tangled hair back from her face, his heart clenching a little at the gray pallor of her skin, the deep hollows under her eyes. Had rinsed out a cloth in warm water and had held it on her forehead, trying to make her comfortable.

Except with Nan it had gone on for months. That's what they'd told him afterward, anyway. He'd all but lost track of time near the end, each day stretching into an eternity of pain and grief and rage. People had come and gone and he'd hardly noticed them, ate when something was put into his hands, slept when exhaustion simply overtook him where he sat, became totally focused on keeping the slender, dark-haired woman he loved alive.

Except he'd failed in the end. The doctors had come finally to take her into the hospital, and although she'd begged him to let her stay at home with him, he'd been too numb and tired to argue with them, too...hell, too damned scared. Scared of having to sit there and watch the life fade from her. So he'd let them take her, and then—in grief, in despair, in guilt—he'd gone down to Malloy's Bar and had drunk himself into a stupor that had lasted three days and three nights.

Long enough, he thought coldly. Long enough for him to miss her dying. He'd taken the coward's way out, and she'd died crying out for him. And there hadn't been a night that had passed since when he hadn't heard her. Hadn't begged her to forgive him for deserting her.

He swore wearily and rubbed his stubbled face with his hands, elbows on knees. Cait muttered fretfully and Shay gazed down at her, feeling the anger jolt through him again as he looked at the yellowing bruise on the side of her jaw. In the shower, he'd seen the other bruises—too precise, too intimate to be anything but deliberate. Somebody had manhandled and hurt her, and it damned well hadn't been accidental.

One way or the other, he was going to get some answers. Someone had some explaining to do—Dalkquist for a start. Then Angstrom. And, just for the hell of it, he'd like to know what *had* happened to Cait's mother.

He realized suddenly that she was awake, staring up at him through a tangle of hair with one bloodshot eye. Clutching the sheet and blanket to herself, she sat up very slowly, looking haggard and wan. "You're still here." She made it sound like an accusation.

"Wouldn't miss it for anything."

Cradling her stomach with both arms, she leaned forward to rest her forehead on her upraised knees. "I think I'm dying."

"No. You just wish you were."

Again, that one bleary eye surveyed him. "Do I look as bad as you?"

"Worse."

"I think I want to go back. To the hospital, I mean."

"No, you don't," Shay said wearily.

"I'm serious. I really don't feel very well at all."

"That's the way you're supposed to feel."

"God, I could hate you." She shuddered, turning her face away from him. "I think I do hate you. Why are you doing this to me, anyway? I never did anything to *you.*"

"You got *me* involved in this, remember? Now you're just going to have to live with the consequences."

She shivered again. "Why do you care? What difference would it make to you if I *did* go back?"

A lot, he found himself thinking. He ran his gaze down the silken curve of her bare back, taunting himself a little. "When I start something, I like to finish it."

There was an undertone to his voice that made Cait give him a suspicious, sidelong look. Just what was he talking about, anyway? This whole mess with Dalkquist . . . or her? And why, when he looked at her in that intense, narrow-eyed way he had, did she always feel that same heart-stopping sensation you get when the roller coaster drops out from under you on that last curve?

Or maybe, like so much of it lately, she was just imagining this, too. Feeling worn out and suddenly contrite, she pushed her sticky, tangled hair back from her face, sighing heavily. "I suppose I'll thank you for this one day. If I live."

"You'll live."

She wasn't as sure, but it took too much effort to argue. Looking around the room, she tried to remember . . . could recall bits and pieces of the past...what?...day? Two days? Fear, she could remember that clearly enough. And anger. And confusion. And under it all, the desperate awareness of her vulnerability.

Uneasily, she glanced at Shay again. He was sitting beside the bed, forearms resting heavily on thighs, head hanging between his shoulders, clearly exhausted. His face was stubbled and gray with lack of sleep, and she looked at the four scratches on his left cheek, the dried blood on his shirtfront, the bloody gash along his arm...and felt suddenly chilled, knowing with cold certainty that she'd done that.

And yet he'd stayed. Watching over her. Protecting her, not just from Dalkquist but from herself.

It gave her an odd feeling. One she wasn't certain she liked. She'd learned the hard way that the only person you could depend on was yourself. How many times had that lesson been drummed into her? She'd been disbelieved, humored, laughed at. People who had once been friends had looked pityingly at her when she'd tried to tell them about Dalkquist, had tried to jolly her along, had taken, finally, to avoiding her altogether. The police had at first listened dutifully, then had simply ignored her, writing her off as a nut case.

No one had listened. No one had believed.

Why would Shay McKittrick be any different?

He was in it for something. Money maybe. Maybe he thought Dalkquist would pay him for her return. Maybe he hadn't brought her here to keep her safe at all, but was waiting for Dalkquist to arrive with a reward.

"I...have to go to the...bathroom."

Slowly, as though the effort cost him, Shay lifted his head, nodding wearily. "I'll give you a hand."

"No." She said it a little too defiantly and Cait swore to herself as she saw the veil of exhaustion vanish from Shay's eyes.

He lifted his head, narrow-eyed and suspicious. "Okay," he said with deceptive carelessness.

It wasn't until she'd dropped her legs over the side of the bed that she fully realized she was naked. She stiffened slightly, back to him. "Could I...umm...is there a—?"

"Here." To her consternation, he strolled around the end of the bed and stood beside her, too near, too tall and broad-shouldered, too strong and quick. He unbuttoned his shirt and pulled it out of his jeans, then handed it to her.

Cait pulled the shirt on and buttoned it, then eased herself out from under the covers and onto wobbly legs that threatened to deposit her none-too-gently onto her backside on the cold plank floor. But they didn't. Grimly, she made her way down the corridor and into the small, rustic bathroom.

Not without cost. By the time she'd gotten the door closed and locked behind her, she was shivering and nauseated and drenched with icy rivulets of perspiration. But there was a window—a big window, easily opened. Easily gotten through, if you were agile.

She stared at it, wondering if she was just being as paranoid as Angstrom kept telling people she was. There was no reason to be afraid of Shay. He'd done nothing but protect her so far. But then again, why take chances? She'd gotten this far on her own. She was better off doing the rest of it alone, too. After all, if you didn't trust people, they couldn't betray you.

Turning on the tap full blast to cover any noise, she got up onto the side of the tub unsteadily and, after a couple of tries, managed to release the catch and push the casement window up far enough to wriggle through.

Her legs nearly gave way then and she grabbed the towel bar for balance, then stepped back down to the floor, dizzy and sick. The water was still gushing into the sink and she scooped up a handful and splashed her face with it, suddenly realizing that Shay had rinsed out her underthings and had hung them over the small electric heater to dry... and socks. Heavy wool socks!

She pulled them on, then scrambled into her still-damp briefs, decided the bra could wait. A coat... she needed a coat. And shoes.

Grinning a little wildly, she clambered back up onto the edge of the tub again and started pulling herself up and through the window. May as well wish for a golden chariot while she was at it. And maybe a bodyguard or two. For that matter, why not just wish her mother was still alive and that Dalkquist had never even existed?

Dropping out of the window and into the still, cold night was the most frightening thing she could remember ever doing. Feet first, unable to see anything below her, she clung to the windowsill and gingerly let herself down, the shirt catching on something rough and riding up.

Eyes closed, she swallowed hard and told herself to just let go, not knowing what she was dropping into. Please, God, not a pile of scrap metal or the edge of a cliff...

The hands caught her around her bare waist with no warning at all. Large warm hands, callused and a little rough. Cait gave a squeak of fright and tried to pull herself back up, but she wasn't strong enough and the hands holding her captive tightened their grip.

"I've got you. Just let go and drop."

"No!" She kicked out at him, her foot connecting with a satisfyingly solid thump, and she could hear him suck in his breath. "Let me go!"

"I'm just trying to keep you from breaking your silly damn neck," he growled. "Now let go of the window!"

One of Shay's muscular bare arms encircled her waist, holding her tightly against him, and he reached up and grasped the fingers of her left hand and started pulling them free of the windowsill. "Let go of the window, Cait," he repeated firmly.

She tried to kick him again, but he simply swore under his breath and leaned closer to the building so she had no room to maneuver, one knee thrust between her thighs to balance himself against the wall as he continued to pry her fingers off the sill.

She dropped unexpectedly and he grunted, caught off balance, and she nearly slithered right out of his arms. Except he caught her expertly, turning her to face him and catching her flailing hands with no effort at all.

His cold belt buckle pressed against her abdomen and she gave another wriggle, realizing that the shirt had ridden up under her arms so she was all but naked. His bare chest was rough against her breasts and she could feel the muscles in his belly tighten as she tried to wiggle free. And then he was pressing her tightly up against the rough log building, his thigh still between hers, one hand holding her wrists, the other splayed against her bare back.

It was one of those insane moments in time when everything seems to come careening to a stop, and she forgot for a moment or two what she'd been running from or why or even what she was doing out here, mostly naked and in Shay McKittrick's very competent arms.

She felt dizzy and warm and her skin tingled where it was pressed against his. She wondered light-headedly if this was just another symptom of drug withdrawal or something else all together. His cheek was rough against hers, erotically masculine, and she shivered slightly, dimly aware of how suddenly sensitive her breasts were, of how exquisitely gentle the movement of his hand down her back.

"Why were you running away?" His voice was a hum of sound against her ear, and she could hear him swallow.

"Dalkquist..." She closed her eyes, trying to collect her scattered thoughts. "You've called Dalkquist, haven't you? To come and get me. For whatever he'll pay."

"No," he said roughly. "I'm not doing this for money."

"Then...why?" She managed to lift her head and look into his eyes.

He was gazing down at her with a wolfish hunger, narrowed eyes glittering with something dark and dangerous. And then, abruptly, he stepped away and let her drop to the ground. She staggered and nearly fell; he caught her by the forearm and held her while he tugged the errant shirt down.

"Try a stunt like that again, and I'll tie you down," he told her tightly, not meeting her eyes as he turned, grim-faced, and led her around the end of the cabin and toward the front. "How far do you think you'll get in the shape you're in? You want to die of exposure?"

"I don't want to d-die at all," she mumbled, suddenly half-frozen and shivering and on the verge of tears for no reason at all.

He pushed the cabin door open and shoved her inside, then gave her another shove toward the bedroom, where she sat numbly on the side of the bed while he brushed pine needles and grass from her bare legs and peeled the socks off her feet. Then he wordlessly lifted the sheet and blankets and she crawled under them, too miserable to even protest as he pulled off his jeans and joined her a moment later, wrapping strong arms around her and holding her close.

"No one's going to hurt you, Cait," he said quietly, tucking the sheet tightly around her shoulders. "Just go to sleep, all right?"

"I'm cold," she murmured, shivering as she burrowed more tightly against his solid male warmth. "Cold..." And the last thing she remembered as she fell tumbling in a downward spiral into darkness was the touch of his lips against her cheek. And the realization, dim, half-formed, that she felt safer here in a stranger's arms than she had for years.

He didn't know how long he'd been asleep. The fire had burned down to embers and the room was distinctly cold, but he was warm—warmer than he'd been in a long, long while. Cait lay sleeping against him, streamers of dark hair lying like silk ribbons around her, one arm draped loosely around his waist. And he found himself just lying there looking at her, telling himself he had no right being there. No right at all.

He could feel the feminine curve of her belly pressing against his hip, the feathery weight of a breast on his arm, the pressure of her thigh on his. Intimate invasions of his sleeping space he wasn't used to anymore.

For two years, he'd slept alone. More than two years. When Nan's illness had gotten worse, he'd moved into the spare room and his nights had been endless and empty. Strange, how easy it was to fall into old habits again, arms lying just so, body angled this way, legs that way to accommodate the sleeping form at his side.

Not that he'd intended to stay. Once she'd calmed down and had fallen asleep, he'd planned to slip out of the bed and catch some shut-eye in the big armchair by the hearth. But every time he'd eased away from her she'd become restless and distressed, and finally it had just seemed easier to stay.

She murmured something in her sleep, frowning slightly, and he wondered if she was dreaming of Dalkquist. He was thinking about that, about her stepfather and murder and a dozen other unrelated things when he heard the noise in the main part of the cabin.

Footsteps. Soft, almost stealthy. The creak of a floor-board.

He was on his feet in the next breath, moving silently and quickly to the door, swearing fervently to himself as he realized his small gun was on the table in the other room. Looking swiftly around the darkened bedroom, he spied the hatchet leaning against the fireplace, where he'd left it after splitting a handful of kindling.

It wasn't very big, but the smooth pine handle fit his hand comfortably and he gave it an experimental swing as he moved soundlessly back to the heavy wooden door.

It was open about an inch and he eased himself against the frame and took a quick glance out into the corridor. Seeing nothing. The fire in the living room had all but burned out, too, but there was enough of a glow from the remaining embers for him to make out the shadow of someone moving around. And then suddenly a dark form stepped into the corridor, paused and started stealthily toward the bedroom door.

Shay's fist tightened around the handle of the hatchet and he braced himself, planting his bare feet solidly against the cold split-pine floor. He could see the shape of a hand as it lifted to push the door open, and in that moment he moved, kicking the door wide with his foot as he reached out and grabbed the intruder by his throat—

And in the next instant found himself flat on his back on the floor, landing so solidly it knocked the wind out of him and made him see stars, right hand numbed to the elbow where his assailant had savagely struck the hatchet from his grip. There was a knee braced across his throat and the small, ice-cold muzzle of a gun pressed against his temple and he lay there, dazed, thinking a little stupidly that as far as heroes went he wasn't doing very well.

There was a savage oath, then the pressure of both gun and knee vanished and in the next instant he was being hauled groggily to his feet. The overhead light flicked on and he winced, squinting. And then he swore himself, dully and with disgust, and eyed the intruder warily. "You."

"That's a real good way to get yourself killed," Rick Jarvis snarled, kicking the hatchet across the room. "What the hell did you think you were doing, coming at me like that?"

"A better question might be why you were creeping around outside my bedroom door in the middle of the damned night!"

"It's six in the morning," Jarvis replied with icy calm. "You said you were in trouble and needed help. My kind of help. So when I got here and you weren't around, I took the normal precautions." His lip curled and he looked across to the bed where Cait lay, still sleeping fitfully. "Some trouble, McKittrick. Wouldn't mind a little like it myself."

"It's not what you think," Shay muttered sullenly.

Rick gave him an evil smile. "Of course not. I see you standing around in your shorts, a beautiful and—if I'm not mistaken—very naked woman, a double bed that's obviously been well used . . ." He gave a snort. "Save it for your mother, McKittrick. And get some clothes on." He picked up Shay's blue jeans and flung them at him. "I'll put the coffee on. Good thing I brought some up. By the way your lady's still sleeping, I'd say you two haven't taken much time off for grocery shopping."

Shay's reply was earthily pungent as Rick turned and limped from the room.

Rick had found the ancient drip cone and filter, and the scent of fresh, hot coffee wafted around Shay as he walked back into the living room. He'd pulled his jeans on but hadn't bothered with his shirt, not wanting to risk waking Cait to get it. Stirring up the embers of the dying fire, he added some kindling to get it going again. It caught finally, and he coddled it for a minute or two, then added a birch log and pulled the screen closed.

"Here." Rick came in just then and handed him a cup of the steaming coffee. "You look like you could use this, McKittrick. Have you gotten *any* sleep in the last week?"

"Give me a break, Jarvis," he muttered, sitting on the wide stone hearth and scrubbing his hair with his free hand. "I told you, it isn't what it looks like."

"No?" Rick dropped into a nearby chair, straightening his left leg with a slight wince.

"That leg still bothering you?"

"Breaking in a new model." Rick reached down and rapped his knuckles on his plastic thigh. "The prosthetics manufacturers use all us old crippled Vietnam vets to test their new hardware. This one's made of some new polymer plastic that's supposed to be lighter, stronger and more flexible—all it's done so far is rub what's left of my damn leg raw."

Shay nodded, realizing a little remotely that it had been almost two years since he'd seen Rick. He looked older— older than just two years could account for. And very tired. His light brown hair was threaded with gray around the temples now, and there were lines around his mouth and eyes that hadn't been there before. "How are your parents?"

Rick glanced up, eyes cool. "Ask them yourself. You know the phone number. They haven't moved."

"I said give me a break, Jarvis."

"I miss her, too, damn you," he said in a low, angry voice. "Do you think you have some God-given right to grieve more than the rest of us? Some special prerogative to hurt more?"

"She was my wife!"

"She was my kid sister!"

The air was suddenly static and Shay glared across at the other man, fingers whitening around the coffee mug. Then, abruptly, the anger vanished, leaving him empty and very tired. "I know that," he finally managed to get out, his voice ragged. "Damn it, I...know that."

"They ask about you all the time. Mom and Dad, I mean." Rick's voice was quieter, almost subdued. "You should drop by, Shay. They'd like that."

Shay nodded. "Yeah, I know. I..." He shrugged.

"I'm sorry."

Rick's voice was so soft, it took a moment for his words to sink in, but Shay finally looked up. "For?"

"Hell, you name it." Rick made a fleeting attempt to smile. "For not being there when you needed it. For not cutting you a little more slack after the funeral. For...all the things I said. At Mom and Dad's. After."

He stared into the coffee mug cradled between his palms. "Nan was always just my little sister, you know? And then you came along and she married you...it's like you came between us." He glanced up, away again. "I told myself you were no good for her, but that was bull. You..." He shook his head, managing a rough smile. "You made her happy, man. You loved her."

Shay stared into the fire, surprised at feeling so little pain. "Yeah. I did." Oddly, he found himself thinking of Cait.

"And...her?"

Shay blinked and looked up.

Rick inclined his head toward the bedroom. "The 34B in there. She something special, or just passing through?"

"Her name's Cait Sawyer," Shay said with irritation.

"And?"

"And?" He held Rick's stare challengingly.

Rick's face darkened, then he swore explosively and nodded, holding up one hand as a sign of capitulation. "All right, all right, it's none of my business. But *you* called *me*, bro."

Shay flushed slightly, wondering why he felt so suddenly protective. "It's a hell of a story," he finally said, almost reluctantly.

"So tell it." Rick leaned over and lifted his left leg onto the ottoman, wincing again. Then, idly massaging what was left of his upper thigh, he leaned back and watched Shay through the steam rising from the mug of coffee. "And make it good, McKittrick. I'm out here on my own time, not the government's."

It took longer than Shay expected. For one thing, Cait had told him her story in bits and pieces and in no particular order and it took a while to put it together. And for another, Rick kept interrupting to ask questions or have some detail clarified or the more obvious contradictions straightened out.

By the time he was finished, it was almost eight o'clock and a sickly pall of sunshine was trickling through the front window. Rick was leaning forward, elbows planted on knees, a deep frown incised between his brows. Shay got up and poked the fire again, tossing on another birch log, and when he straightened, Rick was looking at him thoughtfully.

"You believe her."

"Yeah." His certainty surprised Shay. He wondered when he'd made up his mind. "You would, too, if you'd spent the last couple of days with her."

Rick nodded slowly. "Two days isn't a real long time to get to know a woman, buddy."

"Long enough," Shay replied coolly.

"And you're . . . involved."

"No." He said it a bit too emphatically, wondering who he was trying to convince.

"You were in bed with her, bro."

"She was cold. And restless. It seemed to keep her quiet."

A hint of amusement brushed Rick's mouth. "It usually does."

"Damn it, Jarvis, if you—"

"You wanted my help, McKittrick. I'm here. But I have to know the details."

Swallowing his irritation, Shay nodded. "You know everything I do."

"Which isn't a hell of a lot." Rick's eyes glittered slightly. "Everything you're telling me comes from a woman who ran away from a psychiatric hospital. A woman who is—by your own admission—confused, traumatized and addicted to drugs. Whose stepfather just happens to be one of the richest, most influential men in the country. A candidate for the governor's seat. A respected member of his community."

"They tied her down, Rick. She's got rope burns on her ankles and wrists, and that bruise on her cheek is—"

"It's not unusual for patients to be restrained. As much for their own protection as the staff's. You told me yourself that she attacked one of the orderlies and—"

"He was trying to rape her." Shay bit the words out.

"So she says."

Shay opened his mouth to say something, then subsided, breathing a coarse oath between his teeth as he glared at his brother-in-law. Rick's disbelief shouldn't have surprised him: he'd had the same doubts, had asked himself the same questions. "So you're not going to help me."

"I didn't say that. You haven't told me yet what you want me to do."

"Get the heat off Cait, for one thing. Maybe get someone to look into her accusations."

"I don't have the authority to do any of that."

"Then get someone in here who does, damn it!" Shay got to his feet and flung the dregs of coffee into the fire. There was a burst of pungent steam, the crackle of logs, then quiet again.

"I'm going to ask you again, McKittrick, and I want the truth. Are you sleeping with her?"

"What the hell difference does it make if—" He caught himself, breathing heavily, and stalked across the room to stare out the big front window. The cabin was set back in a stand of tall trees, but he could see through a curtain of drooping pine boughs to the distant beach, the sea all but hidden behind a curtain of early-morning fog. "One night," he said in a clipped voice. "And it was...special."

"Done right, it always is, bro. It always is." There was the barest hint of amusement in Rick's voice. Then Shay heard him sigh heavily and mutter an oath under his breath. "Look, I don't give a damn about your sex life—Nan's been dead for two years, and she'd be the first to tell you to get back out there and into action. But a man's judgment gets scrambled when he's thinking below the belt."

"Don't push it, Jarvis," Shay said softly, turning his head to give the other man a cold look.

Rick smiled faintly, his eyes a little too knowing for Shay's liking. "Look at it from my angle, McKittrick. It's been two long dry years, and suddenly this woman drops into your lap, all big eyes and soft hair and tears. She tells you someone's trying to kill her, begs for your help, and without even knowing how it happened, you're a believer. It *happens,* man. I've seen it before."

"This isn't about being without a woman for two years," Shay said between clenched teeth. "It isn't about *sex,* damn it. It's about justice and fair play and maybe keeping someone alive. It's about a frightened woman with no other place to turn. It's about *being* there."

Rick's eyes narrowed very slightly. He nodded slowly, saying nothing, and gave Shay a long thoughtful stare that had less grieving brother in it than hard-bitten government agent. "I'll see what I can find out. See if anything you've told me makes any bells ring in Washington. But I wouldn't hold my breath, McKittrick. Personally, I think you're being hustled."

"And clothes. She needs clothes."

"I brought what you asked for—jeans, blouses, a couple of sweatshirts, running shoes. If they don't fit, sue me."

Shay had to smile at the expression on Rick's face. "I owe you."

"Damn straight," Rick muttered. "How long are you planning on holing up here?"

"Another two or three days for sure. Maybe longer. Depends on how she gets through the next few hours."

Rick looked at him steadily, his gaze lingering on the scratches on Shay's cheek. "If she's been using for a long time, it'll take a while for her to get clean."

"She hasn't been using," Shay said, his look just as steady.

Rick let it go by, although his expression told Shay more clearly than words what he thought—of Cait's drug use and Shay's gullibility.

"And that trailerload of freight you're hauling? You just putting your job on hold for a few days, too?"

"I've called someone," Shay said calmly. "He'll be here this morning to take my load into Eugene. And he'll take over the rest of my schedule."

"You seem to have it all figured out."

"I haven't got a damned thing figured out. I just know she's in trouble and she needs a place to catch her breath and get straight. She's a sitting duck, the shape she's in."

Rick started to say something, his face thoughtful; then he seemed to think better of it and simply got to his feet, hopping a step or two until he caught his balance.

Watching him, Shay smiled. "I'd take that leg back and ask for a refund if I was you."

"I'm taking it back and cracking it over someone's head, is what I'm doin'," Rick growled. "We can invent spy satellites that can count the fillings in your teeth, and smart bombs that can go down chimneys to find the enemy, but we can't invent an artificial leg with a knee that'll bend in the right direction."

Shay nodded, watching his brother-in-law walk across to the door. "Thanks, Rick. I know you think I'm crazy, but...thanks."

"I've gotta be the crazy one, not putting a come-along on you and getting you out of here before the roof caves in." He shook his head, his expression gloomy. "If The Man finds out I'm workin' a free-lance gig, he'll be on me like a dirty shirt. I'll be assigned to cattle-rustling detail in North Dakota or some damn thing. You ever spend a winter in North Dakota?"

"You still working for Spence O'Dell?" When Rick nodded glumly, Shay smiled. "Hell, he tried to recruit *me* once, remember? At my own wedding. This kind of thing's right up his alley."

"Not when there's a woman involved. There's nothing O'Dell hates more than a romantic. He figures the minute a man gets himself involved with a woman, he's a walking time bomb."

"Good thing for me I'm not a romantic, then," Shay said carelessly. "Or involved."

Rick gave him an odd look, then just nodded again. "You got money?"

"Not much, but enough to last until I can get to a bank."

"No bank." Rick reached into his pocket and took out a handful of bills, counted off half and tossed them onto the coffee table. "That should hold you for a while. If Dalkquist *is* looking for you, he'll have your bank accounts and credit cards flagged. You got someone looking after your apartment, checking your mail?"

"A neighbor comes in every few days. She takes the bills to the bank and hangs on to everything else until I get home."

"Good. Don't contact her—the less she knows, the better. What about this guy you've got picking up your load?"

"Red's okay. Dalkquist won't get anything out of him."

"And the others? At the restaurant?"

"They take care of their own."

Rick's gaze was steady. "Sort of like family, I guess."

"I guess."

A smile brushed Rick's mouth, then he turned and pulled the door open and stepped out into the cool morning air. "I'll be in touch, McKittrick. Keep the door locked and your head down. And if Dalkquist turns up and wants the woman back, you might want to think about turning her over to him."

"If Dalkquist turns up," Shay said quietly, "he's going to have to go through me to get her."

Rick paused on the mossy path and glanced around. "Just don't do anything stupid. Dalkquist is a heavy hitter. Get in trouble with him and I might not be able to help you. And I sure as hell don't look forward to trying to explain to Mom and Dad where I was while you were getting yourself put in jail for the next twenty years."

"If I'm not here when you come back, it means Dalkquist found us and I took off. Call Betty at the Amber Hills Truckstop Café—I'll leave word with her how you can reach me. And if she hasn't heard from me..." Shay smiled grimly. "Then you might want to ask Brenton Dalkquist what he did with the bodies."

"Funny, McKittrick." Rick pulled the driver's door open on the dark blue Pontiac parked beside the cabin. "Real funny."

Shay leaned against the door frame and watched until the car vanished up the road in a cloud of dust, then lifted his face to the thin streamers of sunshine working their way through the canopy of pine boughs. The air still smelled of rain, but it was slightly warmer than it had been, and scented heavily of the sea.

He felt different this morning. More determined. More certain. More...alive. As though having a purpose again—even one as off-the-wall as helping Cait Sawyer—had somehow lifted a darkness and chill from him that he'd only been half aware of. He drew in a deep breath of cold air, tasting salt and pine and woodsmoke, and glanced around at the door to the cabin.

It took him a moment to recognize the feeling he was experiencing. And, when he finally had it pinned down, he couldn't decide if it pleased or alarmed him. Anticipation. For the first time in over two years, he was actually looking forward to whatever the day held.

Chapter 6

Cait was standing by the fireplace when he came back inside, cold and sick and frightened, and she watched him worriedly as he closed the door and walked toward her. "I—I heard voices," she whispered, her voice cracking.

She shivered suddenly, the flames crackling behind her not seeming to provide any warmth at all, and she had to fight to stand there as he neared, telling herself fiercely that he was *not* her enemy, that any threat she read in him was just her own skewed perception of reality.

If any of this was real. It seemed impossible... a waking nightmare that wouldn't be shaken off, bizarre and endless.

"I called a friend in to help." Shay's voice was quiet and low. The kind of voice that *they* used when they wanted her to believe they weren't going to hurt her and that everything was going to be all right. "He's a Vietnam vet—came back from his last tour with one leg and enough shrapnel in him to start a scrap-metal shop. He works with some kind of hush-hush government agency he never talks about.''

Cait nodded, the fear hovering in her mind like dark mist. ''H-how do you know him?'' She tried to ask it casually, as though simply curious as to how one would go about meeting such a man, but her voice echoed with mistrust and suspicion.

Shay had reached the edge of the hearth and to Cait's relief made no move to come closer. Instead, he rested his forearm on the fireplace mantel and just stood there, looking relaxed and at ease and unthreatening. *A trick,* part of her mind whispered urgently, and she made herself ignore it.

''He was Nan's—my wife's—brother. I've known him for a long time.'' He smiled gently, his gaze holding hers. ''He's one of the good guys, Cait. He might not be able to help you, but you can trust him.''

''You told him...everything?'' The possibility that someone actually believed her story—not just believed it, but passed it on to someone who might help—surprised her so badly, it took her breath away.

''Everything you told me.''

Cait nodded, not trusting herself to dare even hope. Too often, she'd hoped, believed. Only to have it thrown back at her. ''And he won't go to...*him?*''

''I wouldn't have called him if I didn't trust him, Cait. We don't always see eye to eye, but I'd trust Rick with my life.''

To Cait's surprise, she found she could still actually smile. She'd thought the ability to smile—along with the ability to trust, to hope—had been burned out of her long ago. ''I hope you're right. Because you just might be.''

''How are you feeling?''

''Like I've died and been dug up a couple of times,'' she said quite truthfully, looking down at herself in disgust. Her waist-length hair, once her pride and joy, was dull and sticky and matted and it hung around her like tattered rags of unwashed silk. The man's shirt she was wearing as a makeshift nightgown was wrinkled and none too clean, and she grimaced distastefully. "Maybe I'll have a bath."

"Rick brought you some things." Shay walked across to a blue duffle bag lying by the chair and picked it up. "Let's see what we've got." He dropped onto the ancient green sofa and unzipped the bag, pulling it open. "Okay, we've got... jeans. Tops."

He took out a couple of pairs of neatly folded denim jeans, the price tags still on them, then a blue-and-white checkered blouse and a white one, followed by two sturdy sweatshirts, one blue, the other white. Cait stared at them disbelievingly.

"Socks. Tennis shoes." They joined the growing pile on the coffee table. "A... umm... some other... things."

Cait caught a glimpse of a pale blue bra and a handful of lacy panties, more silken froth than substance.

"A nightie." He held up something pale and shimmering and let it spill from his hands, holding it by the spaghetti straps, his expression mildly perplexed. "Well, sort of a nightie...."

It was a nightie all right, all satin and lace and delicate embroidery, more befitting a new bride than a recent escapee from the local asylum. Cait simply stared at it, then at Shay, who shrugged a little helplessly. "He...uh...I think he has the wrong idea about us."

"Mmm." Cait simply nodded, astonished to find herself on the verge of bursting into laughter. Except, she was afraid if she started she wouldn't be able to stop, so she swallowed it instead, wondering a little desperately if she really *was* going crazy after all.

Shay dropped the negligee onto the coffee table as though it had singed his fingers, then rummaged around in the duffle bag and came up with a matching powder-blue

peignoir. He let it fall onto the pile of clothes with a muttered comment Cait didn't catch, and peered into the bag
almost suspiciously, as though half afraid of what he might
turn up next.

What he found made him swear aloud. He took something small from the bag and tucked it into his shirt pocket,
not looking at her.

Cait leaned forward curiously. "What was that?"

"Just Jarvis's way of getting in the last word," he said a
bit testily.

"About what?"

"Male folly."

"*What?*"

But instead of answering her, he simply lifted out a clear
plastic travel bag filled with toiletries, a pair of blue satin
slippers and, finally, a surprisingly stylish black nylon
Windbreaker.

Cait took a couple of unsteady steps toward him, eyeing
the toiletry bag greedily. "Shampoo," she whispered. "Is
that shampoo? And *toothpaste?*"

Shay glanced up at her, a hint of laughter lifting one corner of his mouth. "Old Rick seems to have a pretty good
handle on what a lady needs for a weekend away from
home."

To Cait's surprise, her eyes filled with sudden tears. It was
such a small thing, a casual kindness most people wouldn't
think twice about. And yet it had been so long since she'd
received even that....

"Hey, are you all right?" Shay's voice, soft as batting,
wrapped around her, comforting, caring. She turned blindly
and suddenly he was there, all solid chest and protective
arms.

Sniffling, Cait nodded and pulled away. Hating the mo-
mentary weakness, the vulnerability. The *neediness*. A
woman could get caught up in needing someone, could get

tangled into the seductive coils of being taken care of until she was lost. Like her mother had, turning bewildered and childlike to the one man she trusted, the snake in Eden, the charmer who lied and connived and ultimately killed....

"Cait?"

"I'm all right," she lied, keeping her face turned away. "I—I'm all . . . all right."

"Yeah, and I'm king of England," he muttered.

And in the next heartbeat he was there again, catching her even as her knees gave way and she started to fall, dizzy and confused as the room dissolved into spangled blackness.

Another day went by, with Cait fading in and out of reality like a bad TV picture. Then a third, not nearly as bad. She slept through most of it, and the few times she wakened, she seemed more rational, more lucid. Shay finally decided they were almost at the end of it. And also decided, with grim resolve, that when he finally got his hands on Dalkquist, he was going to make him pay for just a little of the agony she'd gone through.

It was dark when she awoke. She was in bed again, with no memory of how she got there, garbed in Shay's cotton T-shirt. And it was impossibly dark. Moonlight streamed through the bedroom window, cold as glass, and she lay there and listened to the night. Wind soughed through the tall trees surrounding the cabin and somewhere a night bird called, the cry cutting through the background cacaphony of trilling frogs.

She rolled onto her back and came up against something solid on the bed beside her, startling her so badly she went motionless, hardly breathing. It didn't move and she turned her head cautiously and realized it was just Shay lying there, eyes closed, his chest rising and falling with reassuring steadiness as he slept.

His face was half turned toward her and she let her gaze travel over its rugged contours curiously, liking what she saw. He was what her mother would have called a man's man, handsome in a rough-hewn kind of way. Taken individually, none of his features was spectacular, but together they added up to something that would make any woman look twice.

A tangle of hair had fallen over his forehead and she reached up to brush it back without even thinking of what she was doing—discovering only then that there was a rope around her right wrist.

She stared at it, mind spinning. And in the next instant realized that Shay was awake, watching her.

He held up his left wrist and its matching tether. "I knew I wouldn't be able to stay awake another full night," he said quietly. "But you've been…disoriented. This was the only way I could be sure I'd wake up if you tried to run away again."

"Disoriented?" She sat up and looked at him in despair, combing her hair back with her fingers. "Raving mad, you mean. How long is this going to last?"

"It wasn't as bad this time," he told her gently, untying the cord from first her wrist, then his own. "You're going to be all right, Cait."

"What time is it? Last thing I remember, it was morning. I think. Or maybe afternoon…"

He squinted at his watch. "Almost midnight."

"Midnight!" She tried desperately to remember something—anything—of the past few days. Her thoughts were nothing but a confused jumble, shot through here and there with flickering images that made little sense. "You said run away. Did I try to run away again?"

One corner of his mouth lifted. "A couple of times. You thought you were back in Amber Hills. You kept calling me

Frank, and every time I got too close you'd try to knee-cap me.''

"Frank Bartowski. He was on day shift. Whenever things got slow he'd come into my room and...touch me. My hands would be tied so I couldn't reach him, the little snake, or I'd have clawed his eyes out.'' She raked her hair back with her free hand. "When this is all over I'm going to go back there with a team of cops and lawyers and investigators and take Amber Hills apart. I'm not the only patient that got Frank's *special* attention. Or Crushank's. And there were others...'' She shivered suddenly, her arms breaking into goose bumps.

Shay got a look in his eyes that was hard and cold and dangerous. "I wouldn't mind an invitation to that party myself. Your friend Crushank and I have some unfinished business.''

"From the café?'' Cait looked at him curiously. "I can't remember much from that night. Just running...running until I couldn't run anymore. What happened between you and Crushank?''

"You.'' His gaze held hers, and there was something in it that Cait felt right to her toes.

And for a moment, she actually thought he was going to reach out and pull her down into his arms and kiss her.

The room, this room, vanished. The moonlight, Amber Hills, whatever they'd been talking about—gone in a single heartbeat of time. And just like that they were back in the truck, just as they'd been that first night, eyes locked, the awareness of each other, of self, of need, filling the air like an electrical charge.

If he touched her, Cait thought a bit desperately, if he simply reached out and pulled her down into his arms and settled his mouth warmly over hers, she'd never find the strength to say no. It would be that night all over again, a few hours of fantasy stolen from real life, magical and erotic and slightly dangerous.

If he touched her...oh, God, if he touched her, it would all be over. Yet, even knowing that, Shay couldn't keep from reaching toward her. Couldn't keep from drawing a loop of tangled hair from her cheek, letting his fingertips brush warm, moist skin...seeing by her eyes that she was as aware as he of the sudden shift between them, the taut awareness of a woman to a man and a rumpled bed and a roomful of sudden possibilities.

Maybe it was the moonlight on her hair, or seeing her sitting there in his old T-shirt and knowing she was naked under it, or simply thinking of how her skin had felt against him that night they'd made love...whatever it was, he wanted her. Suddenly. Urgently. *Now.*

And for half a second he was tempted to just say to hell with it and pull her down beside him and get her out of that damned shirt and make love to her with every bit of driving, aching intensity he could muster.

He wanted to kiss her deeply and slowly, wanted to feel her breasts against his bare chest, wanted to run his hand down her flat belly and into the soft tangle below and part the silken flesh there with his fingers and touch her and caress her and plumb the syrupy, hot depths of her.

Wanted to pull her astride his hips and ease her down and around him, but slowly, slowly...relishing every silken inch of the plundering until there was no more to take. Then he wanted to watch her through half-slitted eyes as she took what *she* wanted, moving lithely on him, driving him out of his mind...

Swearing under his breath, Shay sat up and swung his legs over the side of the bed and sat there, teeth gritted, his back to Cait. He was so aroused, it hurt to breathe—even if he could breathe, which was questionable. He couldn't do anything in fact, but sit there trying not to think, trying not to move, the blood pounding in his temples.

"I think," Cait said suddenly from behind him, softly, "that I'm going to have a shower now."

The thought flickered through Shay's mind that he could probably use one himself—long and solitary and bitterly cold—but decided it probably wouldn't be prudent to tell her that. So he simply nodded instead and dropped his head into his hands, trying not to groan aloud as she slipped from between the sheets with the silken sound of flesh on cotton and made her way across the room and out into the corridor leading to the bathroom.

He sat there a moment or two longer, contemplating following her, then reminded himself that even if she did let him into the shower with her, making love to her now was only likely to make things worse.

That night in the truck hadn't counted. It hadn't been real, hadn't meant anything. But if they made love now, it would be a deliberate, conscious decision—and it would shift the dynamics of what they were to each other, what they were to themselves. There would be the sudden need for small talk, for explanations, for idle promises. There'd be expectations this time, obligations, complications. All the things he didn't need. Things *neither* of them needed.

The shower came on, and he thought of her pulling off the T-shirt and letting it fall, could see her standing there, slender body burnished golden by the light reflecting off the pine walls, imagined her reaching forward to test the water, then stepping under it . . .

Damn it to hell, what was he doing! He lunged to his feet and stalked across to the door. Rick was right—he was losing his perspective. None of this had to do with Cait and him. Not as man and woman, anyway. They were just two people with no past and no future and very little present tossed together by a whim of fate.

He rummaged through the box of groceries that Jarvis had brought up, didn't find anything he wanted to eat and settled instead on a cup of instant coffee. Taking it out onto the wide porch, he leaned against one of the support posts and stared into the night, his thoughts atangle.

It was some time later that he became aware that the shower had gone off and that Cait was moving around in the small kitchenette. The window glowed like a beacon in the darkness just to his left and he could see her standing by the stove as she waited for the kettle to boil, her brows pulled together in a frown, her face pensive.

She came out a few minutes later, and even though Shay was expecting her to join him, his gut pulled a little tighter when he heard the door open behind him. It closed again, then she appeared beside him—close, but not too close— bringing with her a waft of steam-scented air.

She'd smoothed her wet hair back into a sleek ponytail and her skin was still moist and slightly flushed from the shower, and she looked fresh and carefree. She was wearing one of the pairs of stone-washed blue jeans Rick had brought up, and a pale blue sweatshirt that played up her dark hair and fair complexion.

Full points to Jarvis, he thought a little irreverently: for all his faults, the man obviously had keen instincts for women's fashion. Those jeans, for instance . . . Shay took a deep breath, struggling to ignore just how well the jeans fit. They hugged her taut little bottom and thighs like a summer tan and he found himself thinking—even more irreverently—of the contraceptives that Jarvis had also tossed into the duffle bag along with the nightie.

She took a sip from the coffee mug in her hand, not looking at him, then took a deep breath of night air, closing her eyes for a moment. "Mmm. You forget what trees and green grass smell like when you live in the city. And the sea. It's been so long since I've been to a beach, I'd almost forgotten you can actually taste the salt in the air."

"There's a path down to the water. If you feel up to it tomorrow, we can go down. The walk would do us both good."

"Am I—?" She looked at him. "I'm so tired I feel like a zombie in one of those late-night horror movies, but I don't feel weird. Not like before, when my mind kept going in all directions and I was jumpy and sick. Does that mean I'm over the worst of it?"

"Probably. The tired part's normal—sleep's the best thing for you now. But I figure you've shaken off most of what they gave you."

"So you don't think I'll freak out again or anything?"

"I doubt it."

She nodded, taking another sip of the coffee. "So we can leave tomorrow."

"Leave?" He looked at her in surprise, then shook his head. "Uh-uh. No point in leaving before Jarvis gets back. And you're not up to taking on Dalkquist yet."

"I have to." She closed her eyes and tipped her head back as though her neck was stiff. "I've *got* to get to Sacramento. Every day I'm up here is a day lost. Dalkquist is going to be running scared, and that means he's going to be looking for the same things I am—a loose end, some bit of evidence, a hole in his alibi, a weakness in his story." She opened her eyes and looked at Shay. "He could be destroying the proof I need to have him arrested even while I'm standing here."

Shay frowned, telling himself that he should be relieved she wanted to go. That the sooner she got on with her vendetta against Dalkquist, the sooner he could get back to work. This wasn't supposed to have been a long-term thing—one night, max. Then it had stretched to a day. Then three, then four and counting...

"I don't think that's such a hot idea," he heard himself saying. "You might be over the hallucinations and the shakes, Cait, but you're not in any shape to be fighting bad guys."

"You've got a fortune in computers you have to deliver."

"They're gone. A buddy of mine came in late this morning and took the trailer. They'll be in the warehouse in Eugene by now."

She looked at him for a long moment. "You did that... for me?"

He shrugged it off. "You weren't in any shape to travel, and I couldn't leave you alone here while I delivered them."

Cait nodded thoughtfully, taking another sip of coffee as she walked across and leaned against the porch railing, looking up at the star-spangled sky. "I don't know how I'll ever be able to thank you for this. Not just getting me away from Dalkquist and Amber Hills, but... this."

She glanced around at him. "Not many men would have put themselves on the line like you have for me. And maybe one in a million would have done what you've done these past four days. Most would have written me off as a junkie and either dumped me off at the nearest hospital, or called Dalkquist to pick me up."

"Don't think I wasn't tempted," he said with a lazy smile.

She laughed. "Are all you truckers such hopeless romantics?"

"What do you mean?"

"Rescuing damsels in distress, fighting impossible odds, righting wrongs. A brotherhood of heroes."

"Not heroes. Just people doing what needs to be done."

"Mmm." She nodded again, her lips curving in a smile as she turned her attention back to the night sky.

"And if you really want to thank me," Shay said quietly, "keep yourself alive. I've got a vested interest in your hide by now—I've gone to enough trouble to keep it in one piece, anyway. So stay out of Dalkquist's clutches, and bring the bastard down. That'll be thanks enough.''

"You really believe me, don't you? You *don't* think I'm crazy."

Shay gave a snort. "You're no crazier than I am. That's not saying a hell of a lot, I know, but yeah—for what it's worth, I believe you."

"You're the first person who's said that—and meant it— in over a year," she whispered, her voice oddly thick. "There have been times I wondered if people weren't right after all."

"But you didn't let it stop you." He looked at her curiously.

"I couldn't." She gazed up at the stars for a long while, then drew in a deep breath. "I keep thinking that if I'd made *one* more try to get my mother to listen to me, she'd be alive now. Or if I'd stayed in California instead of running off to Italy. Maybe if I'd just *been* there..." She rubbed her eyes wearily. "Do you have any idea of what it's like to betray someone? To have someone die because of it and know you might have made a difference if you'd just been there?"

Shay felt chilled to the bone. "Yes," he said hoarsely.

"When Mom finally phoned me in Italy to tell me she suspected Dalkquist of trying to kill her, I promised her I'd make sure that he didn't. That I'd move heaven and earth if necessary to get Dalkquist arrested before he could hurt her." She stared at the sky, her finely boned profile hard.

"I spent hours on the phone, trying to get the local police to do something. They were amused and patient and said my mother had been behaving a little 'oddly' lately and not to worry about it. By the time I got a flight out of Rome and reached California, it was too late." She turned her head to look at Shay, her eyes cold with anger. "At her funeral, I swore I wouldn't quit until I got him put away."

Guilt, Shay thought. That's what was driving her—not just her hatred of Dalkquist. And guilt, as he knew all too well himself, wasn't something you could just get rid of overnight.

"You said Dalkquist killed her after he got control of the money. Why risk killing her if he already had what he needed?"

"I'm not sure. I think he was afraid that she'd found out he was having an affair and would want a divorce. He'd signed a prenuptial agreement which spelled out quite clearly that if they divorced, he'd get nothing."

"And the money? How did he manage that?"

"To understand that, you have to understand about my mother. She was born into money, with an indulgent father who doted on her, and she grew up taking for granted that there would always be a man taking care of her. When she married my father, he doted on her just like her father had. And when he died, she...just fell apart. She couldn't cope—didn't *want* to cope."

She smiled wanly. "The week after Daddy died, I had to lend her money because she didn't know where his checkbook was or what bank he used or even how much money was in the accounts. Bills would come in and pile up because she didn't realize she had to take care of them, and the household staff went for nearly a month without pay. Someone else had always taken care of those details, and she simply didn't know what to do."

"And Dalkquist came along and offered to take care of it all for her."

"He and my father knew each other for years. They belonged to the same clubs, traveled in the same business circles. I can remember Dad telling me that Dalkquist was one of the most brilliant—and utterly ruthless—businessmen he'd ever met. Dalkquist had tried to interest him in a couple of business ventures over the years, but Dad wouldn't have anything to do with him. He didn't trust him. He used to say that Brenton was the kind of man who'd slap your back and call you his best friend even while he was picking your pocket."

"And after your dad died, he put the moves on your mother."

Cait nodded glumly. "Not that it took much effort, heaven knows. Without Dad, Mother was lost. She'd always had a man in her life, had always defined herself through a man's eyes." She smiled wanly. "I know I'm making her sound silly and shallow, but that isn't really fair. Or even true. She was just a product of her upbringing—the perfect corporate wife. And she didn't know how to function in any other role."

"So she married Dalkquist—against your objections."

Cait's expression hardened. "I told Mother he was just after her money, and of course she told me I was being paranoid, that dear Brenton was just being solicitous and kind." She gave a snort of bitter laughter and looked at Shay, her eyes glittering. "I didn't have the heart to tell her that he'd put the moves on me about two years earlier. When he saw that wasn't going to work, he backed right off. But I've often wondered about my father's accident...."

Shay's gut tightened. "Accident? Your father died in an accident?"

"He and his accountant were out on the boat, hammering out the details on some business deal they were putting together. No one really knows what happened—there was an explosion and both of them were killed outright. There weren't enough pieces of the boat left for the accident investigators to really figure out what had happened, but they *guessed* that there was a fuel leak."

"But you said you'd always wondered...?"

"My dad grew up around boats. And there are a dozen alarms on a motor launch of that size. If there was a fuel

leak or if fumes had been building up in the bilge, my dad
would have known about it. And he'd *never* have started the
engine without putting the blowers on to purge the engine
compartment first. That's one of the first things you learn,
for crying out loud! It would be like . . . like you blowing up
your semi because you'd forgotten to do some simple, routine little thing.''

"You think Dalkquist killed your father?"

"Well, I can't help but wonder if, when his play for me
fell through, he didn't decide to go after my mother. After
all, if he wanted access to Sawyer and Ivarson money, it
didn't matter which one of us he married."

Shay gave a low whistle, thinking about it. Not liking the
way his mind kept adding up the numbers and spitting out
the same answer. "If he got rid of your dad, your mother
would be free to marry again. . . ."

Cait looked at him, her expression bleak. "After the funeral, he was all over her like a cat on cream. He can charm
the bark off trees when he puts his mind to it—he has this
way of looking into your eyes when he talks to you, which
makes you feel like you're the most important person he's
ever met. I've seen him walk into a room filled with people
who hate his guts, and within ten minutes they're fawning
over him like lap dogs."

"And you told your mother how you felt?"

"Constantly." She managed a rough, humorless smile.
"But it was a waste of time. Dalkquist knew I knew what he
was up to and he just edged me out. He spent every moment he could with her, keeping her away from me. He in-
sinuated himself between the two of us, telling her I was
upset over Dad's death and didn't want to see her getting
close to another man, that I was jealous of her. I found out
later that he'd told her I'd made a play for him myself and
was mad because he'd turned me down."

She gave her head an angry toss. "When they made their relationship public, Dalkquist would tell people about my antagonism toward him. He'd make jokes about it, playing the bemused but patient stepfather-to-be. He'd make this big show of how he understood how I felt and how he hoped—for my poor mother's sake—that in time I'd come to accept and maybe even like him. Of course all our friends thought he was wonderful and kind and understanding, and that I was a perfect little bitch."

"And your mother believed him."

Cait shrugged. "The prospect of being alone was more frightening than anything Dalkquist might do. About a year after they were married, she did tell me she thought he was having an affair. I told her to toss him out. But she said she had no real proof, and besides, as long as he was discreet, she'd rather have a man in her life, even an unfaithful one, than be alone."

She looked up at the sky again, then sighed and turned to lean on the railing, looking across at Shay. "I'll tell you one thing, though—I'll never be like her. The minute you let someone start taking care of you, you're vulnerable. You start losing part of yourself and pretty soon you're just an ornament on a rich man's arm. And I'm damned if I'll ever be a...a trinket!"

Shay found himself laughing. "Somehow, I can't see that being a problem, sweetheart. I have a feeling that any man who tries to turn you into a trinket is going to think he walked into a tiger's cage."

She looked at him mistrustfully, as though trying to decide if he was making fun of her or just teasing, then made up her mind and gave him a small smile. "That's what I like about you, McKittrick. Most of the men in my life—aside from Dalkquist and his goons—see me in terms of my net worth and my standing in the social register. You don't seem to give a damn."

Shay shrugged. "I haven't had much experience with rich women. But from what I've seen, I figure you're no different from any other except for the toys you can buy."

She smiled. "To a lot of men, those toys are what make the difference." The smile turned faintly bitter, then faded altogether. "I have a feeling I won't be buying many toys with what's left after Dalkquist is finished stripping the family accounts. From what I can tell, my trust fund is financing his bid for the governor's chair. He broke it somehow and transferred the money into a business account. don't know if he convinced my mother to sign trusteeship over to him before he killed her, or if he just forged her signature."

She managed another wry smile. "So, Mr. McKittrick what you may have on your hands is a rich woman with little or no money. I hope you weren't counting on a big reward for helping me."

She said it flippantly, but Shay sensed a hint of challenge in the words, in her eyes. Did she really believe it, he wondered, or did she just want to see how he'd react?

He found himself smiling, and he tossed the dregs of his coffee out into the night as he shrugged away from the peeled pine pole he'd been leaning against. "Honey, the only thing I figure you've got to offer is trouble, and lots of it. If I was looking to collect rewards, I'd stick to looking through the lost and found."

Still smiling, he turned and walked back into the cabin.

Chapter 7

Trouble.

Cait had to smile slightly. Well, she couldn't argue about that. She was trouble. More trouble than most men would risk taking on.

Her smile faded as she pulled the sweatshirt over her head and dropped it across the back of a chair, giving her head a toss to free her hair; she'd already done away with the ponytail holder that had held her hair back earlier. She combed her hair back with her fingers, eyeing her reflection in the spotty old mirror above the pine dresser and not caring much for what she saw. The past couple of months had left their mark—she was too pale, too thin, the dark circles under her eyes too deep, and she looked ... hunted.

Idly she thought of Amber Hills, testing the memories. The fear came and she fought it down, reminding herself that she was safe now. That Dalkquist would *never* catch her by surprise again. Not unless he killed her outright, anyway. But one thing was certain: she was *not* going back to Amber Hills. Not alive.

As she had a number of times over the past few days when she'd been lucid enough to think clearly, she found herself wondering what would have happened to her had she not met Shay McKittrick.

The thought made her shiver and she turned away from the mirror and started unbuttoning the blouse. Heaven alone knew where she'd be right now if it weren't for him. In a police cell, screaming for more of Angstrom's drugs, with *addict* scrawled across her file. In a hospital, strapped to a psych ward bed while the local doctors tried to figure out what she'd been on. Or maybe just in a ditch somewhere, too cold and sick to even call for help, destined to become just one more Jane Doe on a slab in the county morgue.

Dalkquist would identify her as his beloved but troubled stepdaughter, and there'd be an elaborate funeral. People would come to give their condolences and shake their heads and say how awful it was, and how it was a good thing that her mother wasn't alive to see this turn of events, and how terrible for poor Brenton, losing both wife *and* daughter within a year of each other.

And he'd have gotten away with it, Cait thought bitterly. Even if someone got suspicious, there'd be no way to link Dalkquist to her death. It would have been written off as another family tragedy, and he'd have gone ahead with his bid for the governor's office and in time no one would even remember the troubled stepdaughter who'd caused him so much grief.

Annoyed just at the thought of it, she tossed the blouse onto the chair and peeled out of the blue jeans, distracting herself by wondering how Shay's brother-in-law had managed to get such a good fit when he'd never even met her. A *snug* fit, she amended, recalling Shay's frank appraisal of

her denim-clad backside this evening. What he'd seen had
apparently pleased him, because his gaze had drifted in that
general direction time and again.

Which hadn't exactly displeased *her,* Cait reminded herself with an inward smile. Strange. For the past year or
more, a man's speculative stare had never been anything but
a threat. Just seeing the same man more than once usually
sent her running for cover, certain he was one of Dalkquist's.

But there was something about the way Shay looked at
her that brought a lot of feelings back she hadn't experi-
enced—or even thought of—for a long, long while. Good
feelings.

A little frightening, too. Because starting to feel things for
Shay could spell serious trouble if those feelings started distracting her. If she started thinking about Shay when she
should be thinking about how to trap Dalkquist, started
daydreaming about Shay when she should be watching her
back for an ambush.

She pulled the nightgown from the duffle bag and held it
up to herself, then smiled again and slipped it on. It was
silk—real silk—and felt like a breath of mist against her
skin, so light and filmy, it was hardly even there.

An odd choice of clothing, all considered. But then, this
Rick Jarvis seemed to have his own ideas of what she and
Shay were doing up here.

Smiling again, she reached for the hairbrush and started
running it through her hair, glad to see that the expensive
shampoo Jarvis sent up had worked at least a little magic
and had brought some of the shine back. Whoever this
mysterious Jarvis was, he had good taste in women's toiletries, too. Bending over at the waist, she flipped her hair over
her head and started to brush it seriously.

Her arm gave out finally, and she straightened and swept
her hair back with her arm, giving her head a shake to set-

tle it—and found herself staring straight into Shay's lake-blue eyes.

He was standing in the doorway. Lounging, actually, one outstretched arm braced against the frame, looking as though he had nothing better to do. His gaze held hers for a long, taut moment, then he just smiled faintly and pushed himself away from the doorframe to stroll across to the closet, not looking at her.

"I figure you don't need a guardian angel tonight, so I was going to bed down in the living room." He pulled the closet door open and took a pillow and blanket from the shelf. "Do us both a favor and don't lock the door. If you do have a bad spell in the night, I don't want to have to kick it in."

"All right." Cait found herself feeling suddenly self-conscious, telling herself she was being silly. This was the man, after all, with whom she'd made love. The man who'd nursed her through the past three or four days, including tossing her in the shower a couple of times.

"That…uh…nightie pretty much fits, by the look of it."

"Yes. Your brother-in-law's wife must love him—he has great taste."

Shay gave a snort and tossed the blanket over one shoulder. "Rick's the quintessential bachelor. He says it's because of the work, but I suspect it's just because he likes playing the field a little too much. But you're right—he does have good taste." His gaze wandered over her with unnerving thoroughness. "Very good taste."

"He's obviously got the wrong idea about us."

Shay's eyes met hers, amusement shadowing their depths. "How so?"

Ignoring the way her heart kept jitterbugging around, she walked across to the dresser, wishing she'd pulled on the robe. Wishing this damned nightie were about six inches longer. Wishing it didn't dive so outrageously low in front…

She picked up the handful of plastic-wrapped contraceptives and carried them across to him, depositing them in his outstretched hand. "I found these in the duffle bag. I presume they're for you."

Shay gave a bark of laughter. "That makes about two dozen he sent up. I'd say my brother-in-law has the wrong idea about *me,* anyway, or he knows something about stamina that I don't."

In spite of her best efforts, Cait felt herself starting to blush. Determined not to look rattled, she took one of the little disks from his fingers and looked at it curiously. "At least they're not fluorescent green or hot pink. I've always thought that making love with someone who glowed in the dark would be totally unnerving." She dropped it back into his palm.

Shay gave another gust of laughter and tucked them into his shirt pocket, his eyes glinting with mischief. "Distracting, anyway. A man likes his lady to be concentrating on *him,* not on whether anything's glowing or not."

She tried not to laugh, but it was impossible not to, the image his teasing evoked just a little too vivid to be ignored. And for one long wondrous moment they delighted in the utter silliness of it, forgetting Dalkquist and Amber Hills, forgetting the past four days, forgetting everything but the magic of shared laughter.

Still grinning, Shay spontaneously bent down and kissed her lightly on the mouth. "Between this supply, and the ones some joker tossed in the truck a couple of weeks ago, we could stay up here for a month and never get out of bed."

"You seem to have a lot of considerate friends."

"Considerate, maybe, but not very subtle." Some of the laughter faded from Shay's gaze and he looked down at her, standing so close she could see the flecks of gray in his eyes, the hairline scar across his left cheek. "I . . . don't want you getting the wrong idea, Cait. About these." He tapped his shirt pocket with his thumb. "About me. Rick didn't bring them up because he thinks I'll need them, but because he figures I won't. It's his way of telling me I need a woman in my life again."

Cait nodded, smiling gently. "I kind of figured that."

His gaze locked with hers, and she knew he was thinking of that night they'd made love. Something tightened around his eyes slightly and he stepped back, his expression carefully blank, then he turned and walked toward the door. "Good night, Cait," he said quietly. "I'll see you in the morning."

"We've never talked about it," Cait said softly. "Why is that, do you suppose?"

Shay stopped just short of the door, his back stiffening slightly. "Talked about what?"

"You know what, Shay," Cait told him patiently. "That night in the truck."

"What's to talk about?"

She was silent for a moment, then she sighed and turned to put the hairbrush down, watching Shay in the mirror. "We made love, Shay. We've both been acting as though it never happened, but whether we wanted to or not, or meant to or not, we *did*."

"I got the feeling you didn't want to talk about it." He glanced around at her, his eyes meeting hers on glass.

Cait let her gaze slip from his, her finger trailing along the edge of the dresser. "I didn't, I guess. I . . . just never knew what to say. And you seemed to want to forget it."

Frowning, he made his way back to where she was standing. "I guess I probably did." He put his hands on her shoulders and lowered his face to her hair, still holding her gaze in the mirror. "I'm sorry, Cait. We should have talked. It wasn't right, just leaving it like that between us."

"Are you sorry it happened?"

"No." He closed his eyes, then slipped his arms around her and held her close, resting his chin on top of her head. "No, I'm not. And maybe that's what scares me so much." He took a deep breath, opened pain-filled eyes to look at her. "I loved my wife, Cait. In the two years since she died, I've never even looked at another woman. And yet with you..."

He drew her around to face him, gazing down at her intently. "I want you," he told her bluntly. "Day and night, it's all I can do to keep my hands off you. Every time I look at you, all I can think of is that night... the way your skin felt, the smell of your hair, the taste of your mouth. I can't close my eyes without remembering what it was like being inside you and feeling you moving all around me, and loving you..." His fingers tightened on her shoulders. "And it scares the hell out of me, understand? Because I've gone the past two years without wanting anyone, without needing anyone. And I like it that way just fine!"

Cait stared up at him, mute in her astonishment, her mind spinning as it tried to take in what he was saying. And under the confusion, she felt very real alarm. She'd gotten him into this, she thought dazedly. She'd done this to him....

Shay gave a snort of harsh laughter and released her abruptly, turning and walking away. "Sorry. I didn't mean to scare you."

"You didn't scare me," she lied. "I—I'm just wondering what it means. What kind of complications it creates."

"No complications, Cait," he said more quietly, glancing around at her. "That night didn't *mean* anything. Not long-term. It was just two strangers who needed each other for the night." He smiled lazily. "I'm not going to cause trouble, if that's what's worrying you. I've never been a one-night stand kind of guy, but in this case I figure it's best if we just leave it at that."

And then he was gone, the door closing slowly behind him. And Cait, still shaken to the core, walked across to the bed, pulled the covers back and slipped between the sheets, telling herself firmly that it didn't mean anything. Nothing at all . . .

Rick arrived the next morning. Shay was outside, feeling restless and out of sorts for no reason he could figure, when he saw the blue car pull slowly down the laneway leading to the cabin.

He hadn't slept much, his night haunted by nightmares, and he'd gotten up early and had gone for a run along the beach, discovering to his disgust that he was badly out of shape. Before Nancy had gotten sick, he'd put in five miles a day, sometimes more, but during her illness he'd stopped running and had simply never gotten back to it.

And it showed. He'd limped back up to the cabin with a stitch in his side and had done some sit-ups and other calisthenics just to cool down and work off the rest of his restless energy. And he was still breathing hard when Rick got out of the car and walked toward him.

Rick let his gaze run over Shay's running shorts and ragged, sweat-soaked T-shirt, and nodded approvingly. "Glad to see you're back in the groove, McKittrick."

Giving a snort, Shay grabbed his towel and mopped his face. "Far from it."

"Where's your lady?"

Rick asked it just a little too casually, and Shay gave him a sharp look. "Asleep."

Rick nodded. "Having any more . . . problems with her?"

"What kind of problems?"

"Well, you said she was behaving irrationally."

"No," Shay said with precision, "I *said* she was kicking the drugs they were pumping into her at Amber Hills. And she's clean now. Worn-out and a little worse for wear—but clean.''

Rick nodded thoughtfully, his gaze never leaving Shay's. Then he turned toward the cabin. "You got any coffee? I've been on the road since five this morning."

Shay had his mouth open to tell him to cut the crap and say what was on his mind, but he subsided with an inward oath. Rick would do this his way or not at all. Games, that's what it was all about. Secret-agent games.

He'd made a pot of coffee when he'd gotten up and there was still plenty left, so he told Rick to help himself and headed for the shower. Pulling on jeans and one of the two shirts he had with him, he skipped shoes altogether and walked back out into the kitchen a few minutes later, still toweling his hair dry.

Rick was standing by the big window in the front room, leaning against the frame and staring out into the trees, a ceramic mug of steaming coffee in one hand. Shay got another mug down and poured himself a cup of the coffee, adding a splash of cream but forgoing his usual teaspoon of sugar. Maybe it was time to get back into shape. Maybe two years of not giving a damn whether he lived or died was long enough.

"Okay," he growled, walking across to where Rick was standing. "Let's have it. Something's eating you."

Rick glanced around, then pushed himself away from the window frame and walked over to drop into one of the big armchairs framing the fireplace. "What do you know about Cait Sawyer?"

"I told you—nothing. Just what she's told me."

"Did she tell you she's worth about ten mil?"

Shay gave a low whistle and dropped into the chair across from Rick. "I knew the family had money, but..." Ten *million!*

"Problem is, it's not Cait's. It would have been if her mother hadn't remarried. But when Alicia Sawyer married Dalkquist, it put a different spin on things."

"When she was killed, Dalkquist inherited, leaving Cait out in the cold."

"Matter of how you define *cold*. A million and a half can buy a lot of fur coats. That's what's in Cait's trust fund."

"*Was* in Cait's trust fund. She figures Dalkquist has gotten access to that money, too."

"She's been saying a lot of things, Shay," Rick said quietly. "Ever since Dalkquist came on the scene six years ago, in fact, Cait has been doing everything possible to discredit the man. She was vehemently opposed to the marriage and made few bones about it, and she's made a career out of trying to destroy his reputation ever since."

Shay frowned, but didn't say anything.

"When her mother was killed in that car accident, she stepped up her efforts in what can only be called a hate campaign. From all reports, Dalkquist has been more than patient with her, but she's thrown every offer of friendship, of conciliation, back in his face."

"I know all this." Shay's voice was clipped. He was hearing what Cait had been hearing for six years, he thought coldly. Hearing the truth—but after it had been filtered through Dalkquist.

"During the past six months, she's had what can only be called psychotic episodes. She's accused Dalkquist of having engineered her mother's death. She's been harassing the police and the medical examiner's department, demanding that they *prove* her mother's death was murder. When they didn't give her what she wanted, she started accusing them of being in Dalkquist's pocket. She hired a private detective to follow Dalkquist."

Rick shook his head wearily and leaned forward to rest his elbows on his knees, looking across at Shay. "McKittrick, I know you think you know what you're doing, but I've got to tell you—this woman is more trouble than you ever dreamed. The kind of trouble that could ruin your job, your livelihood, your damned *life* if you let her get too close. She is real bad news, no matter how you look at it."

Shay simply leaned back and braced one bare foot on the coffee table, anger spreading hot tendrils through him. "And who did you get all this from? Dalkquist's campaign manager?"

Rick's expression hardened. "It's on public record."

Shay gave a derisive snort. "You think if Dalkquist did murder her mother, he's going to put it on *public record?*"

"Damn it, McKittrick, this woman—"

"This *woman* isn't a raving psychotic out to get her stepfather, and she isn't some greedy daughter trying to cut her mother's husband out of his inheritance. What she is, Jarvis, is the victim of a very clever man who has been methodically discrediting her right from the beginning. He's invented this version of her, don't you understand that? He's *built* this story about her crazy behavior right from the ground up."

"She's sucked you right into her make-believe world, don't you understand *that?* Hell, maybe she believes it herself now. Maybe she's lived it for so long it's become real to her and she does believe Dalkquist was after the family money all along. But it's *not* real, McKittrick. It's all just a sick woman's paranoid fantasy."

Shay's foot hit the floor with a thud. He stood up and strode into the small kitchenette, his jaw aching slightly where he had his teeth clenched. "Thanks for your help, Jarvis. I appreciate it. Now why don't you just get in your car and get the hell out of here. I'll handle things from here on in."

There was a whisper of profanity behind him. "Don't shut me out like this, McKittrick. I'm trying to save you a lot of grief here. Maybe even your damn life. God knows what she's got planned this time. You could be walking into something you'll never get out of.''

"Get out."

Silence. Shay tossed the rest of his coffee into the sink and dropped the mug into the drainer next to it, shrugging his shoulders to loosen the muscles across them.

"I got her medical records," Rick said quietly. "She's been in and out of drug rehab for the past two or three years, hooked on just about any damn thing you can think of—pills, coke, every exotic chemical you can name. She tried to cut her wrists last fall, took an overdose before that—it was a miracle Dalkquist found her in time and got her to the hospital."

"Amber Hills, right?" Shay didn't even bother turning around. "And I'll bet that's where she did her rehab, too."

Rick was silent for a moment. "So?"

"So," Shay said dryly, turning to give Rick a hostile look. "It's all fantasy, all right—but not Cait's. None of that stuff in her so-called 'medical record' is real. It's all just part of the setup."

"Why?" Rick's voice was vibrant with impatient anger. "Why would Dalkquist go to this much trouble to get rid of her? It just doesn't make sense."

"I can think of about ten million reasons, Jarvis. Not to mention a murder charge."

Rick just stared at him, eyes narrowing. Then, to Shay's surprise, he frowned. Sat back, looking thoughtful, tapping his lower lip with his thumbnail as he stared at the toe of his leather boot, obviously mulling it over.

Then, finally, he shook his head. "What are the odds of it being true, Shay? Hell, we're talking about a man who's running for *governor.* A man who—"

"—has one hell of a lot to lose if Cait can prove he murdered his wife for her money." He walked back into the living room and sat down again, elbows on thighs. "Rick, I know it sounds crazy. But that's the beauty of it. That's what Dalkquist is counting on—that people will look at the 'evidence' and come to the same conclusions you have—that Cait Sawyer is a nut case with a chip on her shoulder the size of Nebraska. Everybody's written her off as a drugged-out psychotic, no one will listen to a word she says and now Dalkquist has committed her to Amber Hills and is calling her a suicide risk."

He leaned forward slightly, his voice intense. "But what if she is telling the truth, Rick? What if Dalkquist *is* planning on having her killed in Amber Hills of a drug overdose and calling it suicide?"

Rick continued to stare at him, his expression becoming more and more troubled.

"If she's really as crazy as they say, why hasn't Dalkquist just called the police in and charged me with kidnapping?"

"There could be a dozen reasons. Having his stepdaughter go AWOL from Amber Hills right when his campaign is kicking off isn't the kind of publicity the man would want."

"Maybe. Or maybe he's just a little nervous about having her talk too much in case someone starts listening."

Rick gave a grunt. "You're taking this pretty personally."

"Damn right it's personal. I've spent four days of my life putting that woman back together. I have an investment."

Rick stared at him for a long moment. Then he muttered something under his breath and rubbed his face with his hands, looking tired and angry. "You're really some piece of work, McKittrick, you know that? I don't see you or hear from you for two years. Don't know if you're dead or alive, figure I'll never know for sure. And then one day you crawl out of a hole and call me up and next thing I know, I'm sitting here listening to the craziest story I've ever heard…and I'm starting to *believe* it!''

"Her story might be crazy, Rick, but I'll stake my life on the fact she isn't."

"That could be just what you're doing, you dumb bastard," Rick muttered, pushing himself to his feet. "Where's your phone?"

Shay stood up and wandered into the kitchen to help himself to another cup of coffee he didn't really want. He carried it back into the living room and sat down again, staring across to where Rick was perched on the arm of the other chair, holding the telephone receiver against his ear with one hand and rubbing his eyes with the other.

Shay couldn't hear the conversation, but he caught Dalkquist's name a couple of times, thought he heard his own uttered with an edging of pure disgust. It made him smile slightly and he took a swallow of the hot coffee, thinking he'd go for another run that evening. He felt loose and healthy for the first time in a long while, and it was a good feeling. He'd forgotten how good—

The receiver went down with a click and Rick sat there for a moment or two, staring down at it. Then he turned to look at Shay, an odd expression on his face. "That was O'Dell. He ran Cait's name through our computers just to see what would turn up and found something strange."

Shay's shoulder muscles tightened. "Strange?"

"I told you she hired a private investigator last year to snoop around and see what he could uncover about her mother's death."

"Yeah." Shay was suddenly alert.

"Well, it seems he *did* find something. At least he said he did, although no one seems to know what it was. He talked to a buddy of his on the Sacramento police force, but wouldn't tell him any specifics. Just that he'd talked to someone who knew for a fact that Cait Sawyer wasn't entirely crazy."

"And?"

Rick had an odd expression on his face. "And he died. He was killed in a hit-and-run the day after he talked to his friend."

Shay felt something cold walk down his spine. "And this friend didn't do anything?"

Rick shrugged. "Nothing he could do. It was a jurisdictional thing—Itoya, the investigator, was killed in Los Angeles. And it looked like a clean hit-and-run. It happens."

Shay thought of what Cait had said...that Dalkquist was retracing his steps, making everything pristine and airtight. He looked up at Rick. "So, are you in or not? What did O'Dell say?"

Rick looked decidedly unhappy as he nodded. "Yeah, I'm in. O'Dell was...interested. He ran Dalkquist's name through the computer, too."

"And?"

"And he didn't like what he saw. Nothing specific, nothing you could put your finger on. But O'Dell has this instinct for trouble. In Nam they used to say he could smell an ambush five miles away—and there are a lot of guys alive today who'd swear by it." He smiled faintly, rubbing his ruined leg. "I'm one of them. I don't like O'Dell much, but I'd follow him to hell and back if I had to."

Shay nodded. "But you're still not convinced there's anything to find."

"I think she's tied you into knots and you've got an overload of testosterone where your brains should be," Rick said bluntly. "If it was up to me, I'd toss you in a cold shower and knock some damned sense into you. But it's not up to me."

"You got that straight."

"So I'm going to tell you to back off, instead. Go home. Get back to work and forget Cait Sawyer and Brenton Dalkquist. I'll handle things from here on in."

Shay just smiled. "Forget it. I'm in."

"No, you're not. You're a truck driver, McKittrick. This is way out of your league. Leave it to the professionals."

"Go to hell," Shay replied mildly. He eased himself to his feet and walked across to the kitchen again. "You want breakfast? You bought the groceries, seems only right you should help eat them."

Chapter 8

Shay was just putting the finishing touches to a panful of scrambled eggs when he heard the shower come on. Rick heard it, too. He lifted his head like a stag scenting the wind, then glanced at Shay.

But he didn't say anything, turning his attention back to the small printer that was sitting on the coffee table beside his laptop computer, chattering away like a deranged chipmunk.

It was hooked up—by phone modem—to a computer in Washington or some damned place, from what Shay could figure out, and was spewing information out by the ream. Rick had been sitting there for nearly half an hour now, reading things that made him shake his head and mutter under his breath now and again and occasionally make a note on the pad of paper beside him.

There was no point in asking him about it. Shay would just get a terse "none of your business" if he tried, so he kept his mouth shut with an effort and stuck to making breakfast.

So it was a relief when Cait finally came out of the bathroom, dressed in jeans and a white cotton shirt, sleeves rolled to her elbows, freshly scrubbed cheeks glowing. She'd brushed her hair until it gleamed and it cascaded around her shoulders and down her back like a fall of ebony silk.

She looked serene and normal and so breathtakingly beautiful that Shay was amused to see Rick gape a little stupidly at her for a split second when she walked into the room.

Cait broke into a warm, friendly smile when she saw him and walked across to offer him her hand. "Hi. You must be Shay's brother-in-law, the mysterious Rick Jarvis."

Rick got to his feet and shook her hand, eyeing her almost warily. "I'm Jarvis. And you're . . . ?"

Cait's smile widened, her left cheek dimpling beguilingly. "I'm tempted to say Cleopatra, just to see your reaction, but I somehow don't think you're in the mood for jokes." She looked at him evenly. "Caitlin Sawyer, Mr. Jarvis. Mad woman, paranoid delusionist and all-around troublemaker."

To Shay's amusement, Rick looked discomfited. "No one called you paranoid, Miss Sawyer."

"Cait. And trust me, half the western world is calling me paranoid. 'A sick woman with paranoid fantasies,' I think you said?"

Shay grinned, deciding to stay out of it. Cait could obviously handle Rick Jarvis without his help—and it would do Jarvis considerable good to have some of his assumptions about Cait knocked out of him by the lady herself.

"Hungry, Cleo?" Shay grinned across at her.

Cait grinned back. "Starved. Although I was Cleopatra yesterday, wasn't I? Maybe I'll be Lady Macbeth today. I love all that manic hand washing."

"Come and sit down and dig in. Jarvis, that means you, too."

Rick looked at him, then at Cait, then gave his head a shake and walked across to sit down at the table. "You two practice this routine before I got up here?"

"Nope, we're just naturals." Shay put a plate of scrambled eggs, bacon and toast in front of him, uncharacteristically ebullient for no reason he could pinpoint. Seeing Cait so healthy and clearheaded this morning was part of it. If you didn't look closely enough to see the fading bruise on her jaw or the needle tracks on her arms, and if you ignored the dark shadows under her eyes, you'd think she was just a normal attractive woman without a care in the world.

"Are those my files on the sofa?" she asked Rick casually, picking up her fork and eyeing with relish the mound of scrambled eggs Shay had put in front of her. "The ones that spell out how I've been harassing my stepfather and the police and anyone else I thought could help me? The ones that say I'm a suicide risk, a danger to myself and anyone around me *and* have dabbled in every kind of recreational drug known to man?"

Rick looked across at Shay, but Shay just took a mouthful of bacon and ignored him. "I guess that's the long and short of it."

Cait nodded, setting even white teeth across a slice of bacon and biting it cleanly through, her expression mild. "You'll have the police reports, too, then. The ones that say I tried to run Dalkquist over with my car last year. And set up a fake break-in at my own apartment—during which I was shot—in order to frame him for my attempted murder."

"*Shot?*" Shay nearly choked on a mouthful of toast. "Break in?"

"A man entered Miss Sawyer's apartment last August in what police think was a burglary attempt," Rick said evenly, gazing across the table at Cait. "She woke up and confronted the intruder, whereupon he pulled a gun and fired. The bullet grazed Miss Sawyer's upper arm, police were called, the suspect was arrested and is now serving time for assault with a dangerous weapon, breaking and entering and a slew of other charges."

He looked at Shay. "She maintained that Dalkquist hired the man to kill her and make it look as though she'd been shot during a burglary. The assailant, however, insists he broke in looking for money, she surprised him, he shot her."

"Except the *assailant* has a wife and two kids who disappeared right after he went to jail," Cait said impatiently. "And a neighbor who swears he saw a big white Mercedes parked in her driveway just after the break-in." She looked at Shay. "Dalkquist drives a white Mercedes."

"Thin," Rick said dryly. "Very thin. But while you're at it, tell him the rest of it."

Cait looked down uncomfortably, frowning slightly.

"Miss Sawyer confronted her stepfather at a party a couple of days later and, in front of about a hundred guests, threatened to kill him."

Cait threw her head up angrily. "I told him that if he tried to have me killed again, I'd hire someone to return the favor." Frowning again, she looked at Shay. "It was stupid, I'll admit that. But no one was listening to me and I was so mad I just…" She made a helpless gesture. "The worst part of it was that he just laughed it off, telling everyone there that I'd had a terrible scare and was understandably upset. That I wasn't responsible for anything I said. As usual, I played right into his hands. He came out of it looking like a saint, and I looked like some drugged-out space cadet."

"And when you tried to run him over?"

Cait met his gaze evenly. "That's the only report in the whole file that has any truth in it. I did nearly run him down."

"For the love of God, Cait..."

She shrugged. "He was standing in front of my car, my foot slipped off the brake. I don't know if it was an accident or my subconscious taking over. He jumped back out of the way and my front bumper just brushed his leg." She smiled a little coldly. "I think that's when he realized he had to get rid of me."

Shay felt a chill work its way down his spine. Not at the cool, matter-of-fact way Cait spoke of nearly killing Dalkquist or of her own death, but at the fact she'd managed to survive for this long. "Jarvis," he said quietly, "I want five minutes with this guy. Just five. Then you and O'Dell can have him."

"Getting anywhere near Dalkquist is *not* in the picture," Rick said calmly. "We're fact finding, that's all."

"Fact finding?" Shay didn't even bother keeping the derision out of his voice. "We're hip-deep in *facts* all ready, Jarvis. Just how much more paper do you need before you can make an arrest?"

Cait smiled gently. "Shay, it's not that simple. He's like Teflon—nothing sticks. He has an army of people taking care of business. Any links between him and my mother's death, or between him and anything that's happened to me, are so tenuous they may as well not even exist. Nothing in those files proves that Dalkquist is anything but a loving husband and stepfather. What I need—what I think I've found—is something that *will* implicate him. Something that he won't be able to lie his way out of."

"Such as?"

"Don Mosely."

Rick's head shot up. "Mosely?"

"He's the guy who broke into my house and took that shot at me. I hired an investigator, Lee Itoya, to do some snooping for me, and he talked with Mosely. Lee's dead now—he was killed in a very convenient hit and run down in L.A.—but the night before he died, he called me and told me he'd gone out to the prison and talked with Mosely.''

Shay met Rick's glance for a long, taut moment, then looked back at Cait. ''What did he tell you?''

''Not much.'' She made a face. ''Just that Mosely was jumpy. He asked Lee to check on his wife and sons, to make sure they were okay. Lee said it sounded as though Mosely was on the verge of cracking, that he figured all it would take was a little more pressure and Mosely would come apart like a cheap suit.''

''Except Itoya was killed before he could apply that pressure.''

''You got it, cowboy.''

''And you think you can pick up where Itoya left off?''

''Well, I can hardly go marching in to the prison and talk with Mosely, but I was planning to try and find his wife. She might know something.''

''I could go to the prison and talk with Mosely,'' Shay rumbled. ''In fact, I'd enjoy talking with Mosely. I'd be happier talking to Mosely with a tire iron in my hand and no witnesses, but I'll take what I can get.''

''Don Mosely is dead.''

Rick's quiet voice fell between them like a gust of icy air. He took a deep breath, looking unhappier by the minute. ''It's in the information the computer's kicking out. He was stabbed by a fellow prisoner the day before yesterday. They got him to the infirmary, but he died a couple of hours later.'' Rick lifted his gaze to Cait's. ''He didn't say anything. Even at the end.''

Cait closed her eyes, feeling suddenly dizzy. The room seemed to spin gently around her and then she felt strong, warm fingers folding around hers and she clung to them, to the anchoring they provided. The spinning slowly stopped and when she opened her eyes, both Shay and Rick were looking at her, Shay's expression clouded with concern, Rick's with faint suspicion.

"Dalkquist did it. Dalkquist had him killed."

"People get killed in prison all the time," Rick said impatiently. "It doesn't mean anything."

But he didn't sound convinced, Cait thought dimly. Even she could hear the faint doubt underlying his voice.

"Lee Itoya. This Mosely dude." Shay looked at Rick. "Seems to me a hell of a lot of people involved with this thing are winding up dead."

"I killed him. He's dead because I escaped from Amber Hills." Cait swallowed, her fingers tightening on Shay's. "He has a wife. Two sons..."

"He tried to murder you, Cait." Shay's voice was cold. "He got exactly what he deserved."

Rick didn't say anything, but after a moment or two he pushed his half-finished meal back and got to his feet. "I've got a couple of calls to make."

Cait watched him walk across to where the small computer was still spitting out paper. He disconnected the phone from the modem, then carried it across to the big armchair. In another moment or two, he was in deep conversation with someone.

"He's not buying any of this."

"Don't write him off yet," Shay said mildly. "It's just the way he is. I was married to Nan for over a year before he finally decided maybe I was good enough for her."

"I don't have a year."

She sounded impatient and edgy, and Shay watched her as she poked at her scrambled eggs then shoved the plate aside, combing a handful of hair back. Impulsively he reached across and brushed a toast crumb from her chin, letting his fingers linger on her smooth, warm skin as long as he dared. "It's going to be all right, Caitie," he heard himself say, believing it himself in the moment it took to say the words. "We'll get him."

She looked up in faint surprise at the vehemence in his voice. Her eyes were the color of melted gold in the morning light and he could see flecks of darker brown in them. He wondered idly why he'd never noticed that until now. Or how they seemed to tip, ever so slightly, upward at the outer corners, or how long and thick her lashes were, or how when she looked at him the way she was right now he swore he could feel it clear through to his bones.

He managed, with an effort, to pull himself away, thinking that it had been a long while since he'd dawdled over breakfast with a beautiful woman. He and Nancy had made a ritual of it on those all-too-rare mornings he'd been home, chatting and catching up on each other's news, then more often than not going back to bed for an hour or two of leisurely lovemaking.

Which is what he'd like to be doing right now with Cait Sawyer, he found himself thinking suddenly.

Irritated at how his mind kept taunting him, Shay pushed his chair back and got to his feet. "I'm going out to check my rig."

Cait just nodded, watching him as he walked across to the door. He was easy to watch: tall, but not too much so, wide-shouldered enough to nearly fill the doorway when he stepped through, torso narrowing to hips as lean as a cat's, well-muscled buttocks that filled those faded old jeans to absolute perfection, long legs that carried him with the confident, going-somewhere stride of a man with a purpose.

Different from most of the men she knew. Gym-toned and sartorially perfect, they traveled in tight packs, as competitive as sharks and with little loyalty to anything but their own success. They all moved in the right circles, had the right jobs, married the right women.

Cait had to smile. She'd been one of those women once. Then she'd accused the esteemed Brenton Dalkquist of unspeakable things, and her standing in the ranks of the socially acceptable had hit rock bottom. And the odd part of it was, she honestly couldn't say she cared.

Restless, she got up and cleared away the dishes, stacking them in the sink, then wandered into the living room. Rick was sitting on the sofa, frowning down at a computer printout.

He lifted his head and looked at her, his cool gaze following her as she walked across to the window. "You know anything about Dalkquist's business ventures?"

"Only that he's been financing them with my grandfather's money," Cait said with a touch of hostility. "Why?"

"Nothing specific. Tax evasion, maybe."

"Tax evasion?" Cait turned to look at him in disbelief. "Dalkquist murdered my mother, hired Don Mosely to murder me and then had *him* killed, murdered Lee Itoya... and you think you might get him on *tax evasion?*" She turned away with a snort of derision. "Hell, why not? Maybe you can just audit him to death!"

"Lighten up," he said mildly. "I'm just looking at all the angles, all right? With a man like Dalkquist, you've got to find a hairline crack in the structure he's built up around himself and pick away at it until it starts to open up."

Cait looked at him again. "Do you really believe there's something to find? Or are you just humoring Shay?"

"Trust me, honey, I wouldn't be wasting company time on McKittrick. The guy was married to my sister, that's all."

"But you came up here when he called you."

He shrugged. "Like I said, he was married to my sister. No big deal."

No big deal. Cait nearly smiled. "You don't like me very much, do you?"

"Like doesn't come into it. I just think you're dangerous."

"Dangerous?" Cait lifted one eyebrow.

"Not you—what you're doing to Shay." His eyes held hers, hard as stone. "What you're making him face."

"I'm not *making* Shay do anything," Cait shot back. "I asked him to help me—but only to get me away from the Amber Hills area. Nothing more. He's done the rest of it himself."

"You didn't have to ask. For him, there's no choice."

"What do you mean?"

Rick's eyes narrowed slightly. Then he rubbed his face with his hand, his expression bleak. "He didn't tell you about Nancy?"

"I know he was married. And that she died two years ago."

"She died of inoperable cancer." There was a softness in the words she'd never have dreamed possible coming from this hard-edged man. He drew in a deep breath, a muscle ticking in his left cheek. "The night they took her into the hospital for the last time, Shay went a little crazy. Instead of going with her, he went to the bar. When he managed to drag himself into the hospital three days later, still half drunk, it was too late."

Rick's eyes glittered. "She died calling for him," he said with soft savagery. "I was there with her, but it was Shay she wanted. Shay she kept calling for. And while she was dying, he was drinking himself into a stupor because he didn't have the guts to face it."

He drew in another long breath, swallowing. Cait said nothing.

"Hell, I can't blame him," he said finally, his voice a hoarse whisper. "He'd been there with her the whole time...eight months. I honestly don't know if I could have done it." He lifted his head to look at Cait. "He nursed her through it, one day at a time. For eight solid months he sat by her bed, making her fight it. Making her laugh. Reading to her. Bathing her. Holding her. And, near the end, listening to her begging him to end the pain..."

He closed his eyes, his throat working. When he looked at Cait again, his expression was filled with pain. "He's got more guts than any man I've ever met, but in the end—" He rubbed his face again. "I've tried to hate him for that, but I can't. He's spent the last two years hating himself more than I ever could. It's been killing him, that guilt. A bit at a time."

Chilled, Cait found herself thinking of the gun under Shay's mattress. The unopened bottle of whiskey. "And you think that's why he's been helping me?"

"I *know* that's why he's helping you." Rick smiled grimly. "He figures you're some sort of second chance. If he can keep you alive, he can redeem himself for letting Nan die."

"But he had nothing to do with her dying."

"I know that. He does too, logically. But logic doesn't have a damned thing to do with guilt. With grief."

Cait turned back to the window.

"He's going to play hero for you. And for himself."

"I don't *need* a hero!"

"Well, honey, you've got yourself one, like it or not. He's out there right now polishing up the armor and sharpening the lance and trying to put an edge on the old broadsword."

She looked around in annoyance. "The deal was for him to drive me to Eugene, nothing more. It's still that simple. The only person I see complicating things is you."

"Simple?" He stared at her. "Look around, lady! You call what's been going on for the last four days *simple?*"

Cait's mouth tightened. "I didn't know this was going to happen. And I didn't ask him to stay. He just...stayed."

"He'll help you," Rick said quietly, "or die trying. There's no middle ground this time."

Frowning, Cait stared out the window. Heroes weren't supposed to come burdened with baggage from a past life! They were supposed to ride in, kill the damned dragon and that was the end of it!

"Just try not to get him killed," Rick said abruptly. "I like McKittrick. He was a good man once—still is, if he could start believing in himself again. I'd hate to see him get himself killed trying to prove something that doesn't need proving."

"Trying to save me, you mean." Cait looked at him evenly.

One corner of his mouth might have lifted fractionally and his eyes, as they held hers, were ironic. "Don't take this the wrong way, lady, but you're nothing to me. McKittrick is."

"Well, I guess that's plain enough." She could feel the anger surging through her but held it tightly at bay. She needed that anger—needed its driving heat, its protective shelter. Needed it against Dalkquist. Using it against this man would just be a waste.

He got to his feet and walked into the kitchen, limping slightly, his shoulders slumping from fatigue. "This isn't about Shay, is it?" she said suddenly. "This is about you. About something that's happened to you."

Cait could see him stiffen slightly.

"What was her name?" she pressed softly. "Who were you playing hero for, Rick?"

She didn't think he was going to answer. Then he glanced around. "How did you know?"

"I didn't. You just told me."

He closed his eyes, weaving slightly, then seemed to steady himself. When he opened his eyes, the pain in them was soul-deep.

"You loved her, didn't you," Cait said softly.

"Yeah. Yeah, I loved her." He swallowed, his face haggard. "And it made me sloppy. I got distracted worrying about her when I should have been worrying about an ambush and she died, along with two others."

"I'm sorry," Cait whispered.

"Yeah. So am I." Then, to her surprise, he managed a rough-edged smile. "I've got a feeling I've underestimated you. It's not a mistake I make often."

To her even greater surprise, Cait found she could smile back. "And I have a feeling that you might be a nice guy under better circumstances."

He gave her a slow grin. "Ditto."

"I'm going for a walk. Want to come?"

He shook his head. "I'm waiting for a phone call." As Cait walked to the door and pulled it open, he called, "Be careful out there. Keep your eyes open and don't go too far."

"Not worried about me, are you, Agent Jarvis?"

"You're in my case file now," he said easily. "Get yourself killed, and I have to do paperwork. I don't like paperwork."

"Gotcha." Still smiling, she stepped out into the sunshine.

The cabin was tucked into a stand of tall pine trees and the air was heavy with their scent. She could smell the sea, too, a briny tang that made her lift her head and inhale a deep breath of it, feeling it tingle through her and relishing even that small luxury. How long had it been since she'd just stood and drunk in the world, enjoying something as simple as the sweet, clear notes of birdsong on the wind, or the perfume of tall, sun-drenched pines? How long since she'd felt this relaxed? This safe?

"You always stand around smiling to yourself?" Shay's deep voice startled her and she glanced around to see him strolling out of the shadows toward her, fingers tucked into the hip pockets of his tight-fitting jeans, a lazy grin warming his mouth.

"It's when I start arguing with myself that you should worry."

"Hell, I argue with myself all the time."

"Who wins?"

"Temptation, usually." His grin widened. "Feel up to a walk on the beach?"

"Absolutely."

They walked side by side in silence, meandering down the path leading to the beach. Cait concentrated on each step, on each bird call, on each complex array of scents the wind brought to them, not thinking of Dalkquist. Of Lee Itoya, a gentle man she'd genuinely liked. Of Mosely.

"He thinks I'm going to get you killed." She turned her head to look at Shay. "Rick, I mean."

He gave a casual shrug, looking very relaxed and comfortable striding along at her side, as though he belonged there and neither of them had a care in the world. "It's his job to worry."

"Why is he here, anyway? Besides trying to convince you that you're overdosing on testosterone?"

"You heard that?"

"I wasn't eavesdropping, exactly." She thought about that, then laughed quietly. "That's a lie. I *was* eavesdropping."

"He's here because I called him. He stayed because someone in Washington ran Dalkquist's name through a computer and bells started ringing. And if it makes you feel better, I'm not. OD'ing on testosterone, I mean." He flashed her a lazy grin. "Although that could be a lie, too, come to think of it. You've been giving me *and* my testosterone quite a workout for the past few days. I've been thinking things I haven't thought in a lo-o-ong time."

To her surprise, Cait felt herself blush. "No one's been arrested for thinking."

"Only because mind reading hasn't been perfected."

Cait had to laugh. "Good point."

Shay glanced down at her, seemingly casually. "This is going to sound like a hell of a strange question, all things considered, but you're not...married or engaged or anything, are you?"

"Married?" Cait looked at him in surprise. Then she laughed softly, combing her hair back from her temples with her fingers. "I keep forgetting we're strangers." Her smile faded after a moment and she looked down at the spongy path, kicking at a pine cone. "You'd think making love with someone would change that, wouldn't you? Strange, how you can share intimacies like lovemaking, yet not know a thing about a person."

"Bad question?"

"Not really. I was planning to be married. About three years ago."

"Second thoughts?"

"Double-cross," she replied bitterly, lifting her face to the leaf-speckled sunshine filtering through the tall trees around them. "I met Mark at a yachting party—he was a lawyer on the fast track, making a name for himself. He was strong and supportive and sympathetic, and being with him was like finding shelter from the storm."

Cait smiled, remembering. "By that time, my suspicions about Dalkquist's motives for marrying my mother had jelled. Harry Frost, senior investment manager at her bank, had told me privately that he was getting concerned about the way Dalkquist was handling some of my mother's investments, about the advice he was giving her, about the fact he seemed to be slowly taking control of things.

"Harry's known my family—and Mom's family—for years. He's handled Mom's finances since her father died.

She'd wanted to turn them over to Dad, but he'd said no way…he didn't want people thinking he'd married her just to get his hands on all that Ivarson Oil money.''

Her smile was fleeting. Painful. ''After Dad died, Mom just handed the whole thing over to Harry, told him to take care of the investments and the bills and any other expenses and not to bother her about it. Harry set it up so she received a monthly allowance—I was getting one from my trust account, too, which was separate—and we both thought things were taken care of.

''But Dalkquist kept telling my mother that Harry was too old and too conservative, that he wasn't taking care of her best interests, that her money should be working harder for her. And he kept talking about my trust fund—that it wasn't being handled properly, either.''

''And that he was the guy to do it.''

''Exactly.'' Cait gave her head a toss. ''It took him a while, but he finally wrested control of Mom's portfolio—and my trust fund—away from the bank. By the time I found out what was going on, most of Mom's money had been transferred out of the rock-solid investments that Harry had made for her over the years, and into Dalkquist's hands. I went absolutely nuts! When I told Mark, my fiancé, about it, he was just as upset. He promised he'd look into what was going on and, if necessary, start some kind of legal proceedings to keep Dalkquist from getting his hands on the rest of the family holdings.''

''Seems to me this Mark had a thing or two at stake himself.''

''I figured it just gave him some added motivation.''

Shay laughed. ''There's that.''

''Anyway, Mark went charging off into the fray like one of Arthur's knights, all ready to do battle. But instead of getting angry, Dalkquist turned his charm up full blast and welcomed Mark with open arms. A week later Mark was walking around in a daze, convinced that Dalkquist was the most wonderful man who's ever walked the earth and that I was just being spiteful and silly."

Shay muttered something under his breath.

"I remember the evening he came over and sat me down, all very serious, and told me how mistaken I was about Dalkquist. How Brenton had only my mother's good—and my good—at heart. How much Brenton loved both of us. How devastated he was by my constant attacks on his honesty and his motives. How his one enduring hope was that I would one day realize he wasn't my enemy and we could become friends." Cait gave a snort. "Dalkquist's one enduring hope in those days was that I'd fall in front of a fast freight car, but, as I said, he can charm the moss off rocks."

"So Dalkquist turned this Mark right around."

"Like a weather vane on a barn roof. And the worst part was that Mark really did believe—I mean, he absolutely *believed*—that Dalkquist was this sincere, good-hearted, caring, generous man who had tried everything to win me over and was heartbroken at failing." Cait's throat tightened. "I probably don't have to add that we disagreed. I called him a toadying, double-crossing sycophant and he called me an irrational, back-biting bitch and things sort of went downhill from there."

Shay gave a bark of laughter and, to her surprise, Cait had to join in. "It put a pall on the romance. I gave him his ring back, he went to work for Dalkquist and we avoided each other like plague carriers whenever we couldn't help crossing paths."

Shay grinned, a lazy, good-natured grin that made her feel warm and special, and dropped his arm loosely around her shoulders, tugging her against him. "He didn't deserve you, lady. You can do better."

"One day, maybe." It was comfortable in the curve of Shay's arm and she let herself just relax against him as they meandered slowly along the path like two old friends sharing good times. She laughed suddenly.

"What?" He pulled her against him.

"Nothing." Then she laughed again and flung him a sidelong, teasing look. "It's just that you remind me of someone. A handyman my father hired when I was fourteen. Michael." Her smile widened. "He had that same kind of ready-for-anything, take-me-on-if-you-dare attitude that you have. He was handsome and a little rough and more than a little dangerous, and I fell for him in a big way."

"And I remind you of him."

"He could always make me laugh. No matter how my life was falling apart—and when you're fourteen, it falls apart two or three times a day—he made me feel safe and happy." Still smiling, she met his gaze challengingly. "And he used to look at me the way you do sometimes."

Shay's smile was lazy. "And how do I look at you sometimes?"

"As though you'd like to toss me down on the nearest bed and make love to me until we're both too exhausted to move."

Shay gave a bark of surprised laughter and tightened his arm around her. "It's that subtle, is it?"

"Mmm." Cait's mouth curved in a mischievous smile.

"If he laid a hand on you, I swear I'll hunt him down and break his neck."

"You and my dad, both."

"Are you telling me that little weasel actually—?"

"No! I was fourteen, for heaven's sake. He knew if he did more than look, he'd have a close encounter with my dad's pruning shears. Although..." She smiled reminiscently.

Shay's eyes narrowed. "Although?"

Cait shrugged carelessly. "Well, he did teach me how to kiss properly. But before I worked up the courage to try anything else, summer was over, he went back to college and I never saw him again.''

''Well, you're right about one thing....'' Shay stopped.

Cait looked at him curiously. ''What?''

Grinning, he cupped the back of her head in his palm and lowered his mouth to hers with no warning at all. ''You do know how to kiss properly.''

The touch of him was silk and fire and Cait parted her lips to the bold thrust of his tongue without even having to think about it, the taste of him as welcoming and familiar as good wine. He kissed her slowly and deeply and after a moment or two Cait slipped her arms loosely around his neck and stepped against him, not giving a damn that she'd promised herself this wouldn't happen again.

His hands were on her back, her shoulders, her hair, leaving trails of fire wherever they touched, and she felt a familiar aching hunger shiver through her, wanting more. *Wanting*...

She pulled her mouth from his and leaned against him dizzily. ''I don't think this is a good idea.''

''I think this is a hell of a good idea,'' he murmured, nuzzling the side of her throat. ''Best idea either of us has had all day.''

''Y-you said no complications.'' Hot fire spilled through her at the evocative touch of his tongue, the warmth of his breath, the slow caress of his hand on the small of her back.

''This isn't a complication.'' He drew the collar of her shirt back and started kissing her shoulder.

''Oh, yes,'' Cait whispered, sliding her fingers into his thick hair and pressing his mouth to her, eyes closed. ''Oh, yes, it is....''

''Let's go back to the cabin.'' His mouth was on hers again, hungry and vital.

Again Cait managed to pull away, her heart hammering wildly. ''Rick's there....''

"To hell with Rick," Shay growled, his eyes glittering. He combed her hair back from her flushed cheeks with his fingers, gazing down at her fiercely. "You know what I want, Cait. You said it yourself...."

She nodded, feeling weak-kneed and dizzy. "A w-walk on the beach," she stammered. "I...I think that's what you said."

Shay's gaze narrowed dangerously, then he gave a wry smile and tugged her into his arms, burying his face in her hair. "You're driving me crazy, lady, you know that? I haven't given sex more than an idle thought in nearly two years—now it's the only thing on my mind twenty-four hours a day."

"I can tell." Laughing, Cait tapped his shirt pocket with her finger. "A woman with a suspicious mind might jump to the conclusion your intentions are anything but honorable this morning, Mr. McKittrick. Or is *that* more of Rick's doing?"

Shay looked at her, obviously not understanding. Frowning, he slid his fingers into the pocket, then broke into a broad grin as he drew out the contraceptive, still sealed in its brightly colored plastic envelope. "I forgot about this one. I found it in the duffle bag when I was taking your things out, and..." The grin widened speculatively. "I'd say fate was telling us something, gorgeous."

Chapter 9

"I don't know what it's telling you," Cait said with a laugh, "but it's telling me I might be smarter to go back to the cabin right now."

"My rig's sitting around back." His smile made her toes curl. "We could slip into the sleeper and spend the next couple of hours playing house."

"Or we could go for a walk on the beach." She gave him her sweetest smile. "I think you need some exercise, Mc-Kittrick. And a cold swim probably wouldn't hurt, either." Slipping her hand into his, she started down the path.

"What I have in mind could be considered exercise," Shay murmured, giving her fingers a gentle squeeze. "In fact, I read somewhere that it's some of the best exercise around."

"The only thing you're going to be exercising this morning is your self-control."

"My self-control isn't the part of my body that's suffering."

"Now you *really* sound like Michael," she teased. And laughed at Shay's earthy reply.

The path turned steep suddenly, veering sharply to the left, then swinging around a tight switchback and another steep stretch that ran down to the wide beach. Just offshore lay a jumble of giant boulders and arches and pillars of water-carved stone, and the sun-silvered waves were crashing in and breaking around them in explosions of spray and flying water. The air was smoky with spume and drifts of late-morning mist and the deserted beach looked like something out of a fairy tale, all rainbows and sparkle.

"I'd forgotten anything could be so beautiful," Cait murmured, entranced. She glanced at Shay with a sob of laughter. "I used to be normal once. I can hardly believe it now. It seems as though I've always been like this—suspicious and afraid and secretive. But there was once a time when I had friends and laughed and had fun. When my biggest decision was what shoes to wear with which outfit, and should I play tennis this afternoon or get a massage and which restaurant serves the best scampi." She managed another ragged laugh. "I don't know what's harder to believe—that I could have been that carefree, or that trivial."

She sensed Shay looking at her, and before she realized what he was up to, he'd pulled her toward him and had swung her up and dropped her over one broad, solidly muscled shoulder. And in the next instant he was heading down the steep, sandy path with a whoop befitting a barbarian warrior carrying off the spoils of war.

Cait gave a yelp of alarm and then started laughing as he careened down the narrow trail at a breakneck pace, skating and sliding on loose sand, one hand gripping the waistband of her jeans to keep her from slipping off.

He hit the beach at a run, off balance and out of breath, and he staggered across the sand with a shout of victory, laughing as he swung her down and around.

"You lunatic!" Laughing, Cait caught her balance, scooping her flyaway hair out of her face.

"Only sometimes." He reached for her hand and tugged her into his arms, grinning down at her. "Just when it counts."

Still laughing, Cait shook her hair back and gazed up at him, encircling his waist loosely with her arms and relaxing against him. "They always say it takes one to know one, cowboy."

"If you're crazy, I don't even want to know what the hell that makes me," he murmured, dropping his mouth to hers. "You're the sanest thing that's happened to me in two years." His lips brushed hers, evocative, teasing, promising magic. "I could get tangled up with you in a real serious way...."

Then, just as she was expecting him to kiss her, he drew back, leaving her shaken and wondering, for about the fiftieth time that morning, why she wasn't putting a stop to this once and for all. It couldn't lead anywhere, had no future. They were just two people whose paths had crossed for a brief, whimsical while.

He must have seen some of this on her face, because he gave a soft laugh and kissed her lightly, then braided his fingers with hers and started walking through the sun-warmed sand.

They walked for nearly an hour, chasing each other up and down the windblown, deserted beach, poking in tidal pools and exclaiming at what they discovered, exploring a shallow sea cave filled with starfish and mounds of glittering pebbles as smooth and colorful as precious gems.

It was, inarguably, a brief time of magic. An hour, two, stolen from the nightmare her life had become, shared with a laughing, blue-eyed man who made her pulse race every time he looked at her. It wasn't real, of course. Eventually they'd have to leave this fairy-tale beach and go back up to the cabin where Rick Jarvis and reality awaited, and the magic would be over. But, for a little while, Cait simply let herself forget.

She got cold, finally, and they found a sheltered place in the tall sea grass where they could still see the water but were out of the wind. It was a sandy hollow, sun-warmed and private and sheltered by sedge-covered dunes, and Cait lay back on a soft blanket of dried grass and closed her eyes, letting the sun's heat soak into her.

The grass around them rustled like silk, hypnotic and relaxing, and she smiled as some bird in the trees on the embankment above them broke into melodious song, its voice rising like a clarion over the boom and hiss of the breakers washing onto the sand beyond.

"You asleep?"

Shay's lazy baritone made her shake her head. "Not yet."

"You've got some color back in your cheeks." He brushed a tangle of hair off her forehead. "You look almost healthy."

Smiling, Cait opened her eyes and looked up at him. He was lying beside her, propped up on one elbow, chewing a stem of grass and looking relaxed and comfortable. "I have you to thank for that." Drowsily she reached out and ran a fingertip down his cheek. "I couldn't have gotten through this if it hadn't been for you. I wouldn't even have known what was happening to me, let alone had the strength to fight it off."

Shay ran a strand of her hair through his fingers. "It's been my pleasure, ma'am."

"Liar!" Laughing, Cait clasped a handful of his wind-tangled hair and gave it a mock tug. "I put you through hell." Gently she ran her thumb over the scratches on his left cheek, almost healed now. "Most people wouldn't go through what you did for a stranger."

"You weren't a stranger," he reminded her gently, his gaze warm with memories. "I'd made love to you, Cait. More than once, in fact. That meant something."

Cait smiled again, tracing the contours of his smooth, clean-shaven cheek with her finger. "I probably shouldn't say this, but I'm not certain I'd have remembered."

His left eyebrow rose and she laughed, feeling herself blush. "That's not quite what I meant! I *would* have remembered, I'm just not sure I'd have believed it. I mean...looking back on it now, that whole night is like a dream. I was scared and half frozen and drugged to the eyeballs, and although I can sort of remember everything—stumbling into that café, facing Dalkquist and Angstrom down, you—it's fuzzy and unreal."

"What you're saying is that you don't really remember making love," he teased with a chuckle. "Now that's what I call a real ego booster."

"I do...and I don't." Again, she had to laugh, tangling her fingers in his hair and giving his head a gentle shake. "I remember something very nice happening. I remember being in your arms, and being warm and feeling safe. It's just the details that are a little vague."

"Nice?" His eyebrow arched again.

"*Very* nice, I said."

"Mmm." Smiling a little, he reached out and drew his finger along her chin, then down her throat and into the vee of the open neck of her shirt. "You're saying you don't remember anything?"

Lazily, knowing she was probably playing with fire, Cait just smiled back. "Not a whole lot...."

"You don't remember getting undressed?" The first button on her shirt slipped free and he drew his finger in the shallow cleft between her breasts.

Lying very still, Cait shook her head. "Nope."

"Don't remember...this, for instance?"

Cait swallowed as he slipped his hand under the loosened front of her blouse and lightly brushed her breast, his touch like molten fire through the light cotton knit of her bra. "No..."

"Or...this...?" Gently pulling her blouse open, he rolled slowly toward her and dipped his head and in the next heartbeat he'd settled his mouth over her breast.

He massaged the hardening nipple with his tongue, sucking gently, and Cait gave a soft indrawn moan, drawing her knees up reflexively and cradling his head against her, fingers tangled in his thick hair.

He gently slipped the rest of the buttons free and drew the fabric back, baring her to him, and Cait had to struggle to catch her breath as he started kissing her abdomen and stomach. He drew his tongue wetly around her navel, then inside, around it again, then along the edge of her waistband, and Cait heard a soft, broken moan and realized dimly that it was her. Felt Shay's hand at the button of her waistband, felt it part, felt the sly touch of his tongue under the waistband, then along the concavity of her belly as it followed the zipper down...

"Shay." Swallowing, she tightened her grip in his hair, holding him still, barely daring to breath. She could feel his warm, moist breath against her stomach, the touch of his lips as he kissed her lightly just at the edge of her bikini briefs, the erotic weight of his fingers resting against her. "Please..."

He moved his thumb, gently, slowly, and Cait gasped, her fingers tightening in his hair, and he lifted his head and moved back up her body, his eyes heavy-lidded and sensuous as he met her gaze. "What about this," he whispered, lowering his mouth to hers. "I know you remember this...."

Cait was going to let him kiss her only once, lightly, then pull free of his embrace, putting an end then and there to any other ideas he might have. But as his mouth settled over hers and she felt the first slippery intrusion of his tongue, seeking, exploring, teasing, she sighed instead, lips parting under his.

And the next thing she knew her arms were around his neck and she was kissing him back, her willpower unraveling like a badly knit sweater as his tongue captured hers and moved against it in slow, wet rhythms as intimate as the lovemaking they mimicked. Desire exploded up through her as her body reveled in the taste of him, remembering that night, remembering the feel of him pressed against her, strong and hard-muscled and wondrously male.

Remembering the rest of it, too... the touch of his hands on her breasts, the erotic sensation of the rough hair on his chest and belly against her smooth skin, the way his hand had cupped the aching warmth between her thighs, touching, caressing.

"I want to make love to you," he growled against her mouth. "Right here, right now."

"You *are* crazy," Cait gasped.

He ran his hands up into her hair and tipped her head back so she was looking up at him, his expression intent and hungry. "I want more than that night in the truck, lady. I want to lay you out in this grass with a whole afternoon ahead of us, and I want to make love to you like a man should love a woman. I want it slow and deep and lasting for hours, and I want to see your face while I'm inside you and I want to hear you telling me what you want."

"Shay..." Cait clasped the shoulders of his denim shirt and closed her eyes, dizzy with desire. "This... this is insane...!"

"Tell me you don't want me to make love to you, Cait," he whispered in a tight, gritty voice, his eyes glittering. "Say it out loud and that'll be the end of it."

She whispered something, then she was lifting her mouth to his and Shay was kissing her again. But not gently this time, not teasingly—this time it was with a fierce and desperate hunger, and he could feel her shiver as she responded to it, to him, her limber body seeming to melt against him, all softness and warm willing curves.

And then he was tugging her shirt out of her jeans so he could run his hands up under it, caressing the warm contours of her bare back. "I hate him ..." he groaned against her mouth.

"Hate who?"

"Michael the handy young man. I think of him touching you and I want to kill him."

Cait kissed his mouth, his chin, his throat. "He had hard hands," she murmured, lifting one of his hands to her mouth and kissing his palm, then slowly drawing the tip of her tongue along one finger. Her lips closed around it and Shay had to swallow, breathing unsteadily as she sucked it gently, then ran her tongue down to his palm again. "I've always loved a man with hard hands...."

He whispered something earthy and erotic and to the point and she gave a soft, throaty laugh. Her breasts were surprisingly lush and he could see the full, dark nipples through the white cotton knit of her bra, touched one, rubbed it gently, watched as she bit her lip and let her head fall back, eyes closed, breath catching.

Lowering his mouth, he suckled one taut nipple greedily, hearing her moan softly above him, her fingers clutching at his shoulders. She arched her back and he slipped his hand under her, freed the clasp of her bra with one expert flick of his fingers, and then her breasts were free, their rose-brown tips swollen, nipples hard.

Half-drunk with desire, Shay sat up, his heart racing. Carefully he reached out and cupped Cait's shoulders with his hands, looking down into eyes as warm as buttered taffy. "Cait, you have to be sure about this. Once it's done, we aren't going to be able to say it never happened. Not this time. It's going to change things. Between us."

Her smile was as old as Egypt, as old as womankind, as she slipped the contraceptive from his shirt pocket and tucked it into his palm, folding his fingers around it. "I am very sure," she whispered, reaching up and placing her fingers across his mouth. "I want to make love with you, Shay McKittrick, because you're good and generous and you make me feel safe. Because I'm so tired of being frightened and alone, and when I'm with you all that goes away...." She let her gaze trace his features one by one, as though memorizing them. "Because you make me feel like a woman, and it's been a long, long time since I've felt anything at all...."

He reached for her and she was there, warm and urgent and uncomplicated. Clothing that was between them one moment was gone the next, and then she was naked and a moment later he was, too. He spread his shirt on the grass and lay back on it and drew her down beside him and began the long and wondrous journey of building want to need, and need to hunger.

Her skin was flame-licked satin, warmed by the sun and desire, and she moved like a cat as he caressed her, sinuous and lithe. She was shy one moment and boldly wanton the next, breathless with surprise and delight as he showed her things and taught her things and whispered things. And then finally he eased her thighs apart and lowered himself between them and pressed gently in, welcomed, wanted, not hurrying, letting her experience and savor it.

"Do you remember now...?" he whispered.

"Partly." She swallowed, biting her lip to hold back a moan as he moved, pressing deeper. "Some of it. This...oh, I don't remember this...!"

Shay smiled against her mouth. "That night was just a taste, Caitie. But there's more...so much more."

He made it last for a long, long time, bringing her to the bright burning edge of release and easing her back again time and again, each crest taking her higher, each slow descent building the tension within her until she was half-crazed with it.

And finally he didn't bother bringing her back from it, taking her up and over, feeling the first tiny spasms before she was even aware of what was happening, watching her eyes as she realized there was no turning back this time. They widened slightly with surprise and then, suddenly, she arched under him, head falling back, knees drawing up, and he could feel her taking all of it, could almost feel it pulse and throb through her in a tidal wave of pure sensation.

She shuddered, gasping for breath, and then arched her back again with a sharp, quick cry of startled gratification when he moved smoothly and quickly against her and it crested a second time. And only then did he allow himself to let go and tumble down that same endless hot slope, dimly hearing his own voice as he groaned her name, felt her thighs grip him, felt her lift and move, whispering to him, and then it was all over....

She'd wake up in a minute or two and find it had all been a long and delicious dream, Cait thought drowsily. Because nothing—*nothing*—could make her feel as wonderful as she did right now.

Except it wasn't a dream ... if she concentrated, which wasn't easy to do, all things considered, she could feel the weight of Shay's muscled thigh lying casually across hers, the warmth of his breath on the side of her throat, the slow, regular thump of his heart against hers.

"You're smiling to yourself again." He kissed her shoulder.

"Little wonder." She stretched her arms above her head and arched her back, loving the feel of the sun on her breasts, her belly, her legs. Loving being naked in his arms, loving knowing he was looking at her. "And don't try to tell me it was like this that night in the truck. Because there is no *way* I'd have forgotten feeling like this!"

Shay's laugh was just a lazy rumble. "No, that night wasn't like this. That night was two lonely, lost people looking for closeness." He kissed her shoulder again, then lifted his head to look at her. "I figured I owed you something a little special this time."

"You mean it wasn't just . . . well, an accident or something?"

"All it takes is a little time, a little trust . . ." He dropped his mouth to her breast and swirled his tongue around the nipple, teasing it to a peak. "A little know-how."

"And, boy, do you know how," Cait murmured, kissing the top of his head.

Grinning, Shay lifted his head from her breast and stretched out beside her again, cradling her in one arm. "I'm a little out of practice, but it's coming back to me."

Cait nestled against him sleepily. "Do you want children?" She had to laugh out loud at Shay's expression. "Not right now, idiot! Barring equipment failure, I think we're covered this time. I mean someday." Turning serious, she reached across and brushed a grain of sand from his cheek. "For that matter, maybe you already have kids. Strange, how little we know about each other."

"I know you're the best damn thing that's happened to me in a long time," he said with a lazy grin, giving her a brief, one-armed hug. Then the grin faded and he stared up at the sky, his fingers tracing absent spirals on her bare back. "No, Nancy and I didn't have kids. We talked about it once or twice, but . . ." He shrugged, frowning slightly. "I'm on the road too much to be even a half-decent father, for one thing. And Nan wasn't keen on taking the whole load on herself. Not that I could blame her."

"And one day?" She looked at him curiously, caressing his shoulder with her fingertips. He looked so thoughtful, she had to laugh again. "This isn't a trick question, Mc-Kittrick—I'm not proposing marriage or anything here. I'm just curious."

"One day?" He frowned again, thinking it over, then turned his head and kissed her lightly. "Maybe, I guess. To be honest, I haven't given it any thought. I've just been marking time these last two years. Haven't even thought of having a woman in my life again, let alone kids." He turned his head again to meet her gaze. "You?"

"I did once. I just took for granted that I'd have it all. Successful husband, house and acreage, two kids—a boy and a girl—both of them beautiful and brilliant, of course."

"Of course." Shay's teeth glinted in an easy grin.

"Then...I don't know. My dad died and Dalkquist moved in on my mother and nothing else really seemed important. Then, after she was killed, I became so obsessed with getting him arrested and convicted that anything else just seemed irrelevant."

She smiled slightly, resting her cheek on her hand. "Now I can't even visualize being just a normal, everyday kind of woman. One with a husband and kids and a career and a home..." Her smile faded and she looked out across the wind-tossed grass to the rollers sweeping up onto the beach.

"What *do* you want, Cait?"

"I want Dalkquist in prison for murdering my mother."

"No. I mean what do *you* want—what does Caitlin Sawyer, woman, art history major and incredible lover, *want?*"

Cait stared at him, her mind spinning with the enormity of the question. It had been so long since she'd thought of anything in those terms. "I...don't know."

The admission, the bald words hanging between them, frightened her. She'd lost herself, she realized with a sudden, cold feeling. Lost all of the essence that had been

Caitlin Sawyer. She'd been real once—real and alive, able to laugh, able to dream. But the past two years had leeched all of that out of her, like water leeches lime from stone. And as water will wear away stone, so had hate worn her away. Right down to the bare bones so there was hardly anything at all left of the Cait she'd once been.

"I don't know." She turned and looked at him, her heart giving a thump. "When I try to see the future, it's just blank. There's nothing there. Nothing..."

The expression of desolation and fear on her face tore at Shay, and he tightened his arm around her reassuringly. "I'll be there for you," he murmured, kissing her sun-warmed shoulder. And as he listened to his own words fade on the sea-scented air, he realized he wanted them to be true.

Up until a few days ago, the last thing in the world he wanted to think about was the future. It had spread out before him like a barren plain, empty, featureless, as cold as death. He hadn't wanted it and it hadn't wanted him, and just getting through each seemingly endless day had been enough of a chore.

But that had changed somehow. In the past few days something tight had fallen away from around his heart, something that had kept him from feeling anything, wanting anything. Even the colors around him seemed brighter these days, the air warmer.

Smiling, he rolled half toward her and slipped his free arm around her waist, pulling her tightly against him. "Worse comes to worst, you can come and live with me. Have some McKittrick babies, if it suits you." He nuzzled the side of her throat, loving the scent of her skin, the feel of her all warm and sandy against him. "And I can guarantee you that I'll be home most nights...."

He could feel her smile against his shoulder. "Worse comes to worst, I might take you up on it." She lifted her face and smiled into his eyes. "And I can guarantee *you*,

McKittrick, that I won't mind your being home nights one little bit. If making love with you is this good when you're out of practice, I can hardly wait until you remember all the fine points.''

He kissed her leisurely, tasting salt and sand and sunshine, and felt more than heard her breath catch slightly, felt her shift against him, one leg sliding across his, the whiskery weight of her pelvis straddling his thigh. Felt his body stir and nearly pushed her gently onto her back, wanting to settle between her thighs again and make slow and gentle love to her all afternoon.

''I don't have anything else with me, so let's not start something we can't finish,'' he groaned against her mouth, flinching with an indrawn breath as her small, warm hand trailed across his belly and she touched him, caressed him, teased him. ''Cait...Caitie, you are asking for serious trouble doing that.''

''I certainly hope so,'' she murmured back, her voice caught with a throaty laugh. ''Do you suppose Rick would be shocked if we went back up to the cabin and asked him to take a long hike while we—'' She stopped dead, stiffening slightly in his arms.

Shay opened his eyes and found her staring up at the embankment above and beyond them, frowning slightly. A cold chill ran through him for no reason and he took her hand from him and sat up, trying to look casual, trying not to scare her. ''What's wrong?''

She sat up beside him, her hair sweeping around her like a curtain. ''I thought I saw something. A flash—like when sunlight reflects off a bottle.''

Or off the lens of a pair of binoculars. Shay reached across and picked up Cait's shirt and jeans, casually putting himself between her and the embankment as he handed them to her. ''It's probably nothing,'' he said, praying he was right. "But you're starting to pick up one hell of a sunburn. Let's call it a day."

Still casual, he started pulling on his own jeans, daring a quick glance behind him. Seeing nothing along the top of the embankment but grass and low shrubs.

Cait had wriggled into her jeans and had zipped them up and was shrugging into her blouse, frowning a little as her gaze traced the top of the bank. "You don't suppose someone was watching us, do you?" She sounded more indignant than frightened.

"I doubt it."

"I just hope it isn't some hotshot wildlife photographer up there with a close-up lens." She grinned, sliding Shay a mischievous look. "Or, if it was, I hope he got your good side. And mine."

"Honey, you don't have anything *but* good sides." Shay planted a kiss on her upturned mouth, then got to his feet and pulled Cait up with him, reaching down to finish zipping up his jeans.

He actually heard the first bullet pass between them, just a huff of displaced air that made him blink. It hit the sand just beyond them and kicked up a puff of dust even as the crack of the rifle shot echoed up and down the beach.

Chapter 10

Cait was simply standing there with a bewildered look on her face, her mouth still half open with whatever she'd been saying, when Shay finally realized what had happened. He caught her around the waist with one arm and dove hard for the sand just as the second shot splintered the air around them, and she gave a squeak of shock and pain as he landed on her, shielding her body from the treed embankment above them.

Cupping her head against his shoulder, he curled over and around her, his exposed back crawling as he waited for the next shot.

When it came, it wasn't what he expected. This one was a smaller caliber, a handgun probably, the sound of the shot accompanied by a shout, then silence.

Cautiously Shay lifted his head and looked up and down the beach, seeing nothing. "Cait, are you all right?"

"Y-yes." She sounded breathless with shock. "W-what happened?"

"I think the game just got a lot rougher. Come on—let's move!" Shay was on his feet in the next heartbeat, dragging Cait up beside him. Grasping her hand tightly, he sprinted for the cover of the embankment.

Panting, he pulled Cait into the lee of the overhang, trying to shield her with his body...except he didn't know where the next shot would come from. If there'd even be a next shot. Maybe whoever was up there trying to kill her was heading down to finish the job at close range.

"T-that was—" He could hear Cait swallow, her breathing fast and shallow. "Someone shot at us!" She sounded more angry than frightened, still too startled to fully comprehend what was happening. "Sh-Shay, someone just shot at us!"

"Cait, this isn't the time to discuss it, all right?" He tightened his arm around her. "We're going to have to be real quiet—whoever's up there will be looking for us as soon as he realizes we're still alive."

She didn't say anything, then just nodded once, swallowing again. One tough cookie, he found himself thinking admiringly. But what did he expect? She hadn't stayed alive this long by succumbing to panic when things turned bad.

"McKittrick?" It was Rick's voice, angry and loud and edged with worry. "McKittrick, you down there?"

"Yeah!" Shay leaned forward slightly so he could see the top of the embankment. "Here."

There was a heartfelt oath, then an avalanche of sand and loose dirt and an instant later Rick landed beside them, gun in hand, looking cool and competent and chillingly dangerous. He gave Shay and Cait a sweeping glance, then turned his attention back to the beach, his gaze moving restlessly. "Anyone hurt?"

"No." Shay wiped his mouth with the back of his hand. "What the hell happened?"

"Car drove up to the main motel a few minutes ago," Rick said curtly, still scanning the beach and the grass-fringed embankment above them. "I didn't think too much about it, then I realized you two idiots had wandered off— hadn't told me where, hadn't taken any weapons." He swore again, his voice filled with anger and disgust. "Amateurs!"

Shay felt himself flush slightly.

"I went up to the motel to check things out and the proprietor told me two men had come in asking about you. Old fishing buddies of yours, they said. Seems when he told them you were on your honeymoon—" this with a cool look at Shay's naked torso and still-unbuttoned jeans "—they said they'd just pop in and give the happy couple their regards. That's when I came looking for you."

Shay swore under his breath. He should have thought of that himself. Should have told the old guy running the place to let him know if anyone came in asking questions. Amateur. The word stung. "Dalkquist?"

"How many other people you have gunning for you?" Rick gave Shay an impatient look.

"So...are you ready to believe me now?" Cait held Rick's gaze challengingly. "Or are you going to write the whole thing off as a psychotic episode? Just a figment of my imagination?"

"Okay, okay." Rick's expression darkened. "Maybe there is something to what you've been saying."

Which was probably as close to an apology as she was going to get, Shay figured. "But why would he risk killing us out in the open like this? How could he explain her murder? Mine?"

"First, someone would have to find your bodies," Rick said bluntly. "And it's not that hard to make a couple of corpses disappear, take my word for it. Second, it would be even easier to just make it look as though some psychopath grabbed Cait—tortured, raped and murdered her. They'd put a bullet through your head and the cops would figure you'd been killed trying to protect her."

Shay felt Cait shudder. "Take it easy, Jarvis. Someone's trying to kill her, for crying out loud!"

"I *know* someone's trying to kill her," Rick barked. "And in case it slipped your attention, McKittrick, they were trying to kill you, too!"

And then suddenly it hit Shay that something had changed. A week ago, he frankly wouldn't have cared if someone *had* taken a shot at him, the idea of death more a welcomed respite than frightening. But now...he tightened his arm around Cait's shoulders, looking down into her pale, frightened face. Now, more than anything, he wanted to live.

"How d-did he find us?" Cait shivered again.

"That damn rig of McKittrick's is like wearing a neon sign around your neck—all they had to do was check every motel and hotel in southern Oregon until they found you. A man like Dalkquist won't be short of manpower. Or they could have tracked you down through your friend." Rick looked at Shay. "The one who picked up that load of computers you were hauling."

"Red wouldn't tell anyone where I was," Shay said uneasily.

"Not voluntarily, maybe."

He didn't need to say the rest. "We have to call the cops."

"And what are you going to tell them? That you think someone took a couple of shots at you?"

"What do you mean *think*," Shay said angrily. "I was standing right there when—"

"Proof, McKittrick. They'll want proof. I already checked for shell casings—*nada*. Whoever these guys are, they know what they're doing. Besides, there isn't going to be any link to Dalkquist, I can guarantee it. If he was that careless, Cait would have nailed him long ago.''

Shay swore under his breath, knowing Rick was right but not liking it.

"So what do we do now?"

"Now? Nothing. We sit tight until we come up with a plan." Rick gave the beach behind him one last look, then blew a long breath between his teeth and flexed his shoulders. "Now they know I'm with you, they'll have to regroup and come up with a new strategy." He grinned suddenly, an evil little grin that made the back of Shay's neck prickle. "They didn't expect someone to return fire, that's for damned sure. Or for you to have someone watching your back."

Then the grin faded and Rick looked at Cait. "Dalkquist doesn't know who you've got helping you or what he's up against—and that's going to scare him. So the next people he sends after you are going to be professional. And dangerous as hell. And that means no more horsing around on the beach like a couple of oversexed teenagers, got it? If you want to mess around, do it in the bedroom. Or better yet, book into a top-notch hotel, lock the door, get into bed and stay there until I tell you it's safe to come out."

"Now just wait a damned minute, Jarvis," Shay growled. "This isn't—"

"Save it," Rick snapped. "You got distracted, McKittrick—your lady nearly got blown away and you along with her. Until now this has been some kind of game to you, but it just got real."

Shay flushed, his mouth tightening. Then he swore, giving his head a disgusted shake. "You're right. I figured he'd try to get Cait back, all right, but I never reckoned on him coming after her in the open like this."

To his surprise, Rick gave him a companionable smile and slapped him on the shoulder. "Don't sweat it, bro. You did good today—it's been a long time since I saw someone move that fast. You've got good instincts. Your concentration's shot to hell, but your reflexes are on the money.''

Shay tightened his arm around Cait's shoulders protectively, chilled at the thought of how easily they could have picked her off. Jarvis was right: he *was* letting his body do his thinking for him. All he'd been able to think about was holding Cait and touching Cait and loving Cait, and the whole while, they'd been stalked and watched and held in a killer's rifle sight.

"I've got to go."

Before he could stop her, Cait slipped out of his embrace and headed back to the path leading up the embankment, walking fast.

Rick took a couple of steps after her, swearing as his foot caught in the loose sand. "Damn this leg! McKittrick, go after her. And take the gun. I doubt those two goons are still around, but you've taken enough chances for one day."

Shay took it without arguing and lit out after Cait at a dead run, shouting at her to wait. But she didn't slow down or even look back, her dark hair wafting back on the wind like a banner as she half ran up the slope.

And in spite of everything, Shay found himself grinning as he jogged up the steep path after her, thinking—as he had a couple of times in the past two days—that Jarvis might not know a hell of a lot about women, but he did know how to buy a pair of jeans. Coming up behind her like this, it was pretty much impossible not to notice just how perfectly Cait's fit.

"Cait!" He caught up to her finally at the top of the embankment and grasped her upper arm. "Damn it, Cait, slow down! They're gone. You're safe for now. So just—"

"For now." She stopped and turned and the wind caught her hair and sent it billowing around her. Impatiently she swept it to one side and held it back with one hand as she stared up at him, her face pale and tense. "I've got to leave. Right now. Before—" She caught herself, swallowing, and started to turn away again. "I've just got to go."

"Hold it. Hold it...!" Shay caught her arm again, holding her firmly. "Damn it, Cait, where do you think you're going? You have no money, no credit cards, no driver's license, no car."

"I've got to go." She was cold, Cait thought. Chilled right to the very marrow of her bones with a cold so deep the sun's heat and even the memories of Shay's lovemaking couldn't warm it.

Distracted. She'd let herself get distracted, and Shay had nearly been killed. She knew Dalkquist—knew what he was capable of, knew another murder or two wouldn't faze him. He had too much at stake, had gone too far already to get suddenly squeamish now. She should have been ready for anything.

Instead, she'd let her feelings for Shay mess up her concentration and her resolve, had been lying in the hot sun making love when she should have been trying to trap a murderer.

"Dalkquist knows you're up here, Cait. But he also knows I'm still with you and that now we've got someone else helping us—someone fast and armed and dangerous as hell. That's going to make him think twice about making another try for you. But if he's smart—and he is—he'll have people watching the banks, the car-rental places, the bus station, the airports...just *hoping* you'll panic and do something stupid."

"Don't try to stop me, Shay. I've stayed here way too long as it is. He's going to be coming after me, and I don't want—" Again, she didn't finish. Pulling her arm free, she started toward the cabin again.

Shay stepped in front of her to bar her way. "Come on, Cait, think about it for a minute! Dalkquist isn't going to come up here after you again. You're safer here than—"

"You still don't get it, do you!" She glared up at him furiously. "He'll kill you, Shay. As quick as look at you. And Rick. And anyone else who gets in his way."

"He's not going to come gunning for you a second time, Cait, trust me. For all he knows, Rick could be some cop we've managed to convince to listen to your story. Even Dalkquist isn't crazy or desperate enough to risk killing a cop."

"All he has to do is make it look like murder-suicide," Cait said with chilling calm. "With my medical records, do you think anyone's going to question it? The police will just figure I finally went off the deep end, killed you and Rick, and then turned the gun on myself."

"They won't get by Rick," Shay said flatly. "Or me." His expression turned even more grim. "I got careless today, Cait. God knows, I knew better! I had no business taking you down on that beach, and even less making love to you in the open like that. But it won't happen again, I promise you."

"This isn't about me anymore!" She gestured angrily. "It's about you, don't you understand that? I don't want you killed!"

"I'm not that easy to kill."

"Shay, it's not—!"

"Why are you running, Cait? What's the real reason?"

Something may have flickered deep in her eyes. "I'm not running away. In fact, I'm doing the opposite. Dalkquist is—"

"To hell with Dalkquist! This isn't about him, it's about me. And maybe yourself."

"I've got to go." She turned and walked away, back rigid.

"Forget it." Shay strode after her and caught her upper arm, swinging her around to face him. "We made love this afternoon, and suddenly you're scared to death. Scared enough to risk your life. And I want to know why."

"I am *not* scared!" She gave her head an angry toss.

"The hell you're not. You're scared we're going to start meaning something to each other, that you might start caring. And you're afraid that if that happens, you're going to lose yourself—lose that bloody-minded independence that makes Cait Sawyer what she is."

He thought for a moment that she was going to deny it furiously and stalk off. And wondered, not altogether idly, how the hell he was going to stop her if she did.

But some of the fight seemed to go out of her suddenly and she let her gaze slide from his. "Partly true," she whispered. "But I'm afraid for you, Shay. Afraid that you'll do something heroic and stupid and get yourself killed and—"

"For crying out loud, Cait, you're starting to sound like Rick!"

"Maybe because what he says makes sense."

"And maybe it doesn't," he growled impatiently. "And besides, it's too late to worry about it. I'm in too deep already."

She looked up at him uncertainly. "What do you mean?"

"Dalkquist can't afford to let me live, Cait. He knows if something happens to you, I'll be raising hell—and that people will listen. I can cause him more grief than you ever could." Gently he put his hands on her shoulders. "I passed the point of no return with you days ago, Cait. Running away from me won't keep me alive. It'll just make us both easier to kill."

It wasn't until they were back at the cabin and safely inside that the reality of what had just happened hit Cait.

Shay made her stand just inside the door while he checked the place out, and it was watching him prowl from room to room, gun in hand, his lean face hard and dangerous, that made it all suddenly, brutally real. And then Rick was there, and the two of them stalked around with cold, predatory expressions, talking in low tones as they checked window catches and escape routes and talked strategy.

It hit Cait like a fist in the belly then, and she startled both of them as she suddenly bolted for the bathroom to be violently sick to her stomach. She sat huddled on the cold tile floor for a long while, forehead resting on the side of the tub, then got up and had a long, hot shower, trying to scrub away the horror.

Images kept flickering through her mind, nightmare on fast forward: Shay, catapulting across the sand to knock her down and out of harm's way. Shay throwing himself over her, shielding her with his own body from the sniper hidden in the trees above them.

Rick was right. As long as she was around, Shay was at risk. And she'd realized something today while lying in that nest of soft grass: what she was feeling for Shay wasn't just infatuation anymore, not just a frightened woman's reaction to the man who had saved her life. It was real. And— for the man she loved—almost as dangerous as Dalkquist himself.

And one thing was certain. She was *not* going to stand docilely around while Brenton Dalkquist killed someone else she loved.

Shay was there when she pulled the curtain back, looking drawn and worried. Wordlessly, he wrapped a big towel around her and started to rub her dry. "You okay? You look like hell."

"I feel like hell," she muttered, catching an unwelcomed glance at herself in the vanity mirror.

"This is your first day up and around since you started coming off that junk Angstrom was pumping into you, remember." His large hands were warm and competent as he dried her back and shoulders. "Get some sleep. Rick and I'll hold down the fort."

"Sleep? How can I sleep?" She pulled away from him irritably, holding the towel around herself. "Quit mothering me! I'm all right."

"Sure you are," he said mildly. "Here." He pulled a cotton T-shirt over her head before she could protest, then tugged it down to modestly cover her bottom. "Bed, Cait. You've been doing fine all day. Don't let it get away from you now, all right?"

She opened her mouth to argue, then subsided, exhaustion washing through her like a leaden wave. He was right, of course. Her reserves of energy were at rock bottom—she still broke into chills and got the shakes at odd moments, and just the effort of standing here was making her head spin. It would be suicide to go after Dalkquist without at least a few hours' rest.

Because she was only going to get one chance this time. She was on to something, that was clear, or he wouldn't be panicking. That meant he was going to be desperate to find her, to stop her. She'd escaped Amber Hills by sheer good luck, had survived the past few days because of Shay—but she couldn't count on either of them the rest of the way. Luck because it never lasted, and Shay because she couldn't go on if he was hurt. Maybe killed.

She followed Shay as he led her down to the bedroom. Slipped between the cool cotton sheets. Felt the touch of his lips on hers. And then the whole world just sort of melted and started to slide sideways and she was falling... falling...

Cait slept until late afternoon. She got up about five-thirty, drowsy and out of sorts, downed the sandwich and glass of milk Shay handed her without saying more than three words, then wandered back off to bed again.

He checked on her a few minutes later but she'd fallen into a deep sleep again, so he just tucked the bedspread under her chin and left her alone.

When he walked back into the living room, Rick looked up. "She okay?"

"Yeah. She's asleep again. Went out like a light."

"It'll take a few days for her body to flush out the last of whatever drugs they were giving her." He held Shay's gaze for a long moment. "I figure you were right about that, by the way. If she was using, she wouldn't have kicked it this fast."

"I was right about all of it."

Rick gave a grunt. But he glanced up after a moment or two, a faint smile playing around his mouth. "I'll tell you one thing, though. I'm beginning to see why you're hooked on that lady. They don't make many like her."

And Shay, standing at the window looking out into the late-afternoon sun, only nodded. Was that what had happened? *Was* he hooked on Cait Sawyer? Over the past few days, he'd been feeling things for her he hadn't felt since... God, since he'd first met Nancy. That same breath-caught feeling when he looked up and saw her unexpectedly, the delight he felt at hearing her laugh, the wonderment that anyone could be so perfect, so beautiful.

And this afternoon as he'd lain in that sun-warmed nest of grass with her, there had been a sense of rightness, of completion, that he'd figured he'd never feel again. Then later, hearing the crack of that rifle shot and realizing he could have lost her just like that: an errant puff of wind, a difference in the calibration of the rifle sight, a single step toward him... She'd have been alive in one heartbeat, laughing up into his face with those sparkling eyes filled with mischief, and dead the next.

Because of him. She wouldn't have been on that damned beach in the first place if he hadn't taken her down there. Would have been safely back in the cabin if he hadn't more or less seduced her down in that grassy hollow.

He was putting her at risk. Rick had called him an amateur, and although the accusation had stung like hell, it was right on the money. And amateurs got people killed.

He'd seen it himself on the road time and again when unskilled or unseasoned drivers got behind the wheel of a big rig and found themselves in more trouble than they knew how to handle. And more often than not, they took innocent people with them: braking too hard too fast and jack-knifing across three lanes of heavy traffic; losing control on black ice and slamming into a bridge abutment and bursting into flames; having a poorly balanced load shift and rolling the whole damn rig, taking six, eight cars out at the same time.

He had to get out, now, before he got her killed. He'd done what he could, but it was time to back out and let someone like Rick take over, someone with the training, the weapons and the resources to keep her alive while bringing Dalkquist down. Because the truth was, he couldn't face that kind of loss again.

In the morning, he thought numbly. He'd leave in the morning.

She was gone in the morning.

Shay stared at the empty bed and felt a chill along the back of his neck, remembering all-too-clearly that morning he'd stumbled into the hospital, looking for Nancy, and had found nothing but an empty bed.

He shook it off with a savage oath, then wheeled around and headed for the bathroom, telling himself he was panicking over nothing. She'd gotten up early, that was all. She was probably lying in a tub full of hot water and bubble bath, sweet-scented and drowsy, wondering why he was crashing around.

He flung the bathroom door open, mouth already open to ask her what the hell she thought she was doing, scaring him like that, and felt the chill go a little deeper. It was empty and cold with morning air, the window wide open, towels dry.

"Jarvis!" Spinning on one heel, he bolted back down the corridor to the living room where Rick was still sprawled asleep under a blanket on the sofa. "Jarvis, damn it, she's gone!"

Rick was on his feet, gun in hand, before Shay had even cleared the door. "What's going on?"

"It's Cait. She's gone." Shay raked his hair back with his fingers, still not entirely believing it. "I came in a few minutes ago and decided to check on her—the bed's empty and cold."

Rick's eyes narrowed. "Bathroom?"

"I checked."

"What about your rig? Would she have gone out there?"

"It's locked."

"When was the last time you saw her?"

"About three hours ago, when you woke me up to take my turn at watch. I looked in on her and everything seemed fine."

"Damn it!" Rick swung around, gesturing angrily. "The car? Is my car still here?"

Shay strode across to the window. "Yeah. It's here. So she's out there somewhere on foot."

"No." Rick shook his head, his eyes glinting. "She's too smart for that. She's hitchhiking, or she caught a ride with someone who was staying at the motel. Have you talked with the proprietor?"

Shay gave his head an impatient shake. "She could just have gone for a walk...." Knowing, even as he was saying it, that she'd never have gone out there alone. Not after yesterday. "Money—she needs money." Sprinting for the bedroom again, all he could think of was Dalkquist. He'd be out there somewhere. Waiting for her. And he wouldn't give her a second chance this time.

His wallet was still lying on the dresser where he'd tossed it days ago. Grabbing it, he opened it, his heart sinking. "Five hundred," he said as Rick stepped through the door. "She took that five hundred you gave me the other day. Government money."

And left his, Shay thought with grim amusement. Even desperate, Cait wouldn't steal from him. He drew out the slip of paper she'd left behind and unfolded it. *I.O.U. my life,* she'd written in a hurried scrawl. *If I stay, you'll be hurt. Don't come looking for me. Tell Rick I'll return the money when this is over. I love you, McKittrick—maybe someday I'll*

She hadn't finished it. Shay stared at the words, wondering what she'd been about to say. What she'd been thinking when she wrote them. *I love you.*

He whispered an oath and closed his eyes, feeling sick and empty. "She's going to try to do it herself, Jarvis. And he's going to kill her this time."

Wordlessly, Rick walked across and took the piece of paper from Shay's numbed fingers and read it. An odd expression crossed his face and he breathed a weary oath, suddenly looking gray and worn-out. "We'll find her," he said quietly. "I'll get a team up here to help look for her— she won't get far."

"Sacramento," Shay said in a ragged voice. "She'll be going after the Mosely woman."

"How can you be so sure?"

"I know how she thinks." He swore again, hitting the wall with his palm. "Damn it, I don't know how she got by me! I was wide-awake the whole time, walking the perimeter, checking the house every few minutes, moving all the time. I can't believe I let her slip by me!"

"She's good," Rick said quietly. "The best I've seen in a long while. If she wasn't, Dalkquist would have killed her years ago. She knew you were watching for someone trying to get in, not the other way around." He smiled faintly. "Hell, bro, she knows you, too."

"I'm going after her." Shay shoved his wallet into his shirt pocket and snatched up the truck keys.

"Like hell you are!" Rick grabbed his arm. "Use your head! Go stumbling around out there and you're going to get yourself killed—and maybe her too. I can have a team of trained—"

"Then do it!" Shrugging off Rick's hand, Shay strode to the door. "Get them up here, spend a day coordinating and planning and talking strategy—in the meantime, Cait is walking right into a trap."

"Trap? What do you mean?"

Shay swore impatiently. "Look, Super Agent Jarvis, do you really believe it's coincidence that Don Mosely got whacked in prison two days after Cait escaped from Amber Hills? He didn't take the fall for trying to kill Cait because he wanted to go to prison—not with a wife and two kids to worry about. He took jailtime instead of turning Dalkquist over to the cops because someone paid him to."

"Why didn't Dalkquist just kill him when he messed up the hit on Cait?"

"Because as long as Mosely was alive to swear he'd shot Cait during a burglary attempt, her accusations that Dalkquist had arranged it could be discounted as just more of Cait Sawyer's psychotic fantasies."

Rick gave a grunt. "So what's the wife got to do with it?"

"A family man like Mosely wouldn't go to jail without leaving some insurance."

"Insurance?"

Shay smiled wolfishly. "Say I hire you to kill someone and you mess up. I convince you to take the fall, figuring you're more use to me alive and talking than dead. I tell you that in appreciation for what you're doing, I'll make sure your wife and kids get everything they need. Now, wouldn't you make damn sure someone knew about the deal we'd made just in case I decided to get trigger-happy?"

Rick thought it over, his face turning even more grim. "And I'm supposed to believe Dalkquist would leave a loose end like Mosely lying around."

"As long as Dalkquist had control of the situation, Mosely was no problem. But when Cait threw a spanner in the works by getting out of Amber Hills, Mosely became a liability. And Mosely's dead."

"It's a hell of a long shot, McKittrick. If you're wrong, we could be wasting time going in one direction while Cait's headed in the other."

"Do you have any better ideas?"

There was a grudging pause. "No."

"I didn't think so." Shay strode across to Rick's computer and started riffling through the pile of paper it had spun out. "There was a page here with information on Mosely's wife—I was looking at it last night. She's holed up with her sister, just outside Sacramento...without the kids."

"Yeah, so?"

"So it sounds like she's running scared. Which may mean she's got something to hide. Like information."

"And it may mean nothing."

"It's gone." Swearing, Shay straightened, holding up two ragged ends of computer printout. "The page with the sister's address on it is gone." He gave Rick a hard look. "Do you believe me now, Jarvis?"

Rick nodded glumly as he eyed the mangled sheets of paper that Cait had ripped apart, taking what she'd wanted and discarding the rest. "Yeah, I believe you," he muttered. "Take my car—that rig of yours stands out like a sore thumb. And this." He handed Shay his automatic revolver, along with the car keys. "There's a double-action semiautomatic in the trunk, along with extra magazines for both. Just don't get stopped by the cops—I don't want to have to explain why a civilian is carrying government issue weapons with *my* name on the permits."

"Thanks." Shay shoved the weapon into the back waistband of his jeans, but tossed the keys back to Rick. "You'll need this. Besides, I feel safer in my own rig. Call me a man of habit." He look at Rick curiously. "You're giving in awful easy, Jarvis."

"Do you love her?"

"I don't know," Shay replied truthfully. "I thought I still loved Nancy."

"Nancy's dead," Rick said with quiet brutality. "But Cait's not. Yet, anyway. She's out there somewhere trying to do the impossible, and she needs your help."

Shay nodded again, heading for the door. "Don't be too far behind," he growled. And then he was out the door and into sunshine, grinning suddenly, feeling reckless and unafraid. Adrenaline, probably. *I love you, McKittrick.*

"I loved him. And he loved me. Or he said he did." Diane Mosely gave Cait a nervous smile.

She was a thin woman with stringy brown hair and a sallow, lifeless complexion, and as she stubbed her cigarette into the overflowing ashtray, Cait couldn't help but feel sorry for her.

"It was silly." Diane gave another of those nervous smiles, winding a strand of hair around her finger. "Donny wasn't good for much, I know that. He was always getting

into trouble, couldn't hold down a job, never had no money
But he was all I had, you know? I just...I just wasn't no
good on my own."

She looked up, her eyes glazed with tears. "But he was
good with the boys." Another smile, sad this time. "He was
always real good with the boys."

Cait rubbed her forehead wearily, thinking of her mother.
She and Diane Mosely were a generation and a world apart,
yet they could have been one and the same, preferring the
wrong man to no man. It had gotten her mother killed, and
Diane Mosely hiding out in this ramshackle house that
didn't even belong to her, widowed and scared to death.

"I know what Donny done to you," Diane whispered
suddenly, her voice thick with shame. "Or tried to do. When
he told me, I nearly walked out then and there." She lifted
her head and gazed at Cait miserably. "My Donny was no
saint, but he wasn't a bad man. Not killing bad. Not until
he got mixed-up with that stepfather of yours."

Cait's heart literally skipped a beat. "Dalkquist? Mrs.
Mosely, are you telling me that you know for a fact that
Brenton Dalkquist hired your husband to kill me?" The fear
on the other woman's face tore at her. "Look, can I make
you some tea or coffee or something?"

Diane gazed around the dirty kitchen vaguely, as though
not able to gather her thoughts enough to even answer that
simple a question. "I...I guess I shoulda' offered you
something when you got here. My sister's at work and I..."

"It's all right." Cait got to her feet and started rummaging through one filthy cupboard after another until she
found tea bags, a pot and two reasonably clean cups. She
rinsed them under the hot water tap, trying not to look at the
piles of greasy plates and cutlery stacked in and around the
sink, then filled the kettle and put it on the stove. "Where
are your two sons, Mrs. Mosely? Are they staying here at
your sister's with you?"

"Diane, just call me Diane." She pushed a handful of dirty hair out of her eyes and sat up a little straighter, smoothing her wrinkled blouse. "My boys are with my mother." She looked at Cait swiftly. "You won't tell anyone that, will you? They won't be safe if...if *he* finds out."

"He?" Cait looked around sharply. "You mean Dalkquist?"

Diane swallowed. "He's evil, that man. Evil as can be. You can see it in his eyes."

"He was here?"

"No. He...he don't know I'm here. Least I don't think he does. But he was at the house. Before Donny went to prison."

"Has he threatened you?"

"He hasn't come out and said it. But I know he told Donny if he said anything, something would happen to the boys and me."

Cait nodded, terrified of pushing too hard and having Diane close up or simply fall apart. "Would you...make a statement to the police?"

"Police?" Diane's face went as white as bone. "I go to the police, I'm dead. My boys lost their daddy last week. I'm not going to make them orphans!"

The kettle gave a screech, making Cait jump, and she took it off the burner, tossed the tea bags into the teapot and then poured boiling water over them.

"Mrs.—Diane. Dalkquist murdered my mother a year ago and he's been trying to murder me ever since. Everything you're telling me is the first real proof I've got of that." She carried the teapot and cups across to the table. "What about a letter? Would you make a written statement?"

"Writing's same as talking."

Cait sat down again, pressing her fingers against her throbbing temples and fighting to stay calm. What she *wanted* to do was grab Diane Mosely by the shoulders and shake her until her teeth rattled.

"He just did it so's we'd have some money for the kids at Christmas," the other woman said suddenly. She picked at a crack in the plastic tabletop, not meeting Cait's eyes. "Your step-daddy paid Donny lots of money. I've still got some of it." She looked up, her eyes red-rimmed and pleading. "I'll give it to you, if you want. It's sort of yours...."

Cait's stomach twisted. "No. I don't want the money." Her voice was rough.

"Someone's watching the house."

"What?" Cait's head shot up. "Now?"

Diane shrugged. "Been there a couple of days, maybe. They think I don't see them." She smiled wanly.

"Who?"

"How would I know who?" She looked at Cait in irritation. "Your step-daddy, more'n'likely."

Waiting for her, Cait thought with a sudden chill. She should have known Dalkquist would be one step ahead of her, anticipating her every move. Heaven knows how he'd found Diane, but it probably hadn't been difficult. And once he'd found her, he'd have put someone outside, watching, just on the off-chance that Cait would turn up sooner or later.

A wave of panic washed through her but Cait fought it down desperately. There may not even be anyone out there, she told herself tightly. Diane could just be panicking, seeing danger where there was none. "Please, Diane," she whispered. "If you've got something—anything—that I can use..."

"If...if you can get your step-daddy put away, will he stay put away?" Diane looked up. "Or will he just buy his way out?"

"He won't buy his way out. Not out of this."

"He's a rich man. An important man."

"He's a murderer."

Diane nodded thoughtfully. "If that happens—if he goes to jail—can I get some protection for my boys?"

Cait's heart gave a leap but she fought to keep the hope out of her voice. The desperation. "Once the truth is out, Diane, he can't do anything to hurt you or your children. Getting the truth out into the open is what's going to keep us *both* alive."

Diane looked up, startled slightly. Then she nodded slowly. "Yeah," she whispered, more to herself than to Cait. "Yeah, maybe it is at that." She glanced up at the clock. "My sister will be home soon. She won't like finding you here." Her smile was humorless. "She don't like *me* being here. She always said Donny was going to break my heart. . . ."

Cait swallowed, fighting to stay calm. She leaned forward slightly and put her hand on Diane's arm. "Please. Diane, you are my one hope. My last hope, probably. Dalkquist sent two men after me yesterday—I heard the rifle bullet go by my head. I won't be that lucky again."

"Donny would say I shouldn't worry about what happens to you." She looked at Cait a bit defiantly. "He always said you rich people got your own justice. Your own ways. That we have to take care of our own first." She smiled suddenly, just a fleeting twist of her mouth, more bitterness than humor. "But then, Donny didn't know spit, did he? Or he'd be alive taking care of me and the boys, 'stead of getting himself killed." She gave her head a sudden toss, her eyes sparking with anger. "Wait here."

She got up and walked into the living room and Cait looked at the clock, trying not to fidget, trying not to think, to hope. She'd been here too long already. If Diane was right and someone *was* watching the house, they would have seen

her come in, would have called Dalkquist . . . he could have
people heading here right now.

"Here." Diane appeared at her elbow suddenly, startling
Cait badly, and she shoved a once-white envelope toward
her. "Take this. Donny give it to me last time I visited him
in jail. He said it was his insurance policy, but I know
Donny . . . he never had money to spend on anything useful.
So I opened it." She took a deep breath. "It's all wrote up
real tidy and neat. He must've had someone do it for him,
'cause Donny's spelling is worse than mine. *Was* . . . was
worse than mine." Her eyes filled.

Heart thumping, Cait took the envelope, half terrified to
open it in case it turned out to be nothing at all. "Sit down,
Diane—here, drink this." Cait poured tea into one of the
cups and placed it in the woman's hands. Then, breath held,
she lifted the already-torn flap on the envelope and pulled
out the five or six sheets of paper that were inside.

Chapter 11

The first thing Cait saw was the notary seal, complete with a witnessing signature. And the second thing she saw was the letterhead. She stared at it, her breath hissing between her teeth. Donald Mosely hadn't only confessed, he'd confessed, in writing, to his prison priest. And if the word of a man of God didn't count for something, Cait found herself thinking a little hysterically, then there was no hope at all!

Swiftly, she read through it, one page, two, three. It was all there. All of it. Names and dates and even how much Dalkquist had paid Don Mosely to break into her apartment and kill her.

"Thirty thousand dollars," she murmured wonderingly. "That's all my life was worth." And the ironic part was that Dalkquist had probably taken the money out of her own trust fund to do it.

"That was only the first bit," Diane said quietly. "There was more. Each month, money would come for me and the boys. It was supposed to be that way until the youngest was eighteen."

"Or until I was finally dead," Cait told her bluntly. "Once I was out of the way, Dalkquist would have had your husband killed and the money would have stopped." She took a deep breath and put the papers back into the envelope, then shoved it into her purse. "You've got to get out of here. Take this." She opened her wallet and took out almost all of the money she'd taken from Shay and shoved it into Diane's hand. "And go."

"G-go?" Diane stared at the money. "Go where?"

"Anywhere! As far from here as you can get. Just don't go anywhere near your mother. Your kids will be safer if no one knows she has them. When you get somewhere safe, lie low. Don't tell *anybody* where you are except that priest your husband talked to—Father Gautier. I'll contact you through him and let you know when you can come home."

"B-but—" Diane stared at her in bewilderment "—why are you doing this? M-my husband tried to kill you. Why would you care what happens to me . . . ?"

Cait shoved the chair back and stood up, pulling on the black anorak-style jacket that Rick had bought. "Because it's not your fault you fell in love with the wrong man," she said quietly. "And because it's not right that you and your sons should be victims of Brenton Dalkquist's vendetta against me."

She turned toward the door, then paused and looked around. "You've probably just saved my life, Diane. And your decision to give me these papers is going to put a murderer in jail. On those days when you don't think you can make it, remember that. You don't need any more Donny Moselys in your life."

The other woman smiled wanly and nodded, looking at the money in her hands. "It might be nice, being on my own for a while. Just me and my boys." She looked up at Cait.

"I sure couldn't do no worse on my own. Maybe I could use some of this money for a new start some place." Taking a deep breath, she looked around the kitchen slowly, as though just seeing it. "And I can sure do better than this. Funny, how if you live with dirt long enough, after a while you start thinking that's all there is in the world."

They were following him, there was no doubt about it now. It had been hard to tell on the freeway, but here, working his way along this winding, two-lane road that led to where Diane Mosely was staying, there was no mistaking it. It was a late-model, gold colored Buick, and it had been behind him for nearly an hour now.

Shay glanced in his side mirror. The question was, what was he going to do about it? He couldn't outrun it. Even freewheeling along without a trailer to slow him down, he wasn't going to be able to outmaneuver a car. And trying to just blend into surrounding traffic and give them the slip wasn't going to work, either—not when you were driving a black-and-chrome double-stacked Kenworth belching diesel smoke, with Hell on Wheels emblazoned in neon pink across its glossy flanks.

Maybe Rick had been right. Maybe he should have settled for inconspicuous.

One thing was certain—he couldn't just lead them to Cait. Whatever he was going to do, he was going to have to do it fast.

They were in the country now, the road winding its way through dry hills confettied here and there with patches of green.

Think, damn it, Shay told himself. Think, *think*.

The road rose sharply and as he crested the hill, Shay saw that it dropped steeply in front of him, then swung into a tight S-curve. At the bottom of the S, the road swung left and vanished behind a stand of tall, thick timber. And in that instant, Shay knew what he was going to do.

He checked his mirrors again to make sure the car was still with him, smiling a little malevolently. Okay, fellas, he told them silently. The quarry's going to turn into the hunter in about thirty seconds flat.

He wheeled the big truck through the first curve smoothly, adjusting his speed slightly, then brought it into the second curve, already gearing down, not wanting to alert them by using the brakes. And the instant he was around the curve and saw the wide, unobstructed shoulder, he knew his plan was going to work.

Hauling the wheel over as sharply as he dared, he swung the truck off the edge of the pavement and onto the shoulder, braking strongly. Without the worry of jackknifing the rig by braking too sharply or the weight of a loaded trailer behind him, he brought the rig to a skidding, shuddering stop in less than a quarter of its normal distance, air brakes snorting and hissing, gravel and dust spraying from under the big wheels.

Eyes narrowed, he watched his left-hand mirror. One car went by. Then another. Then, just as the gold car swung around the curve, he started picking up speed, still on the shoulder.

The driver of the car saw him, too late. Shay could see him and the other man in the car gape stupidly at him as they hurtled by, then Shay wrenched the wheel and brought the truck back up onto the pavement just behind them, tires screeching at the abuse, already accelerating.

He saw brake lights flare, then the driver must have realized that at this speed Shay would run right over the top of them if they slowed too quickly. The brake lights went out and the car leapt ahead and Shay, smiling, pressed the accelerator down.

He brought the rig right up to their back bumper and gave them a gentle nudge, then another one, less gentle this time. The car bucked and bounced and Shay eased back, giving them a blast with the air horn. There was a side road up ahead, turning right, and he gave them another blast with the air horn and gestured for them to make the turn.

To his surprise, the driver put on his turn signal a moment later and started to slow, and Shay eased off the accelerator. The side road turned out to be little more than a dirt trail surrounded by heavy timber, and as Shay followed the car into the sudden, cool shade, he wondered fleetingly just what the hell he was going to do with these guys now that he had them.

The car rocked to a stop ahead of him and Shay stopped a little back, grabbing the loaded semiautomatic from the seat beside him and pushing the driver's door open, swinging down behind it for cover.

"You're making a mistake, McKittrick," one of the men bawled out the car window.

"Yeah, yeah—just get out of the car and lock your hands behind your head. Slowly!"

Again, to his surprise, they did as he asked. They stood on either side of the car and glared at him as they watched him jump down and walk toward them, gun in one hand, tire iron in the other.

Shay motioned for the one on the passenger side to join his companion. "Keep your hands where I can see them, buddy, because believe me, I'm in no damn mood for anything cute."

"Just take it easy, McKittrick," the driver said quietly. "We're Jarvis's men. I'm Matsui, he's Carlson. We've been tailing you from the Oregon line, watching your back."

"And I'm supposed to believe that."

"Left hip pocket."

"Get it out. Slow."

The man reached around gingerly with one hand and eased a slim leather wallet from his back pocket, tossing it on the ground at Shay's feet. Keeping an eye on the two, Shay knelt down and picked it up, tucking the tire iron comfortably under his arm. The heavy gold-colored shield looked authentic enough—at least it and the plastic ID photo card were identical to the ones Rick had, the name of the agency they worked for the same, one Shay had never heard of before. And God knows they *looked* like government types.

"Do you guys all get your suits from the same place?" Shay tossed the wallet back to the taller of the two, nodding for them to put their hands down. "You could have gotten those from a movie prop shop for all I know."

"You married Jarvis's kid sister five years ago, she died two years ago, you've been messed up some ever since. Your mother's name is Beatrice, maiden name Broward. Your father sells insurance in Roseville, California, where he and your mother have lived for thirty-six years. You got into trucking by accident when you were twenty-two and your uncle James McKittrick died and left you his rig. You bought your present truck five years ago with the help of a sizable loan from Seaboard Savings and Loan." The taller of the two arched an eyebrow. "Want more? I could take you right back into high school if you like. Your first real job was—"

"That's enough." Shay looked at him narrow-eyed. "How the hell do you know all that?"

"You don't think Jarvis let you marry his kid sister without running a security check on you first, do you?"

Disbelief came first. Then white-hot anger. Then, finally, laughter. "*Now* I believe you're working for Jarvis," he said dryly. "Where is he?"

"Checking a few things. You find your lady yet?"

"No, but she's definitely down here. She borrowed a beat-up old blue Chevy from some kid at an auto-body shop just south of the state line—gave him a hundred bucks and some story about being late for her own wedding." Shay had to grin just thinking about it.

"We've got orders to stay with you, give you whatever help you need."

"Who's in charge?"

"You are. Jarvis told us to keep out of your way, that you knew what you were doing. We're just hired help." He didn't sound too pleased about it.

"Don't take this wrong, but I've got some of my own brand of help on its way."

"Our orders are to stick with you."

Shay nodded, already turning back to his truck. "Fine. Just stay out of my way and we'll get along great."

Cait saw the car as she ran down the front steps of the house and across the cracked driveway to where she'd left her own car. Theirs was a dark blue, late-model four-door parked across the street and down a bit. There were two men in it, faces half-obscured by sunglasses.

She swore with sudden fright, wondering how she hadn't seen them when she came in. They'd been there for days, according to Diane. Waiting for her.

The papers . . . she had to protect those damned papers. Even if Dalkquist managed to kill her, she wanted them found. Wanted him to pay. Wanted the past year to have meant *something*.

She pulled the car door open and slid behind the wheel, fumbling with her handbag, her hands shaking so badly, it took two tries to get it open. Pulling the envelope out, she wet her lips and glanced in the rearview mirror, her heart hammering against her ribs. They were watching her, she realized. Were talking to each other. And now the driver was opening his door and getting out.

Fighting panic, refusing to look in the mirror, she held the envelope against the steering wheel with one hand and fumbled through her purse for her pen with the other, finding it, so scared she felt light-headed and sick.

Calm, she whispered to herself. Stay calm . . . don't look behind. Just stay calm.

Wetting her lips again, she started to print Rick Jarvis's name, then realized with a groan that she had no idea where to send it, no idea what mysterious government agency he worked for. Just that it was in Washington . . . my God, every agency in the country was headquartered in Washington! She couldn't just address it Rick Jarvis, Secret Agent, Washington!

A gasp of laughter bubbled up and she swallowed it, refusing to give in to the hysteria creeping around the edges of her mind. Think, damn it, Caitlin. *Think . . . !*

Secret agent . . . CIA . . . they were based in Virginia. A name. She'd heard Rick talking about someone in Virginia, someone important . . . O'Donnell? O'Dowd? O'Dell . . . Spence O'Dell!

Swiftly she printed O'Dell's name, then hesitated, pen poised above the envelope. *Where* in Virginia? What agency was he with? Think, Caitlin!

A quick glance in the mirror . . . the man was crossing the street, looking both ways first like his mother had taught him . . . did killers have mothers?

CIA, FBI, abc . . . what the hell did it matter, anyway, they were all playing the same silly little-boy games of spy and counterspy and secret agent! Finally she just wrote *CIA* in block letters, then hesitated again. Virginia. But Langley or Quantico? The CIA was at one, the FBI the other. But which? *Which?*

Too late! He was going to be at the car any instant...she scrawled *Quantico, VA,* praying she was right, praying it didn't really matter, that if she was wrong, someone would open it anyway and realize that what they were holding was important. Just praying...

A reflection moved in her side mirror and she gasped as a hand appeared, reaching for the door handle. Instinctively she flung herself across the car and pushed the passenger door open and stumbled out, half falling, blood hammering.

"Hey! Wait—*wait!*"

Cait was across the driveway and the strip of lank grass beyond it in a heartbeat, gravel spitting under her sneakers as she turned and bolted up the narrow alley, running as she'd never run before, the envelope gripped in her fist. Left, down another overgrown alley, hearing footsteps pounding behind her, right, then right again.

Something growled beyond the high wooden fence to her left and then she could hear the frantic clatter of clawed paws, the roar of a big dog as it kept pace with her just on the other side of the fence, sounding huge and deadly. A door banged somewhere and a voice shouted at the dog to shut the hell up and who was out there anyway and he had a gun...

Nice neighborhood, Cait thought with another gulp of wild laughter. Another alley opened to her left and she skidded into it, nearly twisting her ankle as she hit loose gravel and skated off balance, caught herself, pelted down the laneway as hard as she could run.

And then, with no warning, she was in the street and there was traffic and horns and people and normalcy. She paused, gulping for air, then turned left and ran hard and fast, gaze darting from one side of the street to another as she looked frantically for a familiar blue box. Mail, mail...surely to God there was a mailbox somewhere!

She saw the dark blue car a heartbeat before the driver saw her. Pausing at an intersection, trying to decide which way to go, she glanced around and saw it cruising up the street not ten feet behind her, her heart nearly stopping on the spot.

She froze for an all-too-crucial instant, and in that moment the driver spotted her. The window on the passenger side started to roll smoothly down but Cait didn't wait to see if they were going to try to grab her or simply shoot her on the spot. Spinning around, she sprinted back up the way she'd come, running right by them.

Tires squealed and there was a shout followed by a stream of irate curses, but she didn't look back. The light in the intersection ahead of her turned red and she turned to cross in the other direction and ran squarely into a man getting out of a white Oldsmobile that had just pulled up to the curb.

She staggered, off balance, and two strong hands caught her shoulders to steady her. "Sorry," she said, panting, daring a glance behind her. The blue car was half a block back, trapped behind a courier van making a delivery.

"That's all right," a male voice purred above her. "We were coming to get you, anyway."

The voice sent ice down Cait's spine and she went very still, not even breathing. And then, slowly, she looked up.

Cal Crushank smiled down at her. "Hi, Caitie. Miss me?"

"What the *hell* do you mean, you lost her?" Shay grabbed a fistful of the man's shirtfront and hauled him closer. "You were following her, and you *lost* her?"

"Man, I'm telling you, I've never seen anyone move that fast." The man—Jon Creasy—wrenched himself free of Shay's grip and stumbled back, looking hostile and defensive. "She was there one minute and gone the next. And she's smart, man! It's like she's got this radar or something."

"She thought you were Dalkquist's men," Shay said through clenched teeth, fighting a nearly overwhelming desire to plant his fist in the man's face. "Why the hell didn't you identify yourselves?"

"We couldn't get close enough to her!"

"And you just sat there while they grabbed her off the street, shoved her in a car and drove off!" He took a step forward.

"Take it easy, McKittrick," Carlson said quietly, stepping between him and Creasy. "It happens. Creasy got a good look at the license on the car that snatched her, and we've got three other surveillance cars out. We'll find her."

"You're damned right you're going to find her," Shay said with deadly calm, "because if you don't, I'm going to take the four of you apart, piece by piece, and then I'm going to take Rick Jarvis apart the same way. And when I'm finished with him, I'm going to start in on Dalkquist."

Unclenching his fists, he took a deep breath. He'd find her in time, he told himself. This time he wouldn't be too late....

"I don't like this," Richard Angstrom was saying, his face tight with disapproval. He gave Cait a hostile look from across the room. "When I let you talk me into this, Brenton, I agreed because I *thought* you had everything under control."

"You agreed because you needed the money." The other man in the room gave Angstrom an icy stare. "You're in too deep now to even think about pulling out."

"I'm not going to kill her. Not now. It's too risky."

"You'll do as you're told."

"Ease up, Allan," Dalkquist said quietly. "Richard's not the only one having problems with this. I..." He shook his head, glancing at Cait, looking troubled and introspective. "When we talked about this last year, you assured me we could handle this entire situation without any more violence."

Allan, Cait thought. Allan Gordon. Dalkquist's old friend and executive assistant, now his campaign manager. And a lot more, if the past few minutes were anything to go by. They'd brought her to the house—the house she'd grown up in, the house where Dalkquist now lived—and if anyone seemed to be in charge of things, it was Gordon.

The campaign for the governor's office didn't appear to be all Gordon was handling for his old boss.

"Violence?" Angstrom gave Gordon a hostile look, wiping his forehead with a handkerchief. "He sent two hoodlums up there to kill her! To shoot her right out in broad daylight!"

"Angstrom, why don't you—"

"Shut up, Allan," Dalkquist snapped. "He's right—it was stupid and careless and you should have cleared it with me before you hired those two...thugs." He swore, his eyes sultry with anger. "I can't believe you'd jeopardize the whole thing—the election, my safety, *your* safety—by pulling such an off-the-wall stunt! God knows, it was bad enough when you hired that small-time hood Mosely to break into her apartment and kill her, but this...!"

"Every minute she was outside, she was endangering all of us," Gordon said tightly. "If those two morons you sent after her had done their jobs and brought her back, I wouldn't have had to take matters into my own hands."

"Take matters into your own hands again," Dalkquist said balefully, "and I'll cut you up into pieces so small there won't be enough to fill a bait box. You are *not* to do anything like that without talking to me first, understand?"

"But, Brenton—"

"But nothing! I can't afford to have a couple of extra bodies lying around, damn it! If she's found dead of a drug overdose in Amber Hills, it'll blow over in a matter of days. If she's found on a beach with a bullet through her head— and that trucker of hers along with her—I'll be answering questions from now until doomsday!"

"Instead," Angstrom put in angrily, "we now have at least one witness to the shooting, plus another person somehow involved—we're not even too sure *who* he is. Not to mention the motel proprietor and—"

"He didn't see or hear anything," Gordon muttered. "And as for McKittrick, no one's going to believe him anyway. Not with his history. He's spent the last two years in a black depression over his wife's death, so the way it looks is—he meets Cait, gets the hots for her, they have a little fling for a few days, she gets tired of it and runs away— probably to get more drugs. She winds up in Amber Hills and later, depressed and drugged-out, she commits suicide. Even if McKittrick tries to cause trouble, he's got nothing."

Cait started to protest vehemently, then shut her mouth firmly. As long as he believed that, Shay was safe.

And Shay? She swallowed, thinking about his finding her gone. Thinking about the things she'd said. Would he even come looking for her? Or would he simply decide she couldn't handle a relationship and wanted him out of her life?

"And the other man that was up there with them?"

"McKittrick's brother-in-law. He just came up to bring the happy lovers some food and clothes. He's even less of a threat than McKittrick."

"And this?" Dalkquist slapped Mosely's confession down on the elegant French desk that had once been her father's. "What the hell do you have to say about this, Alan? I suppose you anticipated this, too, did you?"

Gordon flushed slightly. "No. That was a mistake. I should have taken care of Mosely right at the beginning, but I thought he'd be more use alive—repudiating Cait's accusations against you—than dead. It was a bad decision, I admit it." Carefully he tore the papers in half and tossed them in the ornate wastebasket by the desk.

And Cait felt something tear inside her just as certainly. She had to get out of here, she thought numbly. It was dark now. She'd been here for hours, locked in one of the large upstairs closets for most of the day until Dalkquist and Angstrom had gotten there. Too long. She had to get out....

"I don't know." Dalkquist was pacing now, shaking his head, still looking worried. "That private detective she hired. Then Mosely. This started out clean and smooth, Allan. And suddenly I'm knee-deep in bodies. I don't like it. I don't like it at all."

"Brent, it's going to be okay." Gordon's voice was calming. "I'm taking care of everything. You just worry about the election, I'll worry about this."

"It's *how* you're taking care of it that bothers me, Allan."

Gordon's face turned cool. "Maybe you should have thought of that before you asked me to help you murder your wife, Brent. I did help, remember. I set it up, I paid for it, I cleaned up all the loose ends, I kept your name out of it. You told me you'd take care of Caitlin—and look what' happened. Maybe I should have taken care of her right from the beginning, too."

She was going to faint, Cait thought dimly. The room kept spinning and she was feeling sick and cold and Gordon's voice had receded until it sounded very small and very far away.

"So you did kill my mother." Her voice was just a rasp. She shivered and pulled the windbreaker more tightly around her, huddling in the big armchair where Crushan had shoved her. She felt numbed and cold clear to the bone, wondering why hearing it said out loud brought so little satisfaction.

"She was talking divorce, Caitlin," Dalkquist said quietly. "Lord knows, I didn't want to do it. But she left me no choice. That damned prenuptial agreement I signed was bulletproof. If she'd made good on her threat to divorce me, there would have been a major investigation on where all her money had gone and I just couldn't afford the scrutiny." He smiled. "I'm sure you can understand that, Cait. I think you have a vague idea of how much was involved."

"And my father?" She swallowed, drawing her legs up and wrapping her arms around them, trying to stop the shivers.

"Caitlin, your father was my friend. Of course I didn't kill him." Dalkquist looked sincerely upset by the question. "When it happened, however, I did see the obvious benefits to myself."

"You—"

Crushank reached out and gave her a cautionary rap on the head with his knuckles. "Be nice, Caitie."

"If we're going to do this, let's get it over with." Angstrom looked across at Gordon. "You're sure you weren't followed back here...?"

"Of course we weren't followed," Gordon said impatiently. "Angstrom, you spend too much time in that hospital of yours. You're getting as paranoid as some of your patients."

"How did you know I'd go to Diane Mosely's sister?" Cait asked softly, wanting to postpone whatever they had in mind. She had to get out of here, had to find a way out.

"It was just a good guess," Gordon told her, looking pleased with himself. "I had someone watching the house from the apartment building across the street."

Apartment building. "And the... blue car?"

"What blue car?" Angstrom looked suddenly alarmed, glancing at Cait, then to Gordon. "*What* blue car?"

"There was no blue car," Gordon said soothingly.

And then, abruptly, she was clearheaded and alert, every sense fine-tuned, her mind clicking like a computer. "Rick. It was Rick's men!" She gave a soft laugh, her heart leaping. "You *were* followed, Gordon. They're probably outside right now, waiting for you to make a move."

Angstrom paled. "Outside? Who's outside?"

"No one's outside, you idiot," Gordon snapped, giving Cait a cold glare. "She'd just trying to—"

"You should have checked Shay McKittrick out a little better, Al. You'd have discovered that his wife's name was Nancy Jarvis. And that Nancy's big brother works for an undercover crime unit in Washington." She had his attention; she let her smile widen. "They're on to you big time, Al. Rick dropped Dalkquist's name into an FBI computer and alarms started going off from one end of the country to the other. So it doesn't matter if you kill me or not—you're all toast."

"FBI?" Angstrom's eyes bulged. "*FBI?* McKittrick's brother-in-law is FBI?"

"She's making it up," Gordon said impatiently. "My God, you should know her by now."

"And if she isn't?" Dalkquist said slowly.

"Brenton, it's all taken care of." Gordon spread his hands as though to still troubled water. "Go back to your office, make some phone calls, talk to people—be visible. I'll call you when we have her back up at Amber Hills and you can call a press conference. Play the distraught stepfather angle up for all it's worth—tell them that Caitlin's been found and returned to Amber Hills, that there's been some sort of incident with a man and some drugs...maybe an overdose. That would be a good touch. Say she's receiving proper care, that you're glad she's back, blah, blah, blah. The usual. And just let me take care of the details.''

He looked at Angstrom. "Okay, give her something to keep her quiet and then you and Crushank get her into the car. And, Angstrom, remember that it's a good two-hour drive to Amber Hills from here. Make certain you keep her sedated the entire way, because I swear if she gets away from you again, you're going to regret it.''

"Brenton, this madman has gotten out of control.'' Angstrom looked distraught. "It started out just as a simple cover-up, but it's turning into a nightmare and we're all getting sucked in deeper and deeper.''

"And what would you suggest we do, Richard? Let her go and turn ourselves in to the police?'' Dalkquist gave a snort of disgust. "I don't think so. We're all in this. We've gone this far, we'll go the entire distance. Now give her the damned sedative and get her out of here.''

"Come on, sweetcheeks,'' Crushank purred, reaching for her. "You and me have some catching up to do.''

He leaned forward slightly to grab her wrists, giving her the perfect opening. And without even pausing to contemplate the outcome, Cait lashed out with her left foot and caught him squarely in the groin.

For an instant, she thought she'd miscalculated. He stopped dead, hanging over her, one hand still reaching for her arm . . . and then he turned an unpleasant shade of yellow-green and sank to his knees, doubled over and mewling softly as he fought to draw in one agonized breath after another.

"Oh, for. . .'' Gordon looked across at Crushank in disgust, then walked across and reached out to grab Cait's arm. But she was on her feet in a heartbeat, stumbling back just out of reach, looking around frantically for a weapon, for a way out, for something.

She spotted the brass fire tools just as he made another grab for her and she managed to dart out of his reach again and snatch up the ornate poker, taking a vicious swing at him. It hit him on the side of the head with a satisfying thump and he gave a snarl of pain and staggered back. Then he calmly reached out and grasped the poker firmly and wrenched it out of her hand.

It pulled her off balance and before she could stumble away, he grabbed her by the arms and slammed her back against the wall so hard, she literally saw stars, too dazed to even fight.

"Damn you, I'm tempted to kill you right here just for the satisfaction it would give me."

"Gordon!" Dalkquist's voice snapped around them. "Get her sedated and in the car. Angstrom, when you get her up to Amber Hills, I don't care if you have to leave her in a straitjacket twenty-four hours a day and pump her so full of happy juice she thinks she's died and gone to heaven—just make sure she doesn't get out again. We'll wait a month, six weeks at the outside, then she'll have her little overdose and that will be the end of it."

Still dazed, Cait tried to pull away from Gordon's grip, but he wrenched her right arm up behind her while Angstrom caught the other and pushed the sleeve of the windbreaker up. Before Cait could even collect her senses enough to scream, he'd brought the hypodermic up to her inner elbow.

And then, finally, she did scream.

Chapter 12

Light—an explosion of light filled the room, pouring through the big windows, blinding Cait and making Angstrom grunt in pain and put his arm up to shield his eyes.

"What the—" Still holding Cait's arm, Gordon wheeled around to face the window, squinting against the glare.

"The FBI," Angstrom yelped. "It's the FBI!"

"FBI my—*look out!*" Gordon stumbled aside so violently that he sent Cait staggering against the desk.

She nearly fell but managed to catch herself, turning toward the window in bewilderment. All she could see for a moment was blinding white light and then, very suddenly, she saw what was *behind* the light. Sucking in a startled breath, she stood there transfixed, watching in stupefied astonishment as the big truck hurtled across the wide patio like something conjured up from hell itself, chrome grill glinting like armor, engine roaring.

Air horn bellowing, it hit the wall of glass and came bursting through. Cait flung herself behind the desk, arms over her head. Over the explosion of glass she could hear Angstrom shouting something and Crushank whimpering, then the sound of running footsteps and shouts.

"Cait! Cait Sawyer? You all right?"

"Here." Staggering a little, she pulled herself to her feet and looked around a little stupidly at the destruction around her, trying to see who'd been calling her name.

There were two men there, both peering at her worriedly, and although they were vaguely familiar it took her a moment to place them: Sonny and Billy, from that morning at the truckstop when Dalkquist's men had tried to take her away from Shay. They looked just as big and dangerous now as they had then, Sonny's tire iron held at the ready, Billy armed with his baseball bat. When they saw that she wasn't hurt, they nodded and turned away, their boots crunching through broken glass as they prowled restlessly.

There were a couple of other men there she half recognized from that first morning, too. One was standing over Crushank with clenched fists, looking as though the only thing he wanted in the world was for Crushank to try something so he could belt him, and two others had Angstrom backed into a corner where he was babbling at them to get away. Dalkquist was against the far wall, arguing ferociously with someone in a red and black checked shirt who didn't seem to be very interested in whatever he was saying.

Slowly Cait looked back at the truck that sat with its chromed snout halfway across what had once been her father's den. Snorting and rumbling and belching diesel smoke from the sheered-off exhaust stacks, it reminded Cait of a dragon that had come thundering in looking for battle, its glossy black hood glittering with shards of broken glass, wide grill glinting like bared teeth in the flickering light cast from the still-swinging ceiling fixture.

And then she saw the rest of the trucks, all parked out on the street, engines idling, ablaze with lights. Five of them, maybe six. And even as she was trying to assimilate that, figures detached themselves from the darkness outside and started walking in through the ruined wall. She recognized the two who had been in the car outside Diane Mosely's and felt panic start to rise again.

Then the driver's door on the truck opened and Shay jumped down, tire iron in his fist, and the panic turned to relief.

Shay's first thought, when he saw Cait standing by the desk looking shell-shocked, was that he was too late and Angstrom had already given her whatever had been in the syringe. But then he realized she was just stunned. Not surprisingly, he reminded himself. He'd managed to surprise himself pretty well, too.

"God Almighty, McKittrick," Sonny yelled at him from across the room, giving a bellow of laughter as he surveyed the damage. "I'd say you got their attention!"

"Cait, are you all right?" Shay stepped over the remains of a chair and strode across to her.

She blinked and looked at him, eyes still wide and dark with shock. "Do you always make this kind of an entrance when you call on a lady?"

And in that moment, Shay knew it was going to be all right. Laughing, he tossed the tire iron aside and swept her up into his arms, burying his face in her sweet-scented hair, filling his arms and sense with her. "Damn it, Cait, why did you run? You should have known I'd never let you get away from me."

Her arms were around his neck and she was hugging him fiercely. "You shouldn't have come after me," she whispered in a broken sob. "If you'd been hurt—"

"Of course I came after you," he said with a laugh, lifting her up in a fierce embrace. "Are you all right? They didn't hurt you, did they?"

"I'm fine." Cheeks glittering with tears, she smiled up into his eyes. "And I'm sorry..."

"You're sorry?" He gave a snort of laughter and gazed around the room in disbelief. "I'm the one who should be doing the apologizing. I just drove my truck through your house."

Cait looked around suddenly. "Shay, there's another man. Allan Gordon, Dalkquist's campaign manager. He was behind most of it. We have to catch him before—"

"He's caught." Shay gave her another tight hug. "Billy's got him. He's not going anywhere." He let her slide out of his embrace and gazed down at her, smoothing her hair back from her face. "Are you sure you're all right? I planned to stop before I actually hit the damn window, but..." He looked around again, shaking his head wonderingly. "I heard you scream and I guess I just lost it for a minute."

"I'm all right. I'm fine." She gazed up at him, touching his face with her fingers. "I can't believe it's you. I didn't think you'd come after me. I thought—"

"It's going to take a lot more than Dalkquist to keep me away from you, Caitlin Sawyer." He lowered his mouth to hers and kissed her, the taste of her filling him like a good wine, making his blood sing.

He could hear Dalkquist snapping out orders behind them and reluctantly drew his mouth from Cait's, looking around. Dalkquist was covered in plaster dust and tiny flecks of broken glass and was demanding to know what the hell was going on, who these people were, why they were in his house.

He looked pale and gaunt-eyed, and Shay smiled. "Gotcha."

Dalkquist turned slowly and when his gaze settled on Cait, his face distorted with fury. "What have you—"

"I told you I'd put you away," Cait said very softly, stepping out of Shay's arms and walking across to face her stepfather squarely.

"You have nothing. *Nothing!* And I demand you get these—"

"I don't think you should be *demandin'* anything," Sonny drawled. "I'd say your demandin' days are over."

"Dalkquist, I've been promising this to myself ever since I met you...." Shay stepped closer to the other man, planted his feet solidly in the glass-littered carpet, drew his right arm back and swung his fist around with every ounce of strength he could muster.

It caught Dalkquist squarely and the impact sent a jolt of raw pain right up to Shay's shoulder. But he ignored it, watching in satisfaction as Dalkquist flew back and went sprawling full-length on the floor, dazed and bleeding.

Shay looked around and spotted Crushank, who was still crouched on the floor, looking sick and dazed and confused. He thought of lifting him to his feet and punching *him* across the room just on general principles, then gave a snort and turned away. "I think you took care of him just fine, Cait. Couldn't have done a better job myself."

"And I didn't split my knuckles doing it." She kissed his bruised and bloodied hand, cradling it between hers.

He laughed and flexed his fingers, wincing. "Damn, that hurts!"

"Dalkquist could be right, you know," she said very quietly. "I had proof that he paid Mosely to kill me, but—"

"We have it on tape, Cait." Shay grinned down at her. "We have the whole damn thing on tape."

"Tape?" She blinked and gazed up at him in confusion.

"Tape." Rick appeared from around the grill of Shay's rig just then, looking at the shambles around him as though not believing his eyes. "You ever hear of just using a door, McKittrick?"

"Where the hell were *you?*" Shay glared at him belligerently. "I sat outside in that surveillence van for two damned hours, waiting for you to show up. Finally I just decided to handle it myself."

"You call this handling it?"

"It got the job done."

"Who are these guys?" Rick nodded his head toward Sonny and Billy and the others. Billy was grinning sleepily at Dalkquist, slapping the baseball bat gently into his palm.

Shay shrugged. "You've got your team of experts, I've got mine. I put out a call on the CB and asked for some backup."

"Well, would you get them out of here?" Rick growled. "It looks like a truckers' convention outside, rigs parked all over the street. The cops are going to be here any minute and will want to secure the perimeter."

"Secure the perimeter?" Shay looked at him dryly. "You've been playing secret agent too long, Jarvis. The perimeter's secured, in case you hadn't noticed." Then he looked at his truck and the smashed wall around it. "Or what's left of it, anyway."

"You still haven't told me what you meant about a tape." Cait sounded bewildered and a little lost.

Smiling, Rick reached across and slipped the black windbreaker off her shoulders and motioned for her to take her arms out of it. Mystified, she shrugged out of it and watched as he calmly tore off the elegantly stitched stand-up collar and peeled apart the two halves, showing her what was inside.

"It's a voice-activated recorder, and holds about thirty hours of actual conversation. The microphone is here." He pointed to one of the small decorative medallions worked into the design. "The battery is in the hem of the jacket it-self."

Cait stared at it disbelievingly. "But...how did you know I'd be wearing it when it counted?"

"I didn't. But half this business is blind, stupid luck and the other half is knowing when to take a chance." He smiled dryly. "Knowing how you've handled yourself in tight places before, I figured there was a good chance you'd get him talking sooner or later. I just hoped you were wearing that jacket when you did."

"And...and that's how you found me?"

Shay gave a snort. "Hell, he's got you wired up like a Christmas tree. Everything you're wearing has tiny trans-mitters in it. You've been showing up on tracking devices ever since you left Oregon."

Cait pressed her fingers against her temples, eyes closed. "Are you telling me this was all just some sort of scam? That you used me to catch Dalkquist?"

"No. When Shay called me up to that motel, I figured he was in trouble, all right, but I had no idea what kind or how much. It wasn't until I talked with him that I ran Dalk-quist's name through the computers. And it wasn't until I met you that I decided to rig you up with all this gear. While you and McKittrick were taking your beachside stroll, I was wiring your clothes for sound."

"But...why?"

"Because by then you struck me as a savvy lady who knew how to take care of herself. I figured if anyone was going to get Dalkquist to talk it would be you. I..." He winced, swearing under his breath. "Look, Cait, I owe you an apology. After I looked into it, I was convinced that Dalkquist *was* up to something. But I also figured you were real bad news yourself. That you weren't in Amber Hills just because Dalkquist needed to shut you up, but because you had some serious problems."

A hint of a smile lifted the corner of Cait's mouth. "Just for the record, I wasn't particularly impressed with you, either."

"Can this wait?" Shay drew Cait back into his arms and glowered at Jarvis over the top of her head. "You've got what you need. Now take a hike."

"She has to be debriefed," Rick said quietly.

"Damn it, Jarvis, she isn't one of your agents!"

"It's all right." Wearily Cait lifted her face from Shay's shoulder. "Whatever you need, I'll do it if it means putting Dalkquist away. But first, could somebody *please* get this truck out of my house?"

My house. The words were still singing in Cait's head hours later. Someone *had* backed Shay's rig out of the study and someone else had appeared seemingly from nowhere with sheets of plastic and had covered the hole reasonably well. And then Rick had sat her down in a chair and they'd gone over everything—every tiny detail of the past six years. Then he, too, had left, taking his team of weary men with him, and she and Shay had been alone finally in the vast silences of what had, long ago, been a place of love instead of suspicion and murder.

She wandered through the still rooms, smiling now and again when she saw something that reminded her of happier times, noticing things that had changed or been moved. Shay walked along beside her, saying nothing, just *being* there, his strong presence filling her and the house with a sense of security.

"I want to get his things out of this house," she finally said, standing in the double doors leading to her mother's bedroom.

"Caitie, that's a hell of a big job to take on **tonight**."

"Please." She looked up into his strong, calm face. "I have to do it. The clothes anyway—help me get his clothes out."

And Shay just smiled and nodded, reaching down to touch her cheek.

It took them hours. Cait went through the big walk-in closet and dressing room first, stripping the hangers off the rods and then walking back out to the top of the stairs and dropping them by the armful down onto the floor below. Then she went through the drawers and shelves, stripping them of everything Dalkquist had owned. And finally, nearly crying with exhaustion, she dragged everything out into the garage and heaped it there, gazing at it in satisfaction.

"I'd love to set it on fire, but I guess that's not a good idea." She wiped a trickle of perspiration from her forehead with her arm.

"I wouldn't suggest it," Shay drawled. "Your insurance company's going to have a hard enough time believing someone drove a Kenworth through the side of the house. Burning half the place down might be pushing your luck."

And, incredibly, Cait found she could still laugh. She leaned against him, loving just the sight of him standing there in her family home, and laughed until the laughter turned to tears. And then Shay just picked her up in his arms and carried her back into the house.

She awoke in darkness and moonlight. Groggy, she sat up and looked around, completely disoriented for a panicky moment or two. Then she remembered. And with the remembering came the realization that she was in bed in one of the guest rooms, clad only in bra and panties and tucked between French percale sheets lightly scented with lavender.

Shay was there, too, clothed and unshaven, lying asleep on the top of the blue satin comforter as though keeping watch over her. His face was strong and hard-planed in the moonlight, and she remembered being in the truck that first night, afraid, seeing him looking down at her.

Now? Now she was in love with him, and couldn't even remember when it had happened. Smiling, she put her hand out to brush a lock of wayward hair off his forehead, then caught herself. Let him sleep, she decided. Heaven knows, he deserved a hero's sleep after today.

She slipped from between the sheets and rummaged through the closet until she found a guest robe. He was still asleep when she came out of the shower and she tiptoed out of the room and downstairs to the huge kitchen, wondering where the cook and the rest of the staff were. If there even *was* a staff here anymore. Maybe Dalkquist had fired them all long ago.

But once she was there, she realized she wasn't hungry and instead wandered back out and into the dining room, then through to the huge living room with its wall of glass overlooking the city. It felt strange being here, as though the house she'd grown up in had subtly changed while she'd been gone and she didn't fit anymore. The rooms seemed even colder and more silent in moonlight and she wandered from one to the other like a stranger, feeling colder and more unwanted by the passing minute.

She made her way around to the huge indoor pool finally, switching on the underwater lights so the water glowed like something magical in the darkness. Beyond the glass walls, the city spread into the night like a glittering carpet and she gazed at it, wishing she could feel something.

"Cait?" Shay's soft voice startled her slightly and she looked around to see him standing in the wide doorway of the sunroom. "Are you all right?"

She nodded, smiling, and hugged herself. Then, as he walked around to where she was standing, she suddenly shook her head and swallowed, tears filling in her eyes. "No, not entirely. It just feels so...empty."

"Oh, Caitie." Sighing, he wrapped his arms around her and held her close, his body heat soaking into her. "I wish I could make it better for you, Cait. I wish I could take the hurt away."

"Will you stay with me?"

"Here?" He pulled away far enough to look down at her.

"Just for a few days," she added quickly. "I know you've got commitments and people depending on you, but..." She shivered and nestled closer to him. "This place is haunted, Shay. I don't want to be here alone."

"You don't have to stay," he murmured, tugging her against him again and kissing the top of her head.

"Yes, I do. I have to reclaim my life. Reclaim the memories that he's stolen from me. But it scares me, somehow. It's as though he's still here. Still...taunting me."

"I have a better idea." Shay rubbed her back and shoulders with a large, warm hand. "Come on the road with me. We'll pick up a load here in Sacramento and head north to Seattle, then cut east and head along the Canadian border. Come down through the central states, then back across the south." He kissed her ear, nuzzling the side of her throat. "No Dalkquist. No secret agents. Just you and me and the rig and the open road."

Cait smiled and eased out of his embrace. "You tempt me, good sir." And realized, as she said it, how much she meant it. How tempting not just his offer but the thought of simply walking out and making a new life for herself, unburdened by the horrors of the past or the expectations of a future she didn't even know if she wanted.

"But...?" He tipped her chin with his finger so she was looking up at him.

"But..." She smiled as she said it, seeing the questions in his eyes. "There are parts of me here I have to find again, Shay," she said quietly. "He stole...my life. Who I was. What I was. If I just walk away now, I'll never be whole. I have to end it once and for all, and I can only do that here."

He nodded, idly stroking her cheek with his finger, and then he was dropping his mouth to hers and she was wrapping her arms around his neck, shivering a little as the robe fell open and his arms slipped inside and around her, and then all the fear simply vanished and it was just Shay and her and nothing else.

He carried her upstairs for the second time that night, and for the second time, he eased her between cool percale sheets scented of lavender. Only, this time, he was there with her, his muscled body naked and strong, and Cait simply gave herself over to the magic without even trying to make sense of it....

Shay awoke a little after six the next morning with Cait's warm rump tucked against his belly and her legs all tangled up in his, and he lay there drowsily thinking he wouldn't mind spending the rest of his life like this. He breathed in the scent of shampoo and warm woman and smiled, kissing the naked shoulder in front of him and caressing the curve of her hip, feeling his body starting to stir just at the promise of that silken touch.

Cait stirred, mumbling sleepily, and he half expected her to be startled at finding him there. But she just sighed and turned her head to kiss his arm, and when he slid his hand down the gentle curve of her stomach he could feel her breath catch slightly. He stroked the satiny skin of her belly with his fingertips and she shivered and put her hand on his, pressing it more firmly to her, and when he moved it lower still she moaned very softly.

"You're nice to wake up to," he murmured, easing slow, teasing fingers into the liquid heat of her body and listening to her fighting to catch her breath. He curled around and captured the taut peak of her breast between his lips. "Very nice."

"If I'd known this is how you say good morning," she whispered with a soft, teasing laugh, "I'd never have run away the last time...." She stretched sinuously, breath hissing out as his fingers moved and teased.

"More?"

"Ohhh...more." She bit off a soft cry, her fingers tightening convulsively around his wrist as he caressed her gently, his own heartbeat all over the place just listening to her respond.

And then she was turning in his arms, so ready it nearly caught him off guard and he had to fumble in the drawer of the night table, swearing under his breath, his fingers clumsy with haste.

Giving a throaty laugh that made his blood pound, Cait reached across and took the thin plastic package from his fingers and tore it open, smiling wickedly. "May I?"

"Be my guest," Shay groaned as her small hands touched him, a little hesitantly at first, then more boldly.

"Wise thinking, bringing these in last night."

"Wishful thinking," Shay admitted with a rough laugh, reaching for her.

And a long time later, locked within the hot magic of her body, moving rhythmically, steadily, hearing her moan his name and lift to meet him time and again, he realized he never wanted it to end. That there was a rightness to here and to this woman that he'd never felt before, a certainty that everything was as it should be.

And later still, holding her, murmuring to her, quieting her, when she looked up with love-dazed eyes and whispered *"Stay with me,"* he nodded and kissed her gently on the lips...and told himself it would all work out.

* * *

They awoke a second time a little after nine that first morning to find the estate awash with reporters and cameras, every newspaper and radio station and television news team in five states screaming for an exclusive. She gave an interview that afternoon, hoping it would quell the hysteria, but it only seemed to make it worse.

The next few days seemed endless. She spent hours with the police and members of Rick Jarvis's mysterious agency. And later, more hours with accountants and bankers and investment managers who spoke an arcane language she only half understood.

People came back into her life. Suddenly people she hadn't seen in two years were there, filling up the spaces of her world.

"We always thought there was something odd about him, you know," they confided in dark, mysterious voices, arms slipped through hers, best friends now she was no longer something to be avoided. "Tell us," they whispered, eyes afire with curiosity. "Tell us about it . . . spare us no details, dear."

Her mother's friends, too, came crowding round, everyone so knowing, so supportive, so . . . *kind.*

And through it all, Shay was at her side, solid and protective. He took the media hysteria in stride, his answers short and to the point and completely devoid of anything newsworthy. He stood by her through the hours of police interviews, and the even longer hours of social pleasantries when she tried to smile and make conversation with people she barely knew.

He fielded questions about his marriage, about Nancy's death, about the intimacies of his relationship with Cait, about what it had been *like,* harboring a fugitive and running from Dalkquist's wrath.

And at night, he was there for her, too. Strong, gentle, undemanding, he filled her nights with tenderness and laughter and sweet, uncomplicated sex. And talk. Hours of quiet in-the-dark talk, lying side by side in the humid tangle of sheets, always touching, a hand absently caressing a flare of hip, the curve of a shoulder, fingers drawing idle spirals on a back or thigh.

He talked of those nightmare months of Nancy's illness when he'd thought he was losing his mind, and the two years since, when he was sometimes sure of it. He talked of sitting in anonymous motel rooms with an unopened bottle of whiskey and his revolver in front of him, filled with despair and self-hatred. And he talked of now, of how the memories haunted him less and less and he found himself wakening each morning filled not with dread but with the beginnings of enthusiasm.

And she talked of what it had been like watching people turn away when she walked into a room, of how they'd whisper and smile, of the cool, knowing smile Dalkquist would always give her. She talked of seeing the hurt in her mother's eyes, the bewilderment, the desperate hope that everything would be all right. She talked of her fear and her anger and of how sometimes in the night she'd wake and think perhaps she *had* gone insane, that Dalkquist was good and true and her mother was in no danger at all. And she talked of the months following her mother's death when she'd blamed herself for not being there.

And then, deep in the silences of the night, they'd turn to each other again and make love for a long, long while, sometimes gentle and lazy and relaxed, and at other times with a hot, erotic urgency that would leave them both panting and spent and shivering with the intensity of it.

Beautiful Ivarson Oil heiress Caitlin Sawyer and truck-driver friend S. McKittrick told reporters today they have no comment regarding the upcoming trial of Brenton Dalkquist III...

The newspaper story's lead glared up at him from the table where he'd angrily tossed the paper earlier that afternoon, and Shay whispered something profane and not very creative.

The Heiress and the Truck Driver. Someone would be making a TV miniseries out of it before the month was up.

He glowered at his reflection in the mirror above the dressing table and swore again, adjusting the knot in his tie. The last time he'd worn a tie had been at Nancy's funeral. And his mood this time was just about as jovial.

Cait appeared at his elbow suddenly, and she smiled a little wryly at their reflections. "Looking good, McKittrick. That ravening horde downstairs will eat you alive. Are you sure you want to do this?"

"I'm sure I *don't* want to do this," he growled, shrugging his shoulders under the restricting fabric of the dinner jacket. "I'd rather change a flat on the interstate at high noon on July Fourth weekend in the middle of a damned heat wave." He met her gaze on glass and grinned. "You could go down there and tell them all to go the hell home and we could go to bed and just stay there till morning."

Her lips curved upward, the eyes above sparkling with mischief. "You are a silver-tongued devil, aren't you? Hell on Wheels, indeed...." Then the smile slid from her mouth and she fastened small glittery stones on her earlobes that would probably pay for his semi twice over. "I have to, Shay. Giving this party is just a way of saying, yes, damn you, I'm back, I'm sane and I was right all along."

"And I'm the stud in the background." He gave the knot in his tie an irritable tug. "Hell, you even paid for this damn thing. I'm beginning to feel like a gigolo, bought and paid for right down to my damn jockey shorts."

"Shay, don't." She put her hand on his well-tailored sleeve, her expression pensive in the mirror. "It's not like that. I know people talk, but—"

Smiling, Shay bent down and kissed her full on the mouth, not wanting to hear it. Not wanting to fight. They'd had this discussion for the first time a couple of days ago when his irritation had gotten the better of him and he'd lashed out at something he couldn't even remember about now. And since then, it had been between them—strange, uncomfortable, like a secret both knew but neither would acknowledge.

"I love you, Shay," she whispered, her gaze searching his.

"I know." He kissed her again. "Now let's go downstairs and get this damned thing over with so we can go to bed. Because let me tell you, lady, that dress is starting to give me some seriously bad ideas. . . ."

Her laughter rose like the pealing of small bells and she lifted onto her expensively shod toes to kiss him on the cheek. "I like the sound of that. Keep talking."

He whispered something into her ear that made her blush right down to her all-too-dramatic cleavage and well beyond, and he laughed softly and kissed the side of her throat, the subtle scent of her perfume making his pulse leap.

They went down together and found the party already well under way, and Cait slipped free of his arm and started making the requisite rounds as hostess. And Shay, trying to make himself as inconspicuous as possible, got himself a glass of bourbon and stayed out of the way.

Watching her, he found himself smiling, thinking idly that she was about the easiest thing to look at he'd seen in a long, long while. She'd smoothed her hair back and into an intricate knot at her nape that appeared to be held there by nothing more substantial that faith, and was wearing a black dress that made his belly pull tight just looking at it. It was low-cut and complicated and it glittered when she moved, and there wasn't a man in the room who wasn't thinking exactly what he was thinking.

Difference was, he was going to put those thoughts into action later tonight. That made him smile, too.

She was like the blade of a samurai sword, he thought, watching her work the room. Strong enough to withstand just about anything and yet supple, too. Resilient. She'd settled back into her life here as though those long years between her father's death and now had never really existed, picking up the pieces of a life she'd been born to.

A world that had no place for him in it, he realized with sudden and chilling clarity.

The bourbon turned to acid in his mouth and he set the glass down, feeling the emptiness wash through him like a tidal wave. This *was* where she belonged. These people were her people: the movers and shakers, the politicians, the financial heavyweights, the moneyed and the privileged. There was more money in this one room than he'd earn in a hundred lifetimes. More power than most men ever dreamed of wielding. And she fit into it as smoothly and naturally as she had a right to.

Beautiful heiress and trucker.

He found himself smiling a little for no reason, realizing he'd known it all along but had simply postponed dealing with it for Cait's sake. She'd needed him; it had been that simple. And he'd been there for her.

But that had been nearly ten days ago. She was strong now, competent, capable. He'd been watching her grow back into the woman she'd once been slowly, day by day, a bit at a time. And the closer she got to herself, the farther she'd gotten from him.

And that's the way it should be, he told himself fiercely. He hadn't come into this thinking it could be any other way.

Hadn't promised her anything he knew he couldn't deliver, had never said it would be forever.

Truth was, she didn't love him. Not the way it mattered. He'd come riding into her life like a knight on a black-and-chrome steed, slaying dragons left and right and sweeping her off her feet with deeds of derring-do. But the fantasy was over now. And they both had to go back to who and what they were.

Taking a deep breath, he looked around the room until he spotted her, looking regal and very much in charge as she handled some crisis with the caterer.

And then he turned and walked out the door and up the broad, sweeping stairs.

"...and you're looking *wonderful,* darling. Just *wonderful!*" The tall blonde leaned a little closer to Cait. "You're *so* brave. I don't know *what* I'd have done. Although I must say," she added in a conspiratorial whisper, "I wouldn't have minded the obvious advantages of being a woman on the run. I mean, *darling!* That man is to die for."

I nearly did, Cait felt like saying. We both nearly died, as a matter of fact, but that doesn't seem to bother you. But she simply smiled and murmured something suitably banal and made her escape. *Shay, damn you,* she told him silently, *where* are *you! Get me out of here!*

She glanced around the room, wondering who'd buttonholed him. And why. People seemed to think he was some rare species of animal life she'd brought back from a safari abroad, the way they treated him. The men didn't know how to talk to him, and the women...well, the women didn't have talk on their minds. She'd seen some of the predatory looks following him.

And then, suddenly, she spotted him. And her heart gave an odd little twist when his gaze met hers across the noisy room. He'd changed, was wearing his faded denim jeans and his pale blue chambray shirt and his cowhide jacket, and he had goodbye written all over him.

"No." She said it softly, to herself, her heart splintering right to the core like shattering crystal. "No, not yet...." And realized as she said the words that she'd known it was only a matter of time.

As he made his way through the crowds of chattering, laughing people, his eyes locked with hers and everything else receded and vanished and there was just the two of them.

"You're leaving." How she ever got the words past the aching thickness in her throat she didn't know.

"It's time, Caitie."

He suddenly seemed too tall and rugged and wide-shouldered for this room, too elemental for the crystal chandeliers and the priceless rugs and the ornate furniture surrounding them, as though he'd already distanced himself from them. And her.

She looked up at him without saying anything. Not knowing if she even could.

"I'm picking up a load of freight tomorrow morning and taking it up to Portland. Then north..."

"Shay..." Cait swallowed, hoping she didn't sound as panicky as she felt. "You...you could stay. Find someone else to deliver the freight and stay. With me."

"I'm not part of this life," he said quietly, gesturing around the crowded, noisy room. "I don't fit here, Cait. I'm a truck driver—that's what I do and who I am."

"But...damn it, Shay, I could *buy* you a trucking company if that's what—"

He had to laugh. "Cait, listen to yourself. Listen to what you're saying." He cupped her cheeks in his palms, feeling the silken warmth of her, and bent down to kiss her on the mouth. "Honey, I'd never be happy sitting in an office *playing* trucker. Keeping myself busy while I live on your money, telling myself it means something when we both know it doesn't."

"It doesn't have to be like that!"

"How else *could* it be, Cait?" he asked gently. "You're . . . hell, you're satin and silk, and I'm blue denim. You're evenings at the symphony and French champagne, and I'm football on TV and buddies in for beer. You're expensive German cars, and I'm Detroit steel. We're worlds apart, Caitie. You know it and I know it. Let's not ruin what we've had by pretending it can be more than it is, all right?"

"But, Shay—"

"I love you, Cait Sawyer." He turned her face upward lightly, gazing down into the perfection of her eyes. "And, right at this moment, you love me. Let's be smart and leave it like that. If we try and make it into something more, we'll both wind up miserable. You've got a life to lead here—and it doesn't have a place for me in it. Let's just be happy with what we had."

Somehow, Cait managed not to cry. The ache within her heart was like something had just been torn out of her, but she managed a rough facsimile of a smile, trying not to let him see the desperate hurt in her eyes. He was right, she knew that. Deep down somewhere, she knew it. But right now . . . God, all she wanted right now was his arms around her and his mouth seeking hers in the night, his strength, his certainty.

But he *was* right. Being out there on the road was part of who he was—if he lost that, he'd lose a part of himself. Maybe the very part that she'd fallen in love with. He'd be miserable here, hemmed in by walls and social expectations. And it wouldn't be easy. She knew these people, was part of their exclusive little world. To them, he'd always just be Cait's truck driver, something to smile about over cocktails, a curiosity item.

Beautifully kept women would spend their time wonder
ing what he was like in bed—and one or two would un
doubtedly attempt to find out for themselves—while thei
well-moneyed husbands would simply find him a complet
mystery. He didn't play tennis or golf, didn't toy with th
stock market and he'd rather drive down Wall Street in a
eighteen-wheeler than deal on it.

"I guess you're right," she managed to say, forcing her
self to smile carelessly again. "I wish I could convince yo
to stay with me for a while, though. I'm so far out of m
depth here I feel as though I'm drowning."

He laughed softly, that rough-edged laugh that alway
made her heart miss a beat. "You'll do fine, hotshot. Thi
is your world—there's nothing these people can throw a
you that you can't handle."

She nodded again, knowing if she tried to say somethin
she'd wind up bursting into tears. He bent down again an
let his lips linger against her cheek. "Take care of yourself
Cait," he murmured. "We had magic, sweetheart. An
you'll find it again with someone else. Someone you be
long with . . . I promise."

And then, that quickly, he was gone. He turned an
walked away, not looking back, his broad shoulders carv
ing a path through the crowd. Speculative glances followe
him, moved to her, away again.

"Cait, darling! I'm *so* glad you're back!" Bertrice Well
man appeared in a swirl of expensively scented air and de
signer-label silk and planted a cool kiss on Cait's cheek. "
always knew you were right about Brenton. I told people i
was a *shame,* just a shame, the way you were treated, ev
eryone saying you were on drugs and so on." She waved a
elegantly manicured hand to dismiss the entire crowd. "Bu
you're back now and—"

"Why didn't you say so?"

Bertrice blinked. "Pardon?"

"I said, if you believed me, why didn't you support me? Why didn't you tell the police you knew I was being set up?"

"Why... well...I..." She fluttered helplessly, like a brightly feathered bird caught on a wire fence. Her face turned an unpleasant shade of pink. "That is...I...well, I *couldn't*, could I? I mean, who'd believe me?" She placed a hand on her chest and laughed merrily. "Besides, darling, I *knew* you'd come through it with flying colors. You're *so* like your dear mother. Now..." She leaned closer, her eyes avid. "Tell me all about it! And that man! Darling, where *ever* did you find that man! Shoulders...why, I haven't seen shoulders that wide since—"

"No." Cait stepped away from her, away from the false gaiety, the perfume, the greediness. "No, I'm not like my mother at all. Excuse me—there's someone I have to talk with."

"But...but..."

Others tried to grab her as she walked by, their faces glowing with the same avid curiosity, but she shrugged them off without even seeing them, suddenly sickened by it all. Watson Renfrew, a good friend of her father's and one of the few people here she actually liked and trusted, saw her coming and turned away from the small group he was speaking with, smile in place.

"I want these people out of here, Watson. Now."

The smile stayed in place, but he blinked at her. "Out? But, Cait—these people are all your friends. They all want to—"

"These people aren't my friends," she said bitterly. "They never were. They stood back and watched for six years while Dalkquist destroyed my credibility bit by bit, and they loved it. It was a spectacle, like the Christians and the lions, and they couldn't get enough."

"Cait, I think you're being a little hard on them."

"No, I'm not. And I'm tired of providing free entertainment for them. Get them out of here, or I swear I will. And I'm in no mood to be polite."

He paled slightly, obviously seeing something in her eyes that made him murmur a hasty "right away," drop his drink on the nearest tray and head for the front of the room. Gritting her teeth, Cait fought the tears clawing at her throat. Hang on, damn it, she told herself ferociously. Hang on!

She'd be damned if she'd let any of these people see her cry. Not over Shay. Not over a broken heart. They were going to be talking about her and her blue-eyed trucker for years to come as it was. She wasn't going to give them the added pleasure of seeing her fall apart.

"Well, Caitlin, the good news is that I managed to salvage the house, the cottage and that piece of property in Carmel. The bad news is I had to let the condo in Aspen and just about everything else go." Watson set the elegant teacup on the coffee table and sighed. "You're nearly bankrupt, Cait. We might be able to get some of the money back, but it'll be tied up in the courts for years. And I'll be honest with you—I'm not even certain we'll get it then. It was all done legally. There's nothing to prove that your mother didn't give him free rein over her money. The only place we have some leverage is your trust fund, and I'm not sure we can get a claim there, either."

Cait just nodded, feeling a little numb, sitting ramrod straight in the brocade chair, hands folded in her lap. "And you're saying the house is mortgaged to the hilt and that there are debts outstanding well into six figures."

He nodded unhappily. "He siphoned some of it into the campaign, mixing it in with the legitimate contributions with no records or anything to indicate what's real and what isn't. As I say, it could take years to untangle." He sighed again. "But most of it is simply gone, Cait. Bad investments, venture capital we'll never see a return on, bad loans." He looked at her despairingly. "I'm sorry, Cait. There just isn't anything left."

She should be feeling something, Cait thought. Fury. Outrage. Fear. A wealthy woman one minute and bankrupt the next...that should account for *some* emotion, shouldn't it?

And yet she felt nothing. Absolutely nothing.

She hadn't felt anything for nearly six weeks now. Not since Shay had left.

Watson was speaking again, but she hardly heard him. He left after a while and she was alone again. Alone with the echoing emptiness and the numbness...

She went on like that for another week. People stopped dropping by, undoubtedly hearing that she was flat broke, but it was only a relief. She let the staff go one by one, and sold some of the furniture and rugs and artwork to pay the most urgent of the bills.

And finally, one day, she looked around the big house with its marble floors and its Olympic-length pool and its gilt embellishments and its cold, empty rooms...and she knew. Knew that what she wanted wasn't here; perhaps never had been.

What she wanted was out there on the road somewhere: one truck, one man, one heart. She belonged there—more than she'd ever belonged within these ornate, false walls. These walls had been her mother's prison. And hers. She'd felt safe here, but that safety—like so much in her life—had been just illusion.

With Shay, she'd found something more precious than vindication, more precious even than truth. She'd found herself. Or rather, Shay had found her...had unraveled all the layers and uncovered the core of Caitlin as he might a precious gift.

And she wanted that woman back. And Shay. Maybe, more than anything, she wanted Shay.

Watson Renfrew looked worried when she answered the door smiling. He looked closely at her, frowning a little. "You said it was urgent. I dropped everything and came right over."

"It is urgent, Watson. Come into the den—coffee?"

"Please." He watched as she poured him a cup and took it with a nod, adding cream, then sitting in the gilt-and-brocade armchair by the desk. "I heard via the grapevine that you've sold your father's antique car collection."

"Yes, they came and got them yesterday. I always hated those cars. It seemed like such waste, having all that hardware just sitting around taking up space and collecting dust."

"And you're having an auction?" He looked uncomfortable. "Cait, forgive me for saying this, but are you certain you're doing the right thing? Once people realize you're in financial difficulty, they'll be at your throat like—"

"Financial difficulty?" Cait laughed. "Watson, I'm busted. That's about as *difficult* as it gets. And as for these *people* you talk about—who cares? If I never see any of them again it'll be too soon."

"Now, Cait . . ." He looked shocked now. And worried.

"I'm not the same person I was two years ago, Watson," she said quietly. "I can't just pretend nothing happened. That I haven't changed."

"You're still Caitlin Sawyer," he persisted stubbornly. "That hasn't changed."

"Hasn't it?" She smiled, letting her mind drift back to tall, blue-eyed man in a black-and-silver eighteen-wheeler who'd stolen her heart without even trying. "Hell on Wheels . . ."

"What?" He looked at her in bewilderment.

And Cait had to laugh aloud. "Sell it," she said evenly, looking around the cold, ornate room.

"Sell it?" Watson blinked, looking aghast. "All of it?"

"The whole damned thing." Cait tossed a handful of papers onto the low table between them, suddenly feeling so light she was half afraid to move in case she simply wafted off into space. "Sell the house, the cottage, the Carmel property... all of it."

"Cait...!" He sounded so shocked she had to smile.

"There are a few things I want. Dad's fishing rods and his books, Granddad's rolltop desk and that leather chair he used to sit in when he'd read me my bedtime stories. And some of Mom's things—her silver hairbrushes, her collection of Dresden figurines—I always loved those. Some other things. But as for the rest of it..." She looked around again, as though seeing it for the first time. "I used to think I loved this place, but I see now I only loved the memories it held. But I can take them anywhere. They're a part of me, not of this house." She turned her head to look at Watson. "Sell it."

"But...but where will you live?" He looked horrified and upset. "What will you do?"

"I'm going to be a trucker's wife," she said with sudden satisfaction, loving the feel of the words in her mouth. "I'm going to make cherry pies and babies and be happy for a change."

"B-b-babies?" He mouthed the word in disbelief, as though it were something so foreign, so alien, he didn't recognize it.

"Babies," Cait said with some satisfaction. "McKittrick babies, to be specific."

"And... and the money? From the sale?"

"Will there be any left?"

"A few thousand, perhaps. Not much, granted, but—"

"Put a third of it aside for me—I'll contact you in a fe
weeks and let you know where to send it. The rest will go
a Diane Mosely. I'll give you her address." Grinning, sh
shoved her hands into her pockets. "Be happy for m
Watson," she said with a laugh. "For the first time in m
entire life, I know who I am. And it's the most wonderf
feeling in the world!"

Epilogue

"It's a real bad night out there." The waitress—Betty— smiled as she refilled his coffee cup. As though to prove she was right, a gust of wind and rain hit the front windows of the café and made them shudder. "How about a piece of pie to finish things off?" She leaned against the table and smiled down at him. "The cherry's good tonight."

"No, thanks." Shay returned her smile. "I'll just finish this and be on my way."

She made a face. "But it's awful out there—weather report says we're in for heavy rain and a lot of wind." She looked down at him evenly. "Like I said before, she must be something real special."

"Who?"

"Whoever's put that sad look in those baby blues of yours." She grinned jauntily. "Honey, you've got love trouble written all over you. I can spot it a mile off."

Shay managed another rough smile, not wanting to think about it. Unable not to. All he had to do was close his eyes

and she was there beside him, dark hair aswirl, eyes sparkling with mischief and love, those lush warm lips just a kiss
away....

"You want to talk about it, honey, you just tell me."
Betty reached down and patted his arm. "I'm good with
broken hearts."

Shay took a last swallow of coffee, watching her walk
away. Easy to watch, no doubt about it. But watching was
about all he was interested in doing these days.

The wind caught the door just then and blew it open with
a shuddering crash that made everyone jump. A curtain of
icy wind-lashed rain swept in, glittering from the parking-lot
lights, and it was only when the slender form caught the
door and slammed it closed, cutting off the wailing of the
wind, that Shay realized someone had come in with the
storm.

In the sudden silence, everyone stared at the newcomer.
And Shay, slowly lowering his coffee cup, felt the hair
prickle along the back of his neck.

It was a woman, slender and not too tall, dressed casually in jeans and a heavy fisherman-knit sweater and a
denim anorak, the hood pulled up to protect her from the
rain. She tossed it back and gave her head a shake and black
hair cascaded around her, sparkling with rain.

Her skin was rain-wet and pink with cold, and she stood
by the door for a moment, looking around. And Shay literally felt the earth tremble slightly as eyes the color of good
brandy met his full on.

She smiled a little, then started walking toward him.

"Hey, don't I know you?" Betty gazed at the newcomer
curiously. "You've been in here before, haven't you?"

"A lifetime ago," the stranger said with a smile. "Back
when I was someone different...."

Shay leaned back against the fake leather banquette and grinned lazily at her, then reached out to hook a nearby chair with his booted foot and pull it up to the table. "Looking good, Miss Sawyer."

"And you, Mr. McKittrick." She swung a knapsack off her shoulder and let it drop, then sat down, combing her damp hair back with her fingers. "You're a hard man to find. I've been hitching rides with half the truckers north of the state line for the past three days, trying to track you down. Don't you ever listen to your CB?"

"Are you…uh…staying? Or just passing through?" He had no right to even hope, he told himself dimly. No right.

"That depends on you. How long do you want me to stay?"

His gaze held hers. "You know the answer to that."

A smile played around the corners of her mouth. "I should tell you that I'm broke. More or less, anyway. I managed to salvage a few thousand from the house sale, enough to maybe pay a bit down on the rig, but that's all."

Shay winced. "He got away with it all?"

"All."

"Cait, I'm sorry." He reached for her rain-cold hand and cupped it in his, warming it.

"Don't be. I don't even miss it." She grinned suddenly. "Spence O'Dell offered me a job, can you believe it?" Her laughter spilled sunshine and warm days through the café. "Rick was behind it, I think. One day this tall, lean man with eyes like ice turned up at the door and said he wanted me to work for him. He made it very clear that he didn't recruit many women, and that the training was brutal, and that over ninety percent of the applicants don't make it through, and that even if I made it through the training and the testing and everything he could *still* turn me down flat.

But he managed to make it sound as though those who *do* make it through are something special."

Shay had to laugh. He tightened his fingers around hers, holding her gaze. "Are you going to take him up on it?"

She shrugged. "Well, it's the best offer I've had so far." The words hung between them, filled with challenge. "But I figured before I did anything I might regret, I'd better find out if you meant it when you said you loved me."

His fingers tightened. "I meant it."

She grinned broadly. "You're not getting any kind of a bargain here, McKittrick."

"Can you cook?" He gave her a slow, lazy grin.

"I can cook."

"Can you make a bed?"

"I can make a bed."

"I'll be gone most of the week—weekends, too, sometimes. The bank owns half my rig, I'm not interested in being a corporate man and I'll never be rich. Seems to me you're not getting much of a bargain, either."

"Do you love me?"

He looked at her for a long moment, his heart tumbling around like a kite in a windstorm. "I love you."

"Then I'm already richer than I've ever been," Cait whispered, reaching up and running her finger across his cheek almost wonderingly, as though having to prove to herself that he was real. "Money can't buy how you make me feel."

"Hey, honey, if you need a job, Barney can fix you up." Betty winked at Cait as she walked by. "He's always looking for waitresses."

Shay laughed, then reached across and grasped the front of Cait's jacket in his fist and pulled her toward him, kissing her soundly. Then he was on his feet, tossing a handful of bills on the table. He picked up Cait's knapsack and slung it over one shoulder and waited for her to stand up, then dropped his arm around her and walked her to the door.

"We'll call O'Dell in the morning and tell him you've had a better offer," he drawled. "Maybe he'll come to the wedding...."

* * * * *

HE'S AN

AMERICAN HERO

A cop, a fire fighter or even just a fearless drifter who gets the job done when ordinary men have given up. And you'll find one American Hero every month only in Intimate Moments—created by some of your favorite authors. This summer, Silhouette has lined up some of the hottest American heroes you'll ever find:

July: HELL ON WHEELS by Naomi Horton—Truck driver Shay McKittrick heads down a long, bumpy road when he discovers a scared stowaway in his rig....

August: DRAGONSLAYER by Emilie Richards—In a dangerous part of town, a man finds himself fighting a street gang—and his feelings for a beautiful woman....

September: ONE LAST CHANCE by Justine Davis—A tough-as-nails cop walks a fine line between devotion to duty and devotion to the only woman who could heal his broken heart....

AMERICAN HEROES: Men who give all they've got for their country, their work—the women they love.

IMHER05

1
FREE
BOOK COUPON

TO RECEIVE YOUR COPY OF THE *10th ANNIVERSARY COLLECTION* RETURN SIX (6) FREE BOOK COUPONS PLUS CHECK OR MONEY ORDER FOR $3.00 FOR DELIVERY IN THE SPECIAL REPLY ENVELOPE PROVIDED. PLEASE DO NOT SEND CASH.

SDBP-3A

1
FREE
BOOK COUPON

TO RECEIVE YOUR COPY OF THE *10th ANNIVERSARY COLLECTION* RETURN SIX (6) FREE BOOK COUPONS PLUS CHECK OR MONEY ORDER FOR $3.00 FOR DELIVERY IN THE SPECIAL REPLY ENVELOPE PROVIDED. PLEASE DO NOT SEND CASH.

IT'S YOURS
FREE!

10TH ANNIVERSARY COLLECTION

FREE BOOK COUPON

It's Silhouette Intimate Moments's 10th Anniversary and we'd like to give you a special gift! Save this free book coupon. Six coupons entitle you to receive a free copy of Silhouette Intimate Moments's *10th Anniversary Collection*, three classic novels of love and romance.

YOUR NAME

ADDRESS

CITY STATE/PROV. ZIP/POSTAL CODE

IT'S YOURS
FREE!

081KAR

SAVE THIS COUPON

IT'S YOURS
FREE!

10TH ANNIVERSARY COLLECTION

FREE BOOK COUPON

It's Silhouette Intimate Moments's 10th Anniversary and we'd like to give you a special gift! Save this free book coupon. Six coupons entitle you to receive a free copy of Silhouette Intimate Moments's *10th Anniversary Collection*, three classic novels of love and romance.

YOUR NAME

ADDRESS

CITY STATE/PROV. ZIP/POSTAL CODE

IT'S YOURS
FREE!

081KAR

SAVE THIS COUPON